FORBIDDEN PLEASURES

"They are watching," he whispered. "I am certain of it."

Gulbeyaz, the well-trained odalisque, merely nodded, her eyes properly lowered to her lap.

"Do you understand? We will have to pretend."

"There is no need to pretend," she told him grandly, if still very softly. "I have been well trained. I am ready to do what is expected of me."

Gulbeyaz removed her jeweled *kalpock* and long trailing veil, tossing them aside. She ran her hands through her long silver-blond hair, which shimmered like a waterfall in the torch-light. Jason drew in his breath, even as his arousal, already quickened, strengthened very much against his will.

Then she lifted the duvet and climbed into the bed.

"Penelope . . . Penny!" Jason choked. "What do you think you're doing?"

"Only what I have been taught, my lord," came the muffled reply. "Only what I have been taught."

The Harem Bride

Blair Bancroft

A SIGNET BOOK

SIGNET
Published by New American Library, a division of
Penguin Group (USA) Inc., 375 Hudson Street,
New York, New York 10014, U.S.A.
Penguin Books Ltd, 80 Strand,
London WC2R 0RL, England
Penguin Books Australia Ltd, 250 Camberwell Road,
Camberwell, Victoria 3124, Australia
Penguin Books Canada Ltd, 10 Alcorn Avenue,
Toronto, Ontario, Canada M4V 3B2
Penguin Books (NZ), cnr Rosedale and Airborne Roads,
Albany, Auckland 1310, New Zealand

Penguin Books Ltd, Registered Offices:
80 Strand, London WC2R 0RL, England

First published by Signet, an imprint of New American Library,
a division of Penguin Group (USA) Inc.

First Printing, July 2004
10 9 8 7 6 5 4 3 2 1

To all women with veiled and hidden hearts,
who long for *something more.*

Acknowledgments

This book could not have been written without reference to *Harem: The World Behind the Veil,* by Alev Lytle Croutier; also *Dreams of Trespass: Tales of a Harem Girlhood* and *The Veil and the Male Elite* by Fatima Mernissi. Thanks are also due to the late Sydney Checkland who wrote *The Elgins, 1766–1917* and to William St. Clair, author of *Lord Elgin and the Marbles.*

—Blair Bancroft

Chapter One

Shropshire, England, February 1812

Ping. Ping. Ping.

Penelope Blayne winced. She was already suffering guilt over asking the postboys and the long-suffering horses to forge on through a cold driving rain, and now this audible sign that the rain had turned to sleet lowered her spirits still further. They should have racked up for the night at the last posting inn, but Mr. Farley, her Aunt Cass's solicitor, had given her so little money, she feared she would not be able to pay the shot. So here she was, bowling along in the dark on rough rutted roads through sleet that would likely turn to snow, risking herself, her maid and longtime companion, Noreen O'Donnell, and the well-being of the poor exposed postboys and their team in a mad dash to get exactly where she did not wish to go. Namely, Rockbourne Crest. A Shropshire house undoubtedly as daunting and unwelcoming as its owner.

Ping. Ping. Ping, ping, ping, pong!

Penny stifled a groan. The sleet was worsening. She pulled aside the curtain and peered out the window, searching for a light, any light. She could not allow this journey to continue another moment. If they didn't end up in an icy ditch, the postboys, and likely the horses as well, would fall prey to an inflammation of the lungs, and it would be all her fault.

Only a veil of icy pellets met her gaze. The post chaise and its passengers were as alone as if they were lost at sea or attempting to cross the Arabian desert. Swiftly, ruthlessly, Penny shut out the explosion of memories triggered by her unfortunate stray thought. Now was definitely not the time to remember Arabia or the Ottoman Empire. Indeed, *never* was the proper time for remembering the Ottoman Empire.

Rockbourne Crest. Penny failed to stifle a groan. Noreen O'Donnell stirred in her sleep, then settled once again into the corner of the chaise's one forward-facing seat. Thank goodness for that, Penny sighed. Noreen deserved her much-earned rest, for tonight was yet one more adventure in the long years that the Irishwoman had followed Aunt Cass and herself to the ends of the earth. Well, perhaps not that far. Their travels had stopped short of China, Japan, and New South Wales. And even though Bonaparte had put a bit of a crimp in their plans here and there, they had managed to view a great deal of the remainder of the known world, including Jamaica and the former Colonies in the Americas.

Penny scowled, as for perhaps the thousandth time the iniquity of her situation hit her. This was the first time, the very first time in all their travels, that she had ever had to worry about money. From the time she was sixteen, she had taken over travel arrangements for her peripatetic aunt, Miss Cassandra Pemberton. She had dealt with every sort of transportation, from Russian troikas to Greek donkeys, Indian elephants, and Moroccan camels. It was quite remarkable how far and how fast an ample amount of cash and a winsome smile could take a foreign traveler. Yes, she had always managed well.

Except for that one unfortunate incident in Constantinople.

Jason Lisbourne. Earl of Rocksley. Master of Rockbourne Crest. The name she was trying so hard to avoid echoed through her mind with every turn of the wheels. *Jason, Jason, Jason.*

Penny wrenched her long-ago fantasies back to the unfortunate reality of the moment. It truly wasn't possible that Aunt Cass had left her penniless. She couldn't have. Wouldn't have.

Yet she had. Either Aunt Cass's mind had gone begging

during her long final illness, or Aunt Cass was a hopeless romantic, which Penny sincerely doubted, as Miss Cassandra Pemberton had been a determined spinster all her life. Whatever the reason, Cassandra Pemberton had left her considerable fortune in trust for her niece until her thirtieth birthday. *Thirtieth!* This, the same niece who had not only made all arrangement for their journeys, but who had hired their servants, handled all disputes, domestic and foreign, paid all bills—

Outrageous. Perfectly outrageous!

Every penny of the Pemberton fortune was now controlled by Jason Lisbourne, Earl of Rocksley. Even pin money, Hector Farley had assured Miss Penelope Blayne, would be decided by Lord Rocksley. *After* her arrival at Rockbourne Crest. Until then, there was . . . nothing. Mr. Farley had even committed the final outrage of putting Aunt Cass's home up for long-term lease. This, too, he said, had been stipulated in Cassandra Pemberton's will. When Penny demanded to read this offending paragraph for herself, she had discovered the truth of it. For a roof over her head and food on the table, for the clothes on her back, she was now wholly dependent on Jason Lisbourne, Earl of Rocksley.

If she had been sixteen, instead of nearly six and twenty, she might have run away. But she had seen too much of the world, too many of its ills along with its wonders, to think that she could solve her present problem by childish flight. She would ask Rocksley to provide a modest cottage where she could live out the years until her Aunt Cass's will considered her "of age." Truthfully, she had had enough travel for a dozen lifetimes. A quiet life in a small village would suit her very well.

She would not think about a loving husband and children. Like her aunt, she would be grateful for what life had brought.

Truly she would.

Penny gasped and grabbed for the hang strap as the chaise made an abrupt turn. Its large rear wheels promptly skidded on the icy slush now covering the road, and for a few moments the carriage careened from side to side before coming to a shuddering halt.

Noreen O'Donnell came awake as Penny, losing her grip on the strap, slid across the seat and landed in the older woman's lap. "What? Have we arrived then?" Miss Blayne's maid gasped.

"I am so sorry," Penny said, pushing herself upright and straightening her bonnet. "I fear we may have had an accident. Are you all right?"

"Oh, aye, 'tis indestructible I am," declared Noreen O'Donnell, "and after all these years you should be knowing that."

As indeed Penny did. She had been only thirteen when Aunt Cass rescued a frightened Noreen from the streets of Florence. The young maid had been abandoned after her mistress had, for the sake of her health, come to spend the winter in Italy, only to die as spring was bringing life back to the glorious landscape around her. "As Irish as Paddy's pig," Noreen always said of herself and had made an effort to keep her accent and sprightly, unsubservient attitude intact through all the years of Cassandra Pemberton's efforts to teach her to speak "English."

"Be you all right, misses?" One of the postboys, looking more like a carving at an ice fair than a human being, was peeking through a crack in the door.

"We're fine," Penny assured him, "Are we stuck?"

"Don't think so, miss. Just seeing you're not hurt. Hang on a mo' and I'm thinkin' we'll be off. Nearly there, we are."

Penny thanked him, vowing to give the postboys every last cent she had left when they were safely delivered to Rockbourne Crest.

Horses snorted, the chaise jerked, shuddered, jerked again, and at last they crept forward. By the dim light of their carriage lantern Penny thought she saw a gatehouse, but it was dark. No sign of an attendant. The gates were open. Odd, very odd. Rockbourne Crest was an estate of considerable size, or so she had been told. One would not have thought that the earl would be so careless. But, then, why should she expect any sensible action from Jason Lisbourne? From the gossip she had heard through the years, he was careless of everything and everybody. A cynic's cynic, a rake's rake. The living embodiment of all that was wrong with society in the regency of the profligate George, Prince of Wales.

"Oh, sainted Mary, mother of God!" Noreen wailed as the chaise started to slip and slide once again. Its two passengers were thrown back against the squabs as the chaise struggled up a steep hill, slithering from side to side like the undulations of a snake.

"Shropshire is not at all like our dear Sussex, but I am sure the postboys know what they are doing," Penny declared, attempting to sound calm and reassuring when she was far from feeling either of those emotions. What if Rockbourne's drive were on the edge of a precipice? What if they missed a bridge over one of the many ice-fringed streams they had seen earlier in the day? What if—

What a fool she was! To quail over a bit of sleet and a road that wasn't flat. Surely she had never been so missish, even when she saw her first red Indian. Goodness knows she had endured far worse than bad weather and rough roads. But tonight . . . tonight was different. She had not experienced so many qualms since . . . since the last time she had seen Jason Lisbourne. Viscount Lyndon, he was then. Little more than a boy, he had been doing the Grand Tour . . .

With a great stamping of hooves and snuffling from the winded horses, the post chaise came to a halt. "Stay aboard while I rouse the house, miss," the postboy called through the door.

"Praise be!" cried Noreen O'Donnell. As exhausted and cold as Miss Penelope Blayne was, it was not the phrase she would have chosen.

Four tall lanterns illuminated the steps to Rockbourne Crest, but all Penny could see through the sleet was the vague silhouette of what looked more like a fortress than a home. The ice-encrusted postboy continued to pound on a massive door that remained stubbornly closed. They were expecting her. They had to be expecting her. Mr. Farley assured her all arrangements had been made.

The postboy, who was forty if he was a day, turned and gave her a look, a shrug of his shoulders, then renewed his assault on the front door of Rockbourne Crest. At last, it inched open, allowing a pale ribbon of light to illuminate the icy crystals beating down and forming a glistening carpet underfoot. Penny let out a pent-up sigh of relief, combined with a quaver of apprehension, as the door suddenly swung wide, revealing . . . not the proper butler she had expected, nor even a proper footman. Not that she could see the features of the man in the doorway, but he was leaning against the jamb at a rather precarious angle, as if that were all that was keeping him on his feet.

Oh, dear. The open gate. The lanterns. The Earl of Rocksley was having a party. And a shockingly unconventional one, too, if even the butler was barely able to stand. "Come, Noreen," Penny announced. "It's high time we warmed ourselves by a fire."

Noreen O'Donnell's sniff expressed her disdain for their welcome to Rockbourne Crest. " 'Tis fortunate we'll be if that one can show us the way to our rooms. More like, he'll go crashing down the stairs and break his neck."

"There must be a housekeeper somewhere," Penny said, a bit desperately, as the postboy threw open the chaise door.

The shallow steps up to the house were so treacherous, the gallant postboy had to escort the women up one at a time. When Noreen was safely inside, Penny emptied the meager contents of her purse into the postboy's hands, while offering both her apologies and her thanks. Praying she was telling the truth, she told him to go round to the stables where he, his companion, and the horses would find both food and shelter.

"Aye, miss, thank y' kindly," the man replied before disappearing into the night.

Thank goodness he had not seemed displeased by the amount of his vail. Miss Penelope Blayne had not traveled the world without learning the value and worth of those who served.

Although the entry hall was actually quite chilly, it enveloped both women in a blanket of seeming warmth.

"Ah-h," Penny murmured, swaying slightly on her feet, much too tired to examine the details of her surroundings.

"You the one what was expected?" the butler drawled, now propping himself up with one hand against the wall.

Penny drew herself up to her full five feet three inches, somehow managing to look down her nose at the butler who towered over her even while drooping against the wall. She was aware of raucous noises tumbling down from the open gallery on the floor above. Shrieks of female laughter or purported fright rose over guffaws and excited shouts in a cacophony of male baritone and bass. An orgy? Here? Now? How could he! When he knew she was expected. Or was that perhaps why . . . ? Oh, yes, most likely that was the explanation. This unique welcome had been staged for her delectation.

Monster!

"Mrs. Wilton don't like to be roused out o' her bed," the drunken butler muttered, more to himself than to the two shivering ladies.

"What is your name?" Penny snapped.

For a moment the poor man looked as if he didn't know. "Hutton, Miss," he said finally, responding to her imperious tone by making a futile effort to straighten away from the wall.

"Hutton, you will send for the housekeeper immediately. I do not care if she arrives here in her nightgown or her chemise. I want her here within five minutes, do you understand?"

The two guests watched, fascinated, as the butler shoved off from the front wall and lurched across the hall, careening more madly than the post chaise as it climbed the hill to Rockbourne Crest. When his hands finally found the bellpull, Penny feared he was clinging so tightly, he would pull it from the wall. But after jerking it several times, Hutton merely subsided, sinking slowly down the wall until he was sitting upright, his feet flat out in front him, his head flopping limply to one side.

"Behold!" Penny groaned as the two women sank into a pair of elaborately carved oak chairs, which looked as if they might have been in the entry hall since Jacobean times. More important, the chairs were about as far away from the unconscious Hutton as they could get. "We are soaked through. Our bonnets are in ruins, very like our boots as well. My hair must be as plastered to my head as yours, frost still drips from my lashes, and we are both shivering so hard we could be taken for having an ague."

"Which we surely will if we must spend the night in this entry," Noreen declared roundly. "Do you think the entire household is foxed?" she added on a more anxious note.

"If that is the case—" Penny declared most awfully, her dire tone echoing through the sparsely furnished hall.

"I assure you, miss, I do not imbibe!" A formidable woman confronted them from the far side of the entry hall, her face as stiff with outrage as the uncompromising lines of her black bombazine gown.

"I am glad to hear it, Mrs. Wilton," Penny declared, allowing her eyes to drift to the peacefully oblivious form of Hutton, the butler, still seated haphazardly against the wall.

"That one!" sniffed the housekeeper. "Stackpole, his lordship's London butler, was too fine to come to the wilds of Shropshire, so we're stuck with *him*." She nodded at Hutton's recumbent form. "As heedless as the master and his guests, yet him, foolish soul, not seeming to realize gents may do as they please, while he may find himself out on his ear, without a feather to fly with."

Penny noted this sad prospect did not seem to disturb Mrs. Wilton one whit.

"Well, come, then," the housekeeper commanded, as if to recalcitrant children, "I presume you're Miss Blayne. There's a room ready, though why his lordship should put you there, I cannot conceive. With the house full of rakes and whatall, you'll be wanting to have your maid sleep in your dressing room tonight, and make sure to lock your door." After these rather startling admonitions, Mrs. Wilton turned and headed toward the imposing L-shaped oak staircase leading to the gallery above, clearly expecting the guests to follow.

"One moment, Mrs. Wilton," Penny called, rising to her

feet. "I want to be sure the postboys are properly accommodated, and I should like them to have a hot toddy."

Mrs. Wilton, pausing at the foot of the stairs, turned to glare at Miss Penelope Blayne. "Hot toddies, is it? For the postboys? And me with a houseful of rakehells and ladybirds drinking everything in sight. In truth, 'tis a wonder Hutton found a drop for himself. *Postboys!* Good Lord, miss, are you a radical?"

Penny planted her feet on the diamond-patterned tiles, now well muddied by melting sleet and dirty boots. "I assure you, Mrs. Wilton, if not for the efforts of those two men, Miss O'Donnell and I might be freezing to death in a ditch. You will find someone to make and deliver a cold collation and hot toddies to the stables immediately."

"You heard the lady, Hetty, my love." A new voice boomed through the entry hall. "I suggest you see to it immediately. The lady is merely upholding the hospitality of the house, something I'm sure Rocksley would expect you to do."

Penny, turning swiftly, could only stare. No, it could not be. Jason Lisbourne had not changed that much. His hair had once been the gold of a new-minted guinea, and even if it had darkened through the years, as hers had, he could not have become a redhead. A tall, almost skinny redhead with skin nearly as pale as Noreen's Irish coloring and cheeks nearly as pink. And this man was as cursed as Noreen with that redhead's nemesis, freckles. A second look showed that, although he was smiling, it was a lopsided sardonic grin, the curled lips of a man of the world, bored and disillusioned by the world around him.

"Gant Deveny," he said, sweeping her a bow that was close to mockery. "Lord Brawley. And there's many will tell you the name is apt." Hands on hips, he threw back his shoulders, assuming a belligerent stance. "I have that redhead temper, you see. When I'm not too lazy to indulge it, that is," he added on a wink.

Clearly, this man was nearly as far gone in his cups as poor Hutton. *Brawley. Brawl.* "Oh, I see," Penny said faintly, wishing only to find her room and burrow under a mountain of bedcovers.

"Who can say if there's a footman left standing," Mrs. Wilton grumbled, but she tugged on the bellpull.

"Surely not all the maids are tipsy as well," Penny snapped. The housekeeper shrugged. It was at last becoming apparent that Mrs. Wilton was openly hostile, though the why of it Penny could not imagine.

"Ah, there you are, Rocksley!" Lord Brawley drawled. "Come to greet your guests at last, have you?"

Penny felt a frisson of wind as icy as that blowing beyond the great front door. Behind her. Jason was behind her, and, oh, dear God, she couldn't look up, she couldn't move!

"Come, come, Rocksley," Gant Deveny chided, rather gleefully. "See to your guests."

Unsteady, somewhat shuffling steps approached. *Oh, no, not Jason too!* A large body appeared in front of her. She who had been such an intrepid soul all her life fixed her eyes on the tips of his boots and kept them there. Long fingers reached out, tilted up her chin. She kept her eyes down. A head, topped by waves of golden-bronze hair, bent to peer beneath her bonnet. A pair of fine cobalt-blue eyes regarded her with interest, the effect considerably spoiled by the red lines crisscrossing the whites. His nose was sharper, she thought, and far more arrogant than when he was a young man of twenty-one. But his mouth—ah, that was the same—full and eminently kissable . . .

Horrified, Miss Penelope Blayne jerked her chin out of her trustee's grasp and looked past him, to fix her disapproving gaze on Hutton.

"Looks like a drowned rat," the Earl of Rocksley intoned, "but I daresay that's my Penelope." He sighed. "A bit long in the tooth. Looked considerably better the last time I saw her, but what's a man to do?" He shrugged. "Daresay she'll do. Don't have much choice."

Miss Penelope Blayne managed to keep her countenance, but Noreen O'Donnell's indignant gasp filled the hall.

"So who is she?" Lord Brawley asked, lifting an inquiring brow. "Too far gone for proper introductions, are you, Rock?"

"Not at all, not at all," said Jason Lisbourne, Earl of Rocksley. "Gant, dear boy, I'd like you to meet m'wife."

Chapter Two

Upon the following morning, Jason Victor Granville Lisbourne, Earl of Rocksley, opened one bloodshot eye and surveyed the burgundy velvet hangings at the foot of his bed with considerable loathing. Not that the innocent fabric had offended. Oh, no. It was merely a symbol of the world to which he did not care to return. Of his disgust with himself, his wish that all his party guests, including his closest friend Gant Deveny, had miraculously disappeared, whisked off in a hail of sleet. That his butler had been truly unconscious and that his housekeeper was deaf, dumb, and blind.

Aa-rgh! The earl's eye snapped shut, his lips thinned as his head and stomach threatened simultaneous explosion. He grimaced, groaned, swallowed hard, and managed to croak a faint, "Kirby!"

His meticulous and highly efficient valet, Daniel Kirby, whisked back the bed hangings so fast the earl could only assume he had been standing, patiently waiting, beside the bed. After gulping down the concoction Kirby held to his lips, then disgorging the acidic contents of his much-abused stomach into the basin the faithful valet held to his lips, Jason Lisbourne fell back on his pillows. Alas, he was now fit enough to loathe himself still more.

Nearly ten years he had kept the secret. Ten long years. And then, within moments of seeing Penelope Blayne, he had blurted out their dire secret in front of witnesses. Gant was a friend, of course. In spite of the viscount's cynical outlook on the world, the earl knew he could count on Brawley not to reveal what he had heard. But Hutton, who may not have been as dead to the proceedings in the hall as he appeared? And Mrs. Wilton, who had been sour and straitlaced about his doings even before taking up Methodism? *Hell and damnation!* By now the whole household, and each and every guest, would know he had a wife!

Perhaps the sleet had turned to snow? Mayhap there was a mountain of it outside, trapping the secret within his own walls. Which presently contained at least half the most accomplished tale-bearers in the *ton.* Including Mrs. Daphne Coleraine.

Daphne! The Earl of Rocksley moaned, willing the fiendish pixies banging anvils within his head to cease and desist. "The roads, Kirby, are they passable?"

"Indeed, my lord, I believe they are. The sleet turned to snow, but deposited only an inch or two. The roads this morning are nothing worse than their customary winter state." A slight sniff indicated what Rocksley's fastidious valet thought of country roads. "Any proper coachman should be able to manage, my lord."

To the devil with it then. His guests could go. They could all go, spreading the news to every flapping ear along a beeline back to London, for he could scarcely have his present houseful of guests of dubious reputation in residence with Miss Penelope Blayne.

Penelope Blayne Lisbourne, Countess of Rocksley.

"The basin, Kirby," the earl gasped. "At once!"

"My dear fellow," drawled Gant Deveny a few agonizing minutes later as he strolled into the earl's bedchamber, "I am sorry to see you in such a state. Truly, I had thought you the man of rock-hard head and cast-iron stomach."

"Go away."

"But I have come to see how you go on, dear chap. The house is so ominously quiet I feared everyone had expired. There's not even a sign of the lovely Lady Rocksley."

"Lovely!" Jason Lisbourne sputtered.

"Quite so, I believe, when not dripping icicles onto the tiles. Indeed, I rather thought I caught a glimpse of an elegant figure beneath—"

"Be quiet!" roared the earl. Then, after a groan of misery brought on by his burst of temper, he ground out, "Miss Blayne is none of your concern."

"Not the happy reunion of Ulysses and his faithful Penelope, I take it," Lord Brawley drawled.

"If I could move, I'd darken your daylights."

"Ah-h," Gant murmured, and wisely kept silent.

"Kirby," the earl called to his valet, "is Hutton up and about?"

"I fear Hutton, my lord, is in worse case than your lordship."

"Then send whatever footman is on his feet," Lord Rocksley barked. "My guests are to be gone as quickly as they can crawl out of their beds. Mrs. Wilton may feed any who have the stomach for food, and then they are to be off. The party is over." Weakly, the earl wiggled his fingers to indicate his orders were not yet finished. "What is the hour?" he asked.

"Gone eleven, my lord."

Jason Lisbourne sighed, gritted his teeth. The frown lines on his noble forehead deepened. "Kirby, you will inform Miss Blayne that I will see her in my study at one o'clock. See that Mrs. Wilton provides Miss Blayne and her maid with whatever food or other comforts they desire, but under no circumstances are they to leave their room until the time of our appointment. And since it is doubtful all our guests will be departed by that time, see that a footman, not one of the maids, accompanies Miss Blayne to my study. Is that clear?"

"Perfectly, my lord," intoned the most proper Daniel Kirby. "Does my lord have any further orders?"

"Go." Jason waved an impatient hand, shooing his valet out the door.

"So," breathed Gant Deveny as the valet left the room, "can it be that the most notorious rake in the *ton* is actually *married*?"

"I suppose it never occurred to you that my orders for my guests to leave included you?"

"Not a bit of it," said Lord Brawley, serenely. "I suspect

you are in need of as much support as you can get. That is what true friends are for, are they not?"

Lord Rocksley told his closest friend precisely what he could do with his offer of support.

"Now, now, dear boy, no need to get twitty. You can't blame me for being fascinated. We have been acquainted how long? Seven years, eight? And not one word about a wife hidden about in the bushes. I am agog, old chap, simply agog."

"Then may you strangle on your curiosity, for I shall not assuage it!" With a great heave, Jason Lisbourne sat up, dangling his feet off the side of the high four-poster, his arms stiff, clutching the bedcovers on either side for support. He forced back the bile rising in his throat, then swore, most colorfully.

"Perhaps I should speak to Miss Blayne . . . or should I say, Lady Rocksley," Lord Brawley offered, lips twitching, his fine hazel eyes dancing with amusement.

"Take yourself off," the earl growled. "Perhaps by teatime I shall be able to appreciate what you find so humorous in this situation, but at the moment I wish you in Hades."

Gant Deveny grinned outright. As he left, he proffered a wave of his hand so audacious, Jason picked a candlestick off the bedtable and flung it after him. Fortunately for the fine Persian carpet, the candle was not lit.

The earl and his guests were not the only late risers at Rockbourne Crest. Miss Penelope Blayne, exhausted by her journey across England from her home—Miss Cassandra Pemberton's *former* home—in Sussex, also awakened late. Breakfast had arrived on a tray borne by a pink-cheeked maid who must have been as Methodist as Mrs. Wilton, for she looked as if she had never drunk anything stronger than milk in her sixteen or seventeen years of life. A far cry from the debauchery Penny had glimpsed as she and Noreen were escorted to their rooms last night, for the party had spilled out of the drawing room, the card room, various salons, and, she suspected, even the bedrooms. Mrs. Wilton's basilisk stare had failed to slow the shrieks of painted ladies in various states of undress running shrieking and laughing through the stately halls of Rockbourne Crest, with equally disheveled gentlemen in hot pursuit. Gentlemen. It truly did not seem possible the pack of animals Penny had seen last night could be considered *gentlemen.*

Jason had done it on purpose, of course. If he wished to disconcert her, he had come close to achieving his goal. Bad enough he controlled Aunt Cass's money—*her* money—but never had she thought him so low as to greet her in such a fashion. She had loved him, for heaven's sake. Adored him. He was her hero, her savior. The knight on a white charger with whom she had planned to spend her life.

And here she was, trapped in her room while satyrs and demimondaines roamed the corridors, and her husband of ten years had to drink himself into near oblivion just to greet her at the door.

Penny gagged on her toast and blackberry jam, Noreen swiftly appearing to pat her vigorously on the back. After her coughing subsided and she had wiped away her tears, Miss Blayne waved off the remainder of her breakfast and sat, staring glumly at the very fine pastel embroidery of the heavy quilt on her bed. Eyes narrowing, she looked more closely. Very fine embroidery indeed. She lifted her eyes to survey the room she had barely noticed the night before. Noreen had locked both doors . . . yes, there had been two of them. One into the hall and one at the far end of the dressing room, where Noreen would sleep. Then, too exhausted for curiosity, both women had donned their nightclothes and found their beds, tumbling into sleep on the instant.

But now . . . Penny examined the room with care. Disoriented as she was from the recent upheaval in her life, as well as the prospect of a long-postponed confrontation with her husband, it took some time for the truth to become apparent.

Her bed alone was a work of art, as were the furnishings around her. From what she had seen of Rockbourne Crest last night, it was likely a seventeenth-century edifice, built when stately homes still thought first of defense. But this room has undoubtedly been redecorated during the time of

George II or the early days of George III. Even with its heavy winter fabrics, it was light and airy. From the canopy above her head and at the windows hung masses of rose velvet, fringed and tied back in cream cord. The headboard, footboard, and the underside of the wooden canopy were cream, with a delicate painted pattern of tiny pastel flowers and leaves. A tall chest, a dressing table, and two bed tables were painted in a similar manner, while other, smaller pieces of furniture scattered about the vast room were exquisite examples of chinoiserie, the most ornate piece, a fine cabinet, set against a wall-sized mural of delicate flowers, a stream, and stylized trees done in the Oriental manner. The fireplace, in which a cheery fire was taking the chill off the gray day, was of white marble, finely carved in a design of cherubs, birds, flowers, and grapes.

Penny brushed a crumb from her nightgown, then peeked over the edge of the bed. The carpet was also in the Eastern style, a mix of cream and rose accented with pale green and rich burgundy. Vaguely, she remembered the exquisite softness of it, the depth to which her toes had sunk last night as she had crawled into bed.

Oh, no, heaven help her! The thought struck like the cut of a sword. Her heart did a very queer flip-flop, rushed up to dizzy her head, then plummeted to her toes. She very much feared she was in the countess's suite! In the rooms belonging to the wife of the Earl of Rocksley. There could be no other explanation for the magnificence around her.

"Noreen," she called sharply, "where does the second door go?"

"Into another dressing room, miss. I peeked, you see, and caught the eye from a valet too niffy-naffy for his own good, I can tell you."

"Do you think . . . can it be . . . ?"

"Oh, aye, miss. 'Tis his lordship's own room, his valet told me so in no uncertain terms. Horrid man. Thinks he's so grand, he does."

Penny, shuddering, subsided onto her pillows.

* * *

An hour later, having received the earl's command and dressed accordingly, Penny sank onto the deep-set window seat and looked out the mullioned windows toward the bare beds of the formal gardens, the bentwood trellises stark against the mulched earth and pebbled paths. Beyond was a pond, its graceful curves outlined in drooping willows that managed, in their winter state, to look like a fine charcoal sketch. The pond, of course, was as gray as the bare willow branches, under a sky that exactly matched Penny's spirits. She wished she had never come to Rockbourne Crest. She had all the qualifications to be an outstanding governess. French, after all, was only one of the languages in which she could converse. She could play the piano, sketch, and recite history with all the skill of someone who had seen most of the world's great historical landmarks. And at maps and globes . . . ah, she was quite certain there was not a governess in the kingdom who could better her knowledge.

Penny sighed and ducked her head. She lacked the one quintessential quality of a governess. She was not humble. She had a quick wit and a sharp tongue, well honed by her Aunt Cass's example. She would not last as a governess above a day.

So, since she had become accustomed to eating well and having a roof over her head—and since she had an intimate knowledge of the narrow confines of a kept woman's life—she had come to Rockbourne Crest. She had known, of course, that Jason did not want her. After all, had he ever, in ten long years, given any indication that he wished to live with her as husband and wife? Therefore, she would do as she had planned. She would ask Jason—Lord Rocksley—to provide a cottage in the country and a modest maintenance. Surely, that was not asking too much.

Too much. Too much. Penny Blayne Lisbourne, Countess of Rocksley, stayed on the window seat, her bleak thoughts echoing through her head, until the same pink-cheeked maid brought nuncheon. To any and all efforts Noreen O'Donnell made at conversation, Penelope refused to reply. She simply chewed her food, tasting nothing, and looked off into space.

Her much-traveled Irish maid and companion might as well have been nonexistent.

The Countess of Rocksley saw only a great yawning void as her intelligence, sharpened by Miss Cassandra Pemberton's constant prodding, dictated that she remain independent, while her heart yearned for something else altogether. Except, of course, she had loved him too well and too long to ever be a burden. Therefore . . . the circular trap snapped closed, dictating her ignominious exile to a lonely cottage in the country.

"It's time," Noreen said. "A footman's come to take you to his lordship."

Penny pushed back her chair and stood, nervously brushing down the skirt of her gray silk gown. Fortunately, her trunks had been brought up not an hour since and Noreen had hastily pressed out the wrinkles in this severe mourning gown. Miss Cassandra Pemberton, meticulous to a fault, had specified in her will that no one was to wear black. "I have had a good life," she stated. "I need no crows to herald my passing." Her niece had heeded her instructions. She wore the stark charcoal-gray gown to mourn the passing of her marriage to the Right Honorable Jason Lisbourne, Earl of Rocksley.

He had been right. The glorious golden child he had married was gone. As his wife moved toward him with all the regal bearing of a queen marching toward her execution, Jason Lisbourne rose from behind the barricade of his burled walnut desk and studied her with open interest. Her once silver-blond curls had not darkened as much as his own. The wisps of golden brown that now framed her face could not be called unattractive. If only the mass of her hair were not pulled back into a coif more suitable for a governess or maiden aunt. And the face? He had to concede that far more character now shone from the fine symmetry of her face than from that of the soft, unformed child of sixteen. Child? A misnomer, surely. Cassandra Pemberton had never really allowed Miss Penelope Blayne to be a child.

Her eyes were still that clear remarkable shade of summer sky–blue he remembered so well. Those wide, intelligent blue eyes . . . and the masses of silver-gilt hair that tumbled over his fingers and inflamed his twenty-one-year-old body to a peak of embarrassment from which he had never recovered. He had, in fact, spent the past ten years in riotous efforts in other women's arms to erase his wedding night from his mind.

And her mouth? If it were not pursed into a persimmon pose, as if his mere presence had polluted the room, he judged it, too, would be the same. Magnificently formed, full, inviting, nay, *promising* pleasure to the man bold enough to—

Enough! He was no longer a callow fledgling on the Grand Tour, and she was no schoolroom miss. For better or for worse, each of them had grown and changed, putting childhood behind. Very likely, living so long with Cassandra Pemberton, little Penelope Blayne had acquired as much worldly cynicism as he himself. They were adults now, meeting to discuss something that should have been settled long ago. And now, as then, the power was his. He could do with her as he wished. The trouble was . . . the infinitely vexing trouble was that he had once seen her totally helpless, solely dependent on his actions. This beautiful Golden Girl, raised on the principle of feminine independence by Miss Cassandra Pemberton, had been reduced to a commodity to be bought, sold, or given as a gift. Now he himself had the power of a sultan, the right—the *duty*—to decide her fate.

And he did not want it. Cassandra Pemberton was an evil genie who had cut up his peace and ruined his life. And now was managing to continue her Machiavellian machinations from the grave. There was only one way around this impasse, and he hated it, because it was exactly what the scheming old witch wanted.

Jason Lisbourne, Earl of Rocksley moved out from behind his desk, waving his wife into one of two bergère chairs with caned sides, placed catty-corner to the blazing fireplace, before he sat down opposite her. He was pleased with himself. He had arranged a fine informal setting, rather than speaking to his wife from behind the protection of his imposing desk. Unfortunately, a second examination of Miss Penelope Blayne revealed that her steely, though perfectly composed, features had not softened by so much as an iota.

Annoyed, he said not what he had planned to say, but leaped straight into controversy. "May I ask what spark of madness inspired you to be out on the road on such a night?"

"Lack of funds," his wife shot back. "Your Mr. Farley is such a nipcheese I barely had funds enough to pay the postboys a decent vail. There was nothing left for another night at an inn."

Stunned, the earl opened his mouth, closed it, then said in a completely altered tone, "I assure you he is not *my* Mr. Farley. He is your aunt's solicitor, and he is taking his almighty time settling the many legalities involved in an estate the size of hers. If I had ever dreamed he would not provide you with ample funds, I would have sent you a personal draft on my bank. You have my deepest apologies. As you may have noticed—" Jason paused, cleared his throat while cursing the pixies still pounding anvils in his head. "I did not expect you before tomorrow at the earliest, you see. I had thought my guests would be gone by then." The Earl of Rocksley eyed his wife with some trepidation. There was no sign of whether or not she believed him. Perhaps not, for, as he watched, her chin rose by nearly a full inch.

"My Aunt Cassandra was ill for quite some time," she said. "Until I read her will, I thought she had retained her faculties until the very end. Obviously, I was mistaken."

"I fear that beneath her iron façade your aunt was a romantic."

"Do not be absurd!" Lightning flashed from the clear blue of his wife's eyes.

"Your aunt recalled that you were married, even if you did not."

His countess gasped, half-rose from her chair. One of the hands that had been so tightly clasped together in her lap flew up as if she were about to strike him. Jason raised an eyebrow, but did not stir. "*I* did not recall I was married?" she cried. "*I?* Who is it whose name has been linked to half the ladies in the *ton*, and a vast array of the demimonde as well? Who never wrote to me? Never sent for me? Never acknowledged my exist—"

Jason seized his wife's still-raised arm and lowered it into her lap. "Peace!" he told her, incapable of saying more as long-pent-up emotions warred within. Was it possible she had expected them to live together? All those years while Cassandra Pemberton had urged him to keep his distance, while she had dragged young Penelope Blayne over half the world, the child had thought— The pixies crescendoed into a grand cacophony of thuds; the earl's thoughts deteriorated into profanity.

His inner self rallied, valiantly pushing its way through the pain. Perhaps this revelation was all to the good. The past could not be changed, but it was more easily remedied if she was actually willing—

"All I wish from you," his wife was declaring with the precise enunciation of a barely controlled temper, "is a small cottage in a quiet country village and enough allowance to live in comfort until I come into my inheritance. You may continue to live your profligate life as you please. I will not trouble you further."

Jason Lisbourne leaned back in his chair and regarded his wife from beneath lowered lids. Heaven forbid she should see what he was actually thinking, for he was strongly considering sweeping her off to his bedchamber and finishing what had been started so long ago. She was, he was discovering, rather magnificent, even in her perfectly plain gray dress, her prim hairstyle, and with her arrogant little nose tilted at a deliberately insulting angle toward the ceiling.

"A cottage in the country," Jason mused, stalling for time. "Have you not had enough of country living during the long months of your aunt's illness?"

The chin came down; her eyes as well, though her gaze did not quite meet his. "I have discovered I like the quiet of country living, of waking to the security of knowing one's neighbors, of knowing the routine of the day. I like walking in my own garden, watching the seasons change in the same fields, woods, ponds and streams."

"The world traveler has become a country mouse?"

"Yes," his wife responded on a note of steely determination.

In the sudden silence between them a log hissed, cracked, fell in a shower of sparks. Neither adversary noticed.

Chapter Three

"And now allow me tell you what I have in mind," said Jason Lisbourne to his wife. He settled his hands on the arms of his chair and made a conscious effort to look older and wiser. He *was* older and wiser, dammit, and Earl of Rocksley, a member of the House of Lords (however few times his face had actually been seen there). He was Penelope Blayne's trustee. He had complete power over her. A cottage in the country be damned. She was his wife!

Penelope Blayne Lisbourne, Countess of Rocksley.

It used to terrify him. Somehow, lately, it had come to have rather a nice ring to it. Obviously, the dread age of thirty had scrambled his wits, turned him into an addlepated numskull, a muttonheaded skitterbrain, possibly short a sheet, even queer in the attic.

"I believe," the earl said carefully, "that in her last illness your aunt thought about the things she had missed in her life. She may have regretted never settling down in one place, never marrying or having children. Oh, I don't doubt," he said, holding up his hand to keep his wife from interrupting, "that Cassandra Pemberton treasured her independence, but in the end I think she may have wished something else for *you*. Her infamous will was, I believe, not only an attempt to rectify the harm done to you so long ago, but to secure her own immortality through you."

Jason could see from Penny's blank look that she had failed to understand him, so he plunged inexorably on. "Has it not occurred to you that neither of us is getting any younger? That we should, perhaps, consider the immortality of offspring, for ourselves as well as for your Aunt Cassandra?"

His wife's eyes snapped shut, all color drained from her face. Jason leaped to his feet, striding across the room for the brandy bottle. When she had managed a sip or two, Penelope murmured her thanks, then—quite courageously, he thought—looked him straight in the eye. "You are suggesting, at this remarkably late date, that we live as man and wife."

"In a word . . . yes."

For a moment, Penny's spirit faltered. Her gaze plummeted to the hands in her lap, which were clenched so tightly her knuckles cracked. He dared . . . he *dared* to calmly sit there, after all these years, and tell her he was at last ready to be married. Rakehell was too fine a word. *Beast. Satyr!*

For the first time since her arrival at Rockbourne Crest Penelope Blayne took a good look at her husband. Inwardly, a surge of misgiving swept through her, hopefully unnoticed. There was no doubt about why Jason Lisbourne, Lord Rocksley, had acquired his notorious reputation as a rake. Even with eyes still bloodshot from his dissipation of the night before, he was wickedly handsome. If one did not know of his ill-spent life, it would be so easy to say that the promise of his golden youth had been fulfilled. From his fashionably tousled warm-brown curls down to the shining tips of his Hessians, the Earl of Rocksley was a wonder to behold. He had grown another inch or two, she thought, and filled out, adding as much as two stone, all of which appeared to be muscle. His nose was a bit more aquiline, but his eyes . . . they were still that liquid greenish blue that had hovered so close to her own, making silent promises she had thought she understood, only to discover—

No matter. Here they both were, and the past must be put behind them. They must deal with their world as it was now, not the world of might-have-been.

Penny's gaze dropped lower. There was some satisfaction in noting that he had dressed for the occasion. No country clothes this morning for the Earl of Rocksley. Of course, that was more likely due to the efforts of his valet, who would have heard the tale of her grand disaster of an entrance last night. She flicked another glance at her husband's face. Sadly, Penny concluded that Jason had probably been in no case to choose his own clothes this morning. She could dismiss the thought that the perfectly cut burgundy jacket, the finely embroidered cream waistcoat with gold buttons, or the biscuit-colored pantaloons had been donned in her honor. And, certainly, it was his valet who had fashioned the intricate arrangement of his cravat. Her husband's boots, she noted as her gaze lowered, did not sport the tassels so prized by the dandies of the *ton*.

"Will I do?" the earl inquired in an ominously silky tone.

With as much slow insolence as she could manage, Penny raised her eyes from the earl's Hessians. "I waited, you know," she told him. "I waited until I was eighteen and quite grown up. Then I waited until I was nineteen, certain that you would send for me. And then I made excuses. With all our travels, your letters must have gone astray. Yes, surely that was it. The next time we returned to Pemberton Priory, there would be word. A summons for me to take my place beside you."

Penny plunged on, disregarding the faint sound of the earl drawing a deep breath. "And then, finally, when Aunt Cass told me I must put a stop to my foolish notions, that I must forget you, live my life as if you had never existed, I made a quite determined effort to do so. I presumed"—it was Penny's turn to draw a deep breath—"I presumed you, or perhaps your father before his death, had arranged an annulment. Under the circumstances . . . it would not have been too difficult, not for someone with the wealth and influence of the Earls of Rocksley."

She wanted to tell him more, to twist the knife, recounting the hours she had spent waiting for her hero, her savior, her lover, to remember he had a wife. But she wouldn't, of course. She had too much pride.

"There was no annulment."

"I suppose I made a very fine shield," Penny spat, anger erupting as from a volcano bursting its bonds. "You could rake and riot all you wished and never fear parson's mousetrap. Tell me, my lord, how many times have you waved your marriage lines before an outraged father's face?"

"Nothing quite so dramatic, my dear," the earl responded, calmly enough. "Our marriage lines are locked safely away in the Muniment Room, and I have never actually had to show them. After all, no one would dare question my word."

"You are horrid! I cannot think why I wore the willow—"

"Cut line, dear girl. Oh, I may have been a callow young pup with visions of Camelot, dragons, and fair maidens scrambling what wits I had at that age, but I was not without honor. I, too, fully expected our marriage was a commitment for life. But your darling Aunt Cass—the selfish old witch—warned me off. Evidently, she did not wish to lose you. Or your services. And I, I admit, was glad enough to have a few years of freedom, to rake and riot, as you call it. A man needs to feed his *amour propre,* to spread his wings and preen before the ladies. To allow the gentler sex to knock off the rough edges before we settle down to just one female."

"Ten years, Rocksley? *Ten years?*" Penny sputtered.

He held up his hand, palm out. "Two years ago, all too aware that I had left the business to drag on too long, I wrote to your Aunt Cassandra. And discovered her illness. I could scarce take you away at such a time—"

Fury shook her. "You could not have written to *me*, allowed *me* to make that decision for myself? I was three and twenty, Jason. All of three and twenty."

The Earl of Rocksley stuck out his finely shaped lower lip, much in the manner of a recalcitrant child. People did not respond with anger to Jason Lisbourne. It simply wasn't done. "I remembered you as a schoolgirl, Penelope, looking closer to thirteen than just turned sixteen." Except for that one particular day. And night. A vision of exquisite beauty flashed through his mind, causing his loins to clench.

Ruthlessly, Jason thrust away the image. It did not, after all, bear any resemblance to the woman who now sat before him. "A child, Penelope, that was how I remembered you. Truthfully, it never occurred to me to write to you directly."

"That is it, then," his wife scoffed. "I was an object when you first saw me, and an object I have remained through all these years. And now I am still an object, the only legal device through which you may immortalize yourself. You are saddled with me, a millstone about your neck, and are graciously willing to accept the inevitable. How vastly kind of your lordship to consider my humble self—"

"You are not an *object*!" the earl roared. "Nor were you when we met. You were a sweet and charming child of barely sixteen, all silver-gilt curls and innocent eyes. The epitome of the English schoolgirl."

"Not for long." Unable to continue the battle, Penny sagged back against the rich tan leather of the bergère chair and closed her eyes.

"Penelope. Penny." The earl's fingers closed over hers. His voice was unaccustomedly soft and gentle. "Please remember that this abominable situation was not of our choice. There simply was nothing else to be done at the time. That we are still alive is the miracle. Perhaps we—*I*—might have handled matters in a more proper manner over the past few years since you are grown, but that cannot, now, be rectified. So may we not make the best of the years we have before us?"

"Please—I should like to leave now," Penny whispered, head down. She did not see the earl recoil at her words.

"I thought you had more courage," he taunted, thoroughly stung.

"I do. I have . . . but I must go now. Truly I must," Penny murmured, pushing herself to her feet. "I must *go*!" And she fled the room before hot tears could scald her eyes and run down her cheeks, revealing to all the world what a totty-headed fool she was. Because the thought of being Penelope Lisbourne, Countess of Rocksley, the pinnacle of all her foolish girlhood dreams, was quite too much for that sad resigned spinster, Miss Penelope Blayne, to handle.

* * *

"Hovering, were you?" the earl growled, as, after a single knock, the door inched open and, with exaggerated caution, Gant Deveny peered round the edge.

"Dear chap, the entire household was hovering. Including Mrs. Coleraine, who, I might add, shows no sign of packing her bags and fading quietly into obscurity." Lord Brawley favored his friend with a mocking yet sympathetic grin, then sauntered across the room, neatly flipping up the tails of his jacket before sitting in the chair just vacated by Miss Blayne.

"Daphne?" The pixies returned on a roar of arrhythmic noise, sounding like the triumphant heralding of yet another soul descending into hell.

"The glorious Daphne," Lord Brawley confirmed in sepulcher tones. "Not the best plan to have her here, Rock, if you were expecting your wife."

"I was not expecting Penelope until— Oh, to the devil with it!" Jason groaned. "I've made a rare mull of it, my friend. Nothing to do but brazen it out. Ring for Hutton, will you? I daresay your legs are less like a blancmange than mine."

When the butler appeared, still looking a bit green and bleary-eyed, the Earl of Rocksley told him, "Send Mrs. Wilton and two maids to aid Mrs. Coleraine with her packing. And see that Miss Blayne remains in her room until after Mrs. Coleraine's departure."

"Yes, your lordship." Hutton swayed slightly to the left, his feet remaining planted to the carpet. "Ah, my lord," he inquired, "were you expecting me to put a footman outside her door? And what should he say if miss wishes to leave her bedchamber?"

"Hell and the devil!" the earl bellowed. "Tell Mrs. Wilton to lock the door, if you must."

"Rock!" Gant Deveny hissed. "If you truly wish to be married—of course, it's more likely you do not—then it's best to turn the key on La Coleraine!"

Jason Lisbourne's head dropped into his hands. "Go!" He waved Hutton out of the room.

"*Do* you wish to be married?" Lord Brawley inquired, taking no pity on his suffering friend.

"I am obliged to have heirs," the earl muttered from behind his hands.

"So you married a child, then abandoned her for what—ten years? A fascinating way to set up your nursery, Rock. Don't doubt some academic will wish to write a paper about it."

"You may take your overly long nose and your demmed academic paper and put them both where—"

"Tut-tut, dear boy. I am your friend, if you will recall. Mayhap, if you are particularly kind to me, I might be willing to supervise the lovely Daphne's departure—"

The heavy oak door banged back against the wall hard enough to knock over a brace of candles and send a sheaf of papers on a side table flying onto the carpet. "Daphne's departure, is it?" Mrs. Montagu Coleraine paused halfway across the study, her voluptuous body literally quivering with outrage. Waves of dark hair framed her remarkably patrician face. Her rich chocolate-brown eyes hinted of Italian, or perhaps Spanish, ancestry. As did the generous curves of a figure that could never be called classically English. And yet, the earl would have been the first to state, from his intimate knowledge of the lady, that there was not an ounce of fat on her. Only a year older than Miss Penelope Blayne, Daphne Coleraine had already outlived one husband and was on the lookout for another. She was bright, witty, and usually good-tempered. She was also the great-granddaughter of an earl and considered herself quite eligible to be Countess of Rocksley.

"Is it true then?" the lady demanded. "You are *married*?"

Without looking up, the earl nodded.

"I have given you a full year of my life, and you are married?" Mrs. Coleraine declared most awfully.

Belatedly, Jason Lisbourne rose to his feet. "Believe me, Daphne, my dear, my wife is as angry with me as you are. It would seem I have managed things quite badly all round. I would ask you—indeed, beg you—to return to London.

When I myself know what is happening, I will certainly apprise you of the facts."

"How could you not know *now*?" the lady demanded.

"Believe me when I say I am nearly as confused as you. Until I was named Penelope's trustee, I had nearly forgotten our ancient contract—"

Mrs. Coleraine seized eagerly on his words. "Then you are merely betrothed?"

"No," the earl sighed. "We are well and truly married."

"And you *forgot*?"

Frantically, the earl glanced at Lord Brawley, who was studying the carpet in an obvious effort to hide his thorough enjoyment of the moment. If his friend chose, Jason knew, he could dine out on this tale for the next year or two.

But Gant Deveny was a true friend. He had, of course, risen upon Mrs. Coleraine's grand entrance. He now stepped forward and slipped his arm through hers. "Come, my dear Daphne, you do not wish to remain in a house so much at sixes and sevens. Fly this place, and give the two of them room to tear each other apart. Mayhap you will win out in the end," he added quite mendaciously. "I am certain Rock will not wish to give you up." That sentiment, he felt certain, was not a lie. But it was not as a wife the Earl of Rocksley would keep Mrs. Daphne Coleraine. The lady could, however, take his remark any way she wished.

Fortunately, she seemed somewhat mollified, allowing Lord Brawley to guide her steps from the earl's study. As the door swung closed behind them, the Earl of Rocksley groaned, a loud, tearing growl of frustration and pent-up anger. Why, why, *why* had Fate seen fit to visit him with this disaster? How could one small shopping trip in a faraway land have brought them all to such a pass?

It was, he reasoned, no more his fault than it was Penelope's. They had weathered a true crisis, in which he had shown himself a hero. It was only afterward that he had behaved badly. Filled with a young man's longing for freedom, he had allowed himself to be manipulated by Cassandra Pemberton. And then there was the *other.* He had been mortified by his inadvertent display of lust for a sixteen-year-old girl under his protection as a representative of her family. When the crisis was past, instead of shouldering his new-found responsibilities, he had been so overcome by guilt that he had allowed Cassandra Pemberton's wrath to scare him off. Indeed, he had stood by and let her sail into the sunset with his child bride and felt only a profound sense of relief. The incident in Constantinople was over, with nothing left but to sweep it under the carpet and pretend it had never happened.

Little had he expected to spend the next ten years in the arms of other women, trying to forget the wedding night he had spent in a seraglio under the watchful eyes of Sultan Selim the Third, the grand vizier, the chief black eunuch, and Allah alone knew how many others as well. And yet, in spite of the audience, he had barely left his child bride a virgin.

Jason groaned, as the whole ghastly scene came flooding back.

Above stairs, the thoughts of the Countess of Rocksley matched those of her anguished husband. How, from such a simple, quite innocent, mistake, had things gone so wrong? Each was a member of one of England's finest families; each, intelligent, well educated, and accustomed to the vagaries of traveling in foreign lands. Nothing dire should have befallen them. They were English, were they not? They could travel, inviolate, anywhere, any time.

That day in the Grand Bazaar haunted her. What had she done to bring such disaster upon them all? Was it naivety, random accident, or was it simply because she had been born blond and ravishingly beautiful? A golden child in a land of dark skins, dark eyes, and dark hair?

A tear rolled down Penny's cheek as she remembered, yet again, how it had been.

Chapter Four

Constantinople, August 1802

"Turn about, my dear. Slowly now!" Miss Cassandra Pemberton examined her niece with undisguised satisfaction. The child would do, do very well indeed. Only those far too high in the instep for their own good would question her decision to allow a girl of sixteen to attend an evening reception at the British Embassy. Their many years of travel had fashioned a cloak of elegance and sophistication about Miss Penelope Blayne's slim figure that would be envied by young matrons in their twenties. Ah, yes, Miss Pemberton sighed, a bit embarrassed to realize the emotions she was experiencing were suspiciously maternal.

Briskly, she tweaked one of the tiny white rosebuds woven into Penelope's upswept hair. "You'll do," she decreed aloud, then paused, unable to resist making one last inspection. No, she was not wrong. Penelope Blayne was a vision of loveliness. She wore the white rosebuds nestled in her silver-gilt hair like a proclamation of virginal innocence. Curls, carefully arranged, framed a delicate porcelain face with softly rounded cheeks and small nose. The only flaw was, perhaps, a chin that showed signs of jutting out into what, at best, might be called overconfidence; at worst, stubbornness. This minor imperfection was, however, offset by the stunning beauty of eyes the color of a clear summer sky. Wide and heavily lashed—and surely, Cassandra Pemberton thought, she might be forgiven for allowing the child to darken them slightly so their full beauty might be seen and appreciated.

Because of the peculiar nature of foreign travel, this was not, of course, the first time Miss Pemberton had taken her niece into society. But it was the first formal evening party in the highest circles—albeit in a land far from home—that she had deemed Penelope old enough to attend without censure. Not that Cassandra Pemberton had ever cared a fig for what others thought of her, but Penelope was another matter entirely. Miss Pemberton had plans for her niece that did not include becoming an eccentric spinster forever traveling the globe in search of the Lord alone knew what.

Therefore, she had taken great care in ordering Penelope's dress for the evening. A white muslin of the finest weave, embroidered solely with white rosebuds (with not so much as a pale green leaf allowed to intrude upon the purity). A modest flounce at the hem, with equally modest flounces beneath each puffed sleeve. White satin ribbon, cinched less modestly beneath the bust, emphasized how rapidly the girl was becoming a woman. Penelope's only adornment, other than the white rosebuds in her hair, was a single strand of perfectly matched pearls, glowing softly against her creamy youthful skin.

Breathtaking, Miss Pemberton decided. How fortunate Viscount Lyndon had arrived in Constantinople at this particular moment. Fortuitous, that's what it was.

Cassandra Pemberton turned away to hide her smile. Travel conditions being what they were, even in this new century, it was close to a miracle she had managed to time their arrival in the Levant to such a nicety. As long ago as the previous year she had begun to make discreet queries about which young gentlemen were to make a Grand Tour to whatever parts of the world Bonaparte's visions of conquest had left open to foreign visitors. *Egypt!* Miss Pemberton grumbled to herself, as the iniquities inflicted by the upstart emperor's ambition for conquest diverted her thoughts. How it rankled that they had dared not go to Egypt. All those marvelous pyramids and other wonders of the Nile, lost to them because that monster Bonaparte had the outrageous notion he could bring Western civilization—arts and letters, indeed!—to a heathen land whose days of glory were thousands of years in the past. And yet, as reluctant as she was to admit it, when British troops had helped force the French out, the country had fallen into anarchy and become no fit place for two Englishwomen of gentle birth.

Miss Pemberton sniffed, then recalled herself to the moment. She had turned Penelope out in fine style. Now she need only execute the remainder of her plan. Fortunately, her quest, conducted through voluminous correspondence, had turned up a familiar name among the young men making the Grand Tour in what was left of nations that might be termed "peaceful." Jason Lisbourne, Viscount Lyndon, a distant connection of the Pembertons through his mother's family. The young man's antecedents were impeccable, his prospective wealth prodigious, and he was the perfect age, a scant five years older than Penelope, while she, though a mere miss, could claim a marquess as grandfather. Surely a good enough match for a future Earl of Rocksley, particularly since Penny would, one day, have the Pemberton fortune as her dowry.

But before a proper impression could be made on Lord Lyndon, it was necessary for her niece to negotiate the formalities of an Embassy reception. "Penelope," declared Miss Pemberton in stentorian tones, "you will recall that the ambassador is a Bruce, the seventh Earl of Elgin. I'm told he holds Robert the Bruce's sword at Broomhall, the family seat in Dunfermline. Even though you have heard me—ah—declaim against his rumored destruction of the treasures of the Acropolis, you will grant him the full respect of his title and rank."

"But, of course, ma'am," Penny agreed, all innocence, "for surely he is saving them for posterity, is he not?"

Miss Pemberton sniffed. "And what of Greek posterity, pray tell? If Elgin's men continue at the pace we observed while we were in Athens, there will be nothing left. They were supposed to be making drawings, yet they are loading up every last bit of sculpture they can excavate and have begun to chip the friezes and metopes from the face of the

Parthenon itself. 'Tis little better than rape. It's a wonder only one ship has sunk beneath the weight so far."

Since Miss Penelope Blayne was accustomed to her aunt's plain speaking, she merely offered her aunt an indulgent smile. "I believe we must be off, Aunt Cass. It would not do to keep Lord and Lady Elgin waiting. And I will be good, I promise. Not one single question about his marbles shall pass my lips."

But Miss Pemberton was still standing firm, uncajoled, her stern look very much in place. "Penelope, you will remember what I told you about Lord Elgin's deformity. By not so much as the blink of an eye will you acknowledge that you have noticed. Do you—"

"Aunt! As if I ever would."

"Well," Cassandra Pemberton huffed, "I am sure I cannot imagine how he may look, for dread diseases of the skin are not something with which I am familiar— "

"What of the lepers we saw in Ind—"

"Enough! You will not breathe that horrid word."

"Yes, ma'am," Penny agreed meekly. In a moment the small contretemps was forgotten, with neither lady having the slightest inkling of the major role Thomas Bruce, Lord Elgin, would play in their lives.

Miss Penelope Blayne, eyes shining with delight over her debut into Western society in the exotic city of Constantinople, came close to floating out the door in her Aunt Cass's wake. Her white satin slippers seemed to hover just above the mosaic floor, threatening to launch into a dance at any moment. She was going to a *reception.* Not a musicale, tea party, afternoon card party, lecture, or even an assembly held for the "young ones." She was off to a genuine evening affair at the residence of the "Minister Plenipotentiary of His Britannic Majesty to the Sublime Porte of Selim the Third, Sultan of Turkey."

All was right with the world of Miss Penelope Blayne. There was no frisson of warning, not the slightest hint of a wrinkle in her cocoon of confident security. For how could Penny Blayne, a young bud formed in the gentle confines of

Sussex, England, possibly know she was within days of the end of her innocence?

Jason Lisbourne, Viscount Lyndon, put his quizzing glass to one cobalt-blue eye and regarded Lord Elgin's guests with all the scornful ennui of a young man of one and twenty to a courtyard full of people, most of whom seemed to be twenty or more years his senior. One of the great attractions of his journey to the once great capital of the Byzantine Empire was the tales he had heard of its exotically lovely women. But so far his youthful eagerness had not been rewarded. The women of ancient Byzantium he might have seen, for when the Emperor Constantine moved the capital of the Roman Empire to a city on the Bosphorus—the body of water that divided West from East—he had taken Roman customs with him. But for four centuries now the Ottomans had ruled Constantinople, and Viscount Lyndon found the women swathed from head to toe, all but their huge dark eyes hidden behind curtains of cotton, linen, or fine silk.

There were places he could go to find women, his guides had been quick to reveal, but so far he had not done so. Not that he was unaccustomed to paying for female favors, but somehow a good English tavern wench, or a member of London's demimonde, seemed right and proper. A slave girl in a Levantine brothel did not. He supposed London's light ladies were as close to slaves as made no difference . . . yet he found himself shying away from the local commodities so loudly touted by his guides.

Truly, he had not thought himself so fastidious. What man would not wish to see what was beneath the veil? Certainly, his two traveling companions had been openly eager to embrace the underbelly of Ottoman culture. Arrangements had, in fact, been made. And Jason knew his resolve was weakening. Yet it was possible he might find a rude surprise beneath the veil. Or problems worse than ugliness. The kind that lingered . . . and drove a man mad before they killed. Or caused their noses to disintegrate, as had happened with his Scottish host.

With a curl of his lip, Viscount Lyndon dropped his

quizzing glass. In no hurry to join the milling throng in the courtyard, he leaned against one of the marble pillars supporting the roof of the loggia on which he was standing and continued to examine the scene before him. The foreign residents of Constantinople, unlike their counterparts in England, did not seem to fear the night air. He had to grant there was a certain attraction to an outdoor party, rather like an evening at Vauxhall. The fountains cooled, as well as soothed—some a mere gurgle, others shooting up into the early evening air well above the tallest visitors' heads. And the air was perfumed by flowers, many of which Jason could not name. Marble benches, scattered about in places where one might best view either flowing water or garden flowers, invited intimate conversation.

He would have to leave his refuge soon, get off the demmed pillar and plunge into the crowd, doing his duty as a titled Englishman greeting a host of foreign dignitaries—most of them younger sons—and their plump wives, spotted sons, and ugly daughters. He must smile and shake hands with wealthy merchants and their even more unappealing offspring. Society in Constantinople was far more eclectic than the one to which he was accustomed. But had his father not sent him on this Grand Tour to broaden his education, gain polish in dealing with every type of situation? He must—

Jason straightened off the pillar. Quizzing glass forgotten, he stared at the vision of loveliness who had just stepped out onto the loggia, not twenty feet away. *Exquisite.* The embodiment of the dream every man keeps tucked away in his heart. Hair so pale it might have been made of moonlight. A face to make the angels weep. A gown of virginal simplicity, clinging to the petite but promising figure of budding youth. Stunned, Viscount Lyndon failed to note he was acquainted with the young lady's chaperone, even when the two women turned and walked straight toward him.

The older woman was tall and imposing, an Amazon of a female. Although impeccably dressed in a long column of amber silk, with matching turban, in which gemstones winked in a style a pasha might have envied, her stride was that of a man, strong and confident. Spine straight, shoulders back, she looked more as if she were marching in a military parade than negotiating a marble loggia overlooking Lord Elgin's courtyard. She stopped not three feet from his pillar and looked him up and down. "Lyndon?" she inquired, her sharp gray eyes peering intently up from only slightly lower than his own. In response to his slight bow of affirmation, she flashed a triumphant smile. "I am Cassandra Pemberton. You were naught but a scrubby schoolboy when last we met—Felicity Warrington's wedding, it was. My mother was a Warrington, as was yours. You would scarce remember my dear niece, Penelope, however," she added, turning toward the beauty who hovered like a small moon in the wake of Cassandra Pemberton's sun. "My lord, may I present Miss Penelope Blayne. Penelope, Jason Lisbourne, Viscount Lyndon. Although you are not related by blood, my dear, you are connected to him by marriage."

As the very young lady sank into a deep, and perfect, curtsey, Jason feasted his eyes, even as his heart plummeted to his toes. She was a child, a veritable child. Only a well-known eccentric, such as Cassandra Pemberton, would commit the social *faux pas* of bringing a schoolgirl to such a reception. For although he had not recognized her face from that long-ago wedding, Miss Pemberton's name was legion. Everyone had heard of her unladylike traipsing around the world, dragging her poor niece after her. Into every momentary pause in the *ton*'s scandals Cassandra Pemberton's name would fall. There was always some shocking new story to titillate jaded palates. And, if not, nothing lively minds could invent would be too outlandish to be believed of the peripatetic spinster from Sussex.

Penny stared in wonder at Aunt Cass's previously unknown connection. He was everything her girlish heart had ever dreamed of. From his golden hair and eyes of brilliant azure . . . from his rich brown jacket and cream vest heavily embroidered in gold . . . to his dark breeches, gold-clocked stockings and shiny black evening shoes, he was a young lady's idea of perfection. His face—darkened by what was undoubtedly months in the Mediterranean clime—boasted a regal nose and full inviting lips, though they seemed, as now, all too ready to curl into derision. Oh, dear, what had she done? Why was he looking so . . . so arrogant and withdrawn? Had Aunt Cass presumed, once again? He was, after all, a viscount—

"You must forgive my manners, ma'am," Viscount Lyndon drawled, looking down his nose—though not very far—at Miss Pemberton. "I was startled by Miss Blayne's youth."

"I am turned sixteen!" Stung, Penny interjected herself into the conversation.

And looked a veritable child. The viscount raised his quizzing glass, one enormously magnified, and exceedingly distorted, eye examining her from head to foot. "Are you quite, quite certain, Miss Blayne?" he inquired.

The sweet mockery of his tone was enough to send Penny into battle. There were those who said she had been much overindulged by a doting, though sometimes careless, aunt. It is possible they were correct.

"I saw you standing here, examining the guests," Miss Blayne informed the viscount. "Quite as if you were Zeus himself looking down from Olympus. And 'tis plain Aunt Cass and I are also numbered among the mere mortals attending Lord Elgin's reception. I am quite sorry for you, my lord, for I fear if you scorn the ambassador's guests, you will miss much of the exotic flavor of Byzantium."

Before responding, Viscount Lyndon broke his aristocratic stance long enough to offer Miss Pemberton an adult-to-adult look of condolence. "Byzantium is long gone, child," he announced to Penelope, "its treasures ripped from its palaces and cathedrals and carted off to enrich the cities and manor houses of the greedy, thieving knights of the Fourth Crusade. Most particularly, Enrico Dandolo, Doge of Venice. Did you not know the very walls of St. Mark's are coated in the spoils of Byzantium?"

Penny's chin went up. "Of course I knew, my lord. My Aunt Cass's instruction is never bound by the narrow confines of religious preference. I am well aware that Christians looted Byzantium long before the coming of the Ottomans."

Jason Lisbourne glared, and then his lips, of their own accord, began to twitch. What English schoolgirl could even find Constantinople on a map, let alone have the slightest inkling of its history? Miss Penelope Blayne might look a scant thirteen—except for that figure, of course—but her mind and education might well be the equal of his own.

"Have you just arrived in Constantinople, Miss Blayne?"

"We have barely had time to settle into our villa," she replied eagerly, the clouds clearing from her face as if by magic at this simple offer of a truce, for she was at that age where she could go from child to woman and back to child again in a matter of moments. "We have seen nothing of the city but the limited view from our carriage. I can scarcely wait to see more!"

A slow smile lit the viscount's face. It was like the sun coming out from behind a great black cloud. Penny was dazzled, while Jason Lisbourne was as captivated by her innocent beauty and unfeigned enthusiasm as any other young man might be, particularly one so far from home.

"I believe," he drawled, "that I am able to show you something you would truly enjoy. Miss Pemberton . . . if you and Miss Blayne would be willing to accompany me on a small climb up to the roof? I vow you will find the view most rewarding."

Since Cassandra Pemberton's agile brain could not have devised a better scheme for throwing the two young people together, even if she had sat up half the night attempting to do so, she swiftly accepted Viscount Lyndon's invitation.

"The light is beginning to fade," Jason said as he guided the ladies toward an outside staircase at one end of the loggia, "so we must be quick. I promise you the panorama will amaze you."

" 'Tis not half so high as the tower at Pemberton Priory," Penny scoffed as they shortly found themselves on a flat roof high above the courtyard. *"O-oh!"* Miss Blayne was silenced.

The soft sibilance of a hundred voluble guests drifted up on the sea breeze wafting from the great harbor below. And somehow even the strains of the orchestra had become more mellifluous, magic notes for a night in a land so exotic it seemed almost to be part of a tale in a storybook and not real at all. Beyond the courtyard and the green of the Embassy's parklike setting was a sight even Penny's lively imagination could not have conjured. Not only were they on the roof above the British Embassy, but the entire embassy grounds were on a hill rising steeply above that magnificent harbor known as the Golden Horn at precisely the point where it joined the Straits of Bosphorus.

Enchanted, Penny could only stare in wonder. Everything, as far as the eye could see, was *different*. The shapes of the ships in the harbor, the cut of their sails, made even the familiar sea look strange. And the buildings . . . an undulating array of domes and towers of every size and description spread out before her, solidly covering both sides of the great harbor of the Golden Horn.

"This side of the harbor is the district of Pera," the viscount told her. "Back in the thirteenth century Genoa helped the Byzantine emperors take back the city from invaders and were given this great hill on the far side of the river as a place to live."

"No foreigners to contaminate the city," Miss Pemberton interjected dryly.

"Precisely," Jason agreed. "Thank you very much, we are granting you the right to control our trade, but please live on the other side of the Golden Horn. Soon the Genoese were joined by Jews, Greeks, Armenians, and eventually other Europeans."

"If we are in the foreign quarter," Penny pronounced thoughtfully, "then where is Constantinople?"

"Everything you see on the far side of the harbor is the city of Constantinople," Jason told her. "The capital of Byzantium, the final resting place of what was once the Roman Empire, and now the capital of the Ottoman Empire."

"Very good, Lyndon," Miss Pemberton applauded. "Are you thinking of becoming an Oxford don?"

"Miss Blayne seemed interested," Jason muttered, his youthful pride much stung.

"Oh, I am!" Penny cried. "But are you saying we must cross the harbor to see the city?"

"*Vapurs*—ferries—run constantly," the viscount told her in the superior tone of one who had been in Constantinople for all of two weeks. "Look there"—Jason forgot himself long enough to point—"to the right is the Grand Bazaar. You will, no doubt, be fascinated by the sights there. Though on no account should you go without several footmen to bear you company," he added, turning toward Miss Pemberton. "Constantinople is not the safest place for women, particularly those who go unveiled."

"What are all those grand buildings with the tiny towers?" Penny asked. Not hesitating to follow the viscount's bad example, she pointed toward an elaborate maze of buildings, set on a prominent point directly across the Golden Horn, domes and turrets shining in the red glow of the lowering sun.

"On the left is the sultan's palace, called Topkapi," Jason told her. "The buildings on the right are the Blue Mosque and the Haghia Sophia, which was the cathedral of the Byzantine emperors before the Ottomans converted it to a mosque. And those 'tiny towers,' Miss Blayne, are minarets, where muezzins call the Muslim faithful to prayer."

"Oh, Aunt Cass, when may we go?" Penny burbled. "It is like a fairy tale." She clapped her hands. "We cross the water on a *vapur*"—Penny peeped up at the viscount to see if she had recalled the word correctly—"and, *voilà,* we are in a land of enchantment!"

As Jason Lisbourne looked down at Penelope Blayne, her fragile golden beauty haloed by the brilliant red of the setting sun, he experienced a moment of dizziness, something so foreign to his young but hardheaded nature that he dismissed it as the result of gazing too long at sunlight on the water. He almost offered to escort Miss Pemberton and her charge on their ventures into the teeming streets of Constantinople, but then he remembered the other young men with whom he had made plans. Interesting and intriguing plans.

And Penelope Blayne was so very young. There would

be time, plenty of time, to stand back and wait for her to grow up. Perhaps when she made her come-out, he would take another look. Or possibly not. He would be only three and twenty then and still many years away from wishing to settle down and set up his nursery. A man must, after all, have delicious years of freedom to look back on before he could reconcile himself to being leg-shackled.

He should, of course, suggest that young Penelope cover up her glorious head of spun gilt and her delicate beauty as well. But Cassandra Pemberton would not appreciate his interference, and surely she was tigress enough to protect her innocent cub. With nothing more than a polite social smile, Viscount Lyndon escorted the ladies back down the staircase, where they promptly joined the ambassador's other guests and soon were separated by the inevitable ebb and flow of conversation.

It was a fateful moment, a failure in communication, a fault of youthful carelessness Jason Lisbourne would regret for the rest of his life.

Chapter Five

Before leaving the British Embassy that night, Miss Cassandra Pemberton—who had been called many things, but never a fool—asked Lord Elgin to recommend a guide. And so, on the second morning after the reception, Miss Pemberton and Miss Blayne began their exploration of the ancient city of Constantinople, accompanied by their guide, Faik, who spoke passable English, and a stalwart house servant named Abdul.

As their party approached the array of boats along the edge of the great harbor, Aunt Cass's eyes were sharp, Penny's shining with excitement. For some reason Constantinople seemed so much more *foreign* than India, perhaps because there were fewer European faces, even here in Pera. Perhaps, Penny thought . . . yes, perhaps it was because in India Britain's influence was much greater. Here, it was almost nonexistent. This was the Ottoman Empire, the sultan an absolute monarch. Today they were to drive by the Topkapi Palace, where it was said Selim the Third kept a harem of thousands. Very likely an exaggeration, of course; nonetheless, Penny felt a shiver course through her. Part horror at the mere thought of such a practice; part an almost shameful curiosity, a delicious wonder about what went on in the hidden recesses of that great palace situated at the confluence of the Golden Horn, the Bosphorus, and the Sea of Marmara.

Lately, Penny had begun to wonder with greater frequency about the secret relations between men and women. From what little she had gleaned—mostly from the violent mating of cats, dogs, and farm animals—Penny feared something rather strenuous might be involved. And the thought of the sultan doing whatever it was with so many wives and concubines was perfectly amazing. She should be ashamed of herself for thinking such thoughts, of course. But the day was so lovely, life was so good, Constantinople so exciting. She was on the verge of womanhood . . .

And she had met Jason Lisbourne. Penny cast a quick glance toward her Aunt Cass to see if she had noticed her niece's abstraction. Thankfully, she had not. Miss Blayne heaved a sigh of relief. Aunt Cass was so . . . so *contained.* She could not possibly understand the longings that had insinuated themselves into Penny's life. Not that Aunt Cass had not been a wonder of kindness since her parents had died in a shipwreck on what was to have been a simple sea voyage to Edinburgh when Penny was nine. And she had enjoyed seeing the world—truly she had—but how would she ever find a young man, a suitor . . . a *husband* if Aunt Cass continued to drag her from pillar to post and back again year after year after year?

"You are woolgathering, Penelope," Aunt Cass snapped. "Faik has procured a caïque for us, and you sit there like a lump, as if rooted to the squabs. Come, come, child. If, that is," she added ominously, "you wish to see the city while the sun still shines."

Penny had no problem with distraction on the short trip across the Golden Horn. Surrounded by sails of saffron and bloodred, some jutting out on both sides of a boat like great angular wings . . . with the waterfront echoing with shouts, laughter, and other unidentifiable sounds that cast even the great harbor of Bombay into the shade, Miss Penny Blayne was totally fascinated. Their ferry cast off, the sails snapped up, caught the wind, and they were off, skimming across the harbor as easily as the birds flying high above. *Oh, oh, o-oh!* She was an addlepated nincompoop to think she wished to give this up and settle down. Be ruled by some man, who would control both her fortune and her life. Aunt Cass was right, after all. Freedom was truly marvelous!

If Miss Cassandra Pemberton was surprised to discover,

as they debarked, that their means of transportation was a light English-style carriage, she did not remark upon it. But Penny was, in fact, quite disappointed that nothing more exotic was offered. The vehicle—she was informed through Faik, who acted as interpreter—was the castoff of an undersecretary at the embassy, the younger son of a duke who could well afford to have a spanking new carriage sent out from London. Their driver had been delighted to acquire the young man's breakdown so he could please his many European customers. Ibrahim, the coachman, clad in a striped caftan and somewhat ragged turban, offered Penny a gap-toothed grin and gave his padded leather bench seat a loving pat. Miss Blayne grinned right back. She had long since discovered there were moments when language was completely unnecessary.

Obviously, they were not the only visitors to Constantinople who thought more than one strong male was necessary when exploring the city, for the platform at the rear of their carriage had been expanded to accommodate two. At first glance, Faik and Abdul seemed nearly indistinguishable. Both men sported identical black mustaches and white turbans, and each wore a modest cream-and-tan striped caftan, slit high on the sides, to reveal the very full trousers, called *shalwar,* that were gathered tight to their ankles. They were an awesome, and reassuring, sight, Penny thought, as their two stalwart escorts climbed up behind.

As they drove through the oldest part of the city, Penny hissed, "Look, Aunt Cass—miradors. Like Spain." She nodded toward a series of enclosed balconies that hung out over the street from a row of wooden houses. "Do you think there are ladies hiding behind the lattices peering down at us, even now?"

"It was Moorish influence that brought such a heathen custom to Spain," Miss Pemberton sniffed. "Imagine, enclosing a balcony to keep women from being seen!"

"Surely it is better than keeping them wholly shut inside," Penny ventured.

"Humph-h!" Miss Cassandra Pemberton remained true to her fierce spirit of female independence.

Alas, the closer they came to the Topkapi Palace, the less they could see, for a great crenellated wall cut off their vision, leaving only a view of domes, towers, and an occasional treetop. "We shall have to be content with the mosques, I fear," Aunt Cass pronounced.

At that moment the call of the muezzin echoed from one of the minarets on the Blue Mosque, just outside the palace walls. Their coachman, Faik, and Abdul leapt down from the carriage and bent low to the ground, nearly prostrate, their eyes turned toward distant Mecca. This was scarcely a surprise, as Penny and Aunt Cass had witnessed Muslim prayers many times before, but somehow the ritual took on greater significance as they waited directly in front of the Blue Mosque in Sultanahmet Square, with the once-great church of Byzantium, the Haghia Sophia, directly across the park-like setting. To Muslims, Mecca might be the center of their religion, but Penny felt she would never be closer than this moment to understanding what this foreign religion meant to its people.

In the days that followed, Penny and Aunt Cass drove along the great double city wall, with deep moat, built by Theodosius in the fifth century. Four miles long, fourteen hundred years old, most of its walls, eleven gates and nearly two hundred towers still stood. To Penny, it seemed quite impossible that Mehmet the Conqueror had managed to breach them, bringing a final end to the great Roman-Byzantine Empire. The city's aqueducts, a product of Roman engineering, were nearly as fascinating. They had been bringing water into the city since the fourth century. But after viewing what was left of the Hippodrome, Constantinople's re-creation of the Coliseum in Rome, Penny's interest in antiquities began to wane. Each time they drove by the walls of the Grand Bazaar, Penny would lift her eyes to Aunt Cass in shining hope, and each time be dashed down.

"We will save the Bazaar for last," Cassandra Pemberton pronounced. "If we visit its marvels too soon, we might be tempted to forgo the remainder of Constantinople. And, I daresay, if we go to the Bazaar too frequently, we will need to hire an entire ship to take our purchases back to Pemberton Priory. We might even be as desperate for shipping space as Lord Elgin is for his marbles," she added in a rare display of dry humor. "So we will restrain ourselves, Penelope, my child. We will exercise proper British equanimity and not be so vulgar as to rush to purchase everything in sight."

"Yes, Aunt Cass," Penny sighed, and dutifully turned her attention to yet another grand tomb or mosque or garden or ancient ruin. They were *never* going to get to the Grand Bazaar. Or, if they did, Aunt Cass would rush her through it so fast, the treasures of modern Constantinople would be nothing but a blur.

"Aunt Cass?"

"Yes, my dear?" Miss Pemberton responded absently, intent upon the study of a Byzantine frieze that had suddenly come into sight on the side of ruined wall.

"Have you noticed how everyone stares at us?"

"They are staring at you, child," Cassandra Pemberton returned, not at all disturbed by what was scarcely a revelation. 'Tis not often the people of this city look upon a strange female's face, let alone one of such youth, light skin, and fair hair."

"I have heard that the Circassians in the sultan's harem are fair."

"Wherever can you have heard such a thing?" Miss Pemberton cried. "Who would dare speak to you of harems?"

"Ah . . . I do not remember, Aunt Cass," Penny lied. For only the night before she had shamelessly eavesdropped on Viscount Lyndon and his friends, Mr. Yardley and Mr. Timmons, as they had discussed some of their adventures at a party given by the Dutch ambassador and his wife. The young men had, in fact, teased the viscount about his amorous adventures, for it seemed the women of Constantinople were as enchanted by blond hair, fair skin, and blue eyes, as were the men. There had even been one remark Penny did not quite understand, as it seemed to imply that Jason Lisbourne had been thoroughly shocked to receive amorous offers from men as well as women. Surely, she must have misunderstood.

"I have decided," Aunt Cass pronounced. "Tomorrow we will visit the Grand Bazaar."

Penny threw her arms around her aunt and hugged her.

Through the many years Penny had known her Aunt Cass, there had been more than a few times when she had questioned her aunt's temerity. But reason had always prevailed. She was a child. How could she doubt her aunt's good judgment, the decisions of a head far older, wiser, and more experienced than her own? But within moments after Faik and Abdul had helped them down from the carriage . . . in fact, the very moment they walked through the ornately carved stone gateway into the Grand Bazaar and were confronted by a teeming mass of people unlike anything she had seen before, Miss Penelope Blayne feared they had made a grave mistake.

She had wanted to come—oh, quite desperately she had wanted to come—but the color, the noise, the pungent odors confronted her like some great snarling beast out of legend. Constantinople's Grand Bazaar made London's Covent Garden market look like a quiet day at a village fair. Dutifully, she followed in Aunt Cass's wake, as Faik went before them, clearing a way through the crowd, and Abdul brought up the rear, making a valiant effort to keep the foreign ladies from being jostled.

Penny attempted to take up as little space as possible as she kept her eyes on Aunt Cass's serviceable tan gabardine walking dress and watched the determined swing of Miss Pemberton's equally plain parasol. Gradually, as they moved away from the gate, the crowd thinned a bit, and Penny could see some of the wares being offered along the alleyways of the Bazaar. She even dared raise her eyes to the vaulted ceiling above, which protected both vendors and customers from sun, wind, and rain. When Aunt Cass paused to examine some jewelry, Penny took a deep breath and allowed herself to enjoy the beauty of the intricate gold filagree and the sparkling depths of the gemstones. Yet, in the back of her mind, doubt clung. She would never be as intrepid as Aunt Cass. The Grand Bazaar, despite all its marvels, was not at all like viewing the wonders of Constantinople from the safety of their carriage.

With a wave of Cassandra Pemberton's parasol, their party moved on. Penny's fears disappeared in a welter of sparkling brass and copper, of antiquities ranging from ancient earthenware pots to plates, ewers, trays and goblets that might once have been the property of a Byzantine Emperor. Suddenly, Penny breathed in the familiar odor of leather. But the smell, they discovered as they entered this next section of the Bazaar, was almost the only thing that was familiar. There was no sign of smooth English saddles, belts, and boots. Every bit of leather was crafted into a work of art in designs so intricate Penny could only gape. There were book bindings that took her breath away, and a high-pommeled saddle, every inch embossed in an exotic pattern, that she would have purchased on the instant, if only females were allowed to ride astride. And if such a huge saddle were not so difficult to transport. And if she had any money of her own.

Faik, after finally managing to pry his charges loose from the leather crafts, ushered them into a *han,* one of several open courtyards scattered about the Grand Bazaar. The two women indulged in tea and pastries far sweeter than they were accustomed to, while listening to the soft tinkling rush of a fountain.

"Aunt Cass," Penny inquired after surreptitiously brushing crumbs from her lap, "what was that very odd pipe I saw you examining?"

Penny recognized her aunt's look. It was the one she received every time she asked an awkward question, the one Aunt Cass put on while she thought: *Oh, dear, what shall I tell the child?* Surely, at sixteen, she should be past all that, Penny grumbled to herself.

"That," Cassandra Pemberton responded briskly, "is a hookah. It is for smoking."

"Smoking? How can someone smoke with a device like that?" Penny demanded. Then added, more thoughtfully, "And what do they smoke?"

"I am sure I do not know," Miss Pemberton sniffed, recalling with some anguish the time she had tried it in Morocco, back in the days of her youth and foolishness.

Penny gave her aunt a sharp look and was wise enough to say no more.

As the ladies finished their last cup of tea, Faik and Abdul descended from the gallery above the courtyard, from which vantage point they had been keeping watch. The ladies, after lingering over ancient illuminated texts in the book bazaar, indulged their senses in an orgy of sniffing and tasting as they wandered through an area filled with open sacks of spices and teas. By this time Faik had hired a boy to carry the ladies' packages, but when they arrived at the next section of the Grand Bazaar, it was apparent one child of about twelve years would not be enough. For spread before them were fabrics of every quality and description, from the thinnest, most diaphanous white silk for veils to brocaded silks, interwoven with gold and silver thread. The piles of textiles seemed to go on forever, winding through the labyrinthine corridors of the bazaar in an overwhelming array of color. There were linens and muslins of every weight, velvets of such deep pile Penny could not keep from petting them. Silk satins so heavy they could only be for used for draperies, or perhaps an empress's long, flowing train.

Even Miss Cassandra Pemberton was awed. "We will have to come back," she pronounced. "Obviously, fabrics require a day unto themselves." She waved a hand, which might almost have been described as agitated. "Faik, we will continue on and ascertain what more must be reserved for a special excursion."

"Jewelry?" Penny inquired hopefully.

"Possibly," Miss Pemberton conceded. "I have never cared for it particularly, but you are reaching the age where you will need a few good pieces. And I pride myself that I am knowledgeable enough to tell the genuine article from bazaar fakery." Once again, she waved her parasol, and their small cavalcade moved on.

As they passed by more antiquities, they caught glimpses, through arched colonnades, of sparkling gold, silver, and gems. Yes, there was little doubt jewelry, both antique and newly crafted, would require a separate trip. And then they came to carpets, and Cassandra Pemberton realized it was quite possible she would have to hire at least half the hold of a stout merchant ship to take their treasures back to England. Although carpets, too, would require yet another separate trip, neither Penny nor her Aunt Cass could pass on by. The area was vast, rounded arches dividing the space into smaller rooms, many with domed ceilings. The ladies *ooh*-ed and *aah*-ed and touched the heavy pile, the incredibly tight weave of carpets of every shade from brilliant burgundy and gold to soft pink, blue, and cream.

Penny ran her fingers over a small fringed carpet of primarily azure and biscuit and discovered that it was silk, not wool. Her lips turned up in a whimsical smile. Perhaps this was a magic carpet. If she were to sit upon it and make a wish, where would it take her? Into Jason Lisbourne's lap?

Shocked by such a wayward thought, Penny dropped the carpet, blindly following the direction in which she had been wandering. No pastels in this room. The carpets were dark and masculine, in strong shades of black and red and gold. Carpets for the floors of rooms where only men gathered. They were, somehow, too harsh for female taste.

Penny wrinkled her nose, lifted her eyes from the riotous display of color . . . and found herself alone. She turned, gazing at the many arches lining this particular room. Through which had she come? Which led back to Aunt Cass, to Faik and Abdul? To safety?

The nearest, of course, silly, she told herself, and started toward the rounded arch.

Something descended over her head, over her arms. Rough hands seized her, clamping tight over her mouth and around her waist. The *something* tightened around her face. She couldn't breathe. Her feet lifted off the floor. Penny kicked out wildly and was rewarded with an *oompf* from her captor. And a blow to the back of her head. She knew no more.

Chapter Six

"Faster, man, faster!" Viscount Lyndon barked at his driver, hoping the urgency of his tone would convey his meaning, even if the English words themselves meant nothing. Jason Lisbourne, usually engulfed in the mindless cloak of invincibility common to youth everywhere, was unsure why the urgent tone of Cassandra Pemberton's note should have filled him with dread, but the moment he read it, he had canceled his plans for the evening and set out for Miss Pemberton's villa, situated almost halfway up the southeastern slope of the District of Pera.

The child. Young Penelope. She must be the source of the problem. Nothing else would have reduced Miss Cassandra Pemberton to near incoherence. And he, of course, was the only family connection available. It was only natural she should turn to him, though what he could do—Jason pounded his fist against the carriage frame—he did not know. Surely Lord Elgin . . .

But a half hour later, as Miss Pemberton finished pouring out the whole terrible tale, with wailed interjections—primarily apologies—from Faik, Viscount Lyndon, for the first time in his life, knew despair. He had heard many tales in the last few weeks of the great value placed on beautiful virgins with blond hair and blue eyes. In a city the size of Constantinople, where women were hidden away behind impenetrable walls, the task of finding her was impossible. She was lost.

"Nakshedil, wife of our former Sultan Abdulhamid—may Allah give rest to his soul—is a Frenchwoman," Faik was saying as Jason's attention returned to the conversation. "She was taken by Barbarossa's pirates and given as a gift to the sultan. He was so enchanted with her, he made her one of his wives."

"Aimée de Rivery," Cassandra Pemberton murmured. "I have heard the story. She is still at the palace, then?" she asked, her tone taking on slightly more animation.

"Ah, yes, miss," Faik replied. "She is much respected by the sultan, who has allowed her to teach him her language and bring other ways of the French to the palace."

"Is it possible," Jason asked, "that Miss Blayne might be considered a suitable gift for the sultan?"

Faik shrugged. "Only if she is bought by a man who wishes to gain the sultan's favor." Faik paused, lowered his voice, speaking to the viscount alone. "Miss Blayne is most beautiful, my lord. She would bring a great price. It is more possible her buyer would wish to keep her."

"Should we go to the slave markets?" Jason demanded.

Faik's doleful voice dropped to whisper. "Such beauty would never be sold on the open market."

"Speak up!" Cassandra Pemberton demanded. "She is *my* niece. I wish to know the worst of it."

So Jason told her, somehow finding calm, coherent words to outline the seriousness of the situation, while managing to leave some lingering hope. "I will go directly to Lord Elgin," the viscount assured her. "He will, I know, initiate every diplomatic channel that might be useful. And Faik will begin inquiries among the guides. There have to be rumors about what happened to her. She is too great a treasure for someone not to let a tongue slip, bragging of today's work. I assure you, ma'am, everything possible will be done. I pledge myself to your service."

For the first time in her life, Miss Cassandra Pemberton knew what it was to be grateful to a man. This boy, who had barely reached his majority, was revealed as more of a man than any she had previously encountered. Her eyes filled with unaccustomed tears. Her head dropped into her hands, and the sobs came at last.

Viscount Lyndon, after calling for Miss Pemberton's

maid, took his leave, sweeping Faik along with him. When seated in the carriage, the viscount turned to the guide. "I am a liar, am I not, Faik? There is no hope at all."

"Sometimes Allah is merciful, my lord," Faik intoned.

There were some who might say God had been merciful to Aimée de Rivery, Jason thought, but a position as one of the wives of the Sultan of the Ottoman Empire was far from the life planned for the French schoolgirl. And it most assuredly was not the life intended for Penelope Blayne. Yet any fate for a captured beauty, other than being an odalisque of Sultan Selim the Third, was worse.

Jason Lisbourne closed his eyes, rested his chin on his fist, and wondered if Lord Elgin would be as adept at locating lost maidens as he was at "rescuing" Greek antiquities.

Penny roused to the horror of finding herself encased in a tomb. All was dark, she could not move. Yet she *was* moving. The wiggling and jiggling, the close confinement, brought on a bout of nausea, which she firmly repressed. She was so tightly wrapped up that breathing was nearly impossible, and the thought of being ill under these circumstances was too horrible to contemplate.

Tentatively, she flexed her fingers and toes—ah, they worked!—then forced her mind to *think*. The Grand Bazaar. Carpets. That was it. She was rolled up in a carpet, being carried over someone's shoulder. *She must scream!* But when she tried to draw breath, she encountered carpet fibers that clogged her nose and filled her mouth. She managed little more than a muffled squeal before the effort tumbled her back into unconsciousness.

A thump woke her. The dizzy whirl of the unrolling carpet. The blessed rush of air. She lay quite still, struggling to find her wits; yet, when the world steadied, she was afraid to look. Whatever awaited her here in this room could not possibly be good.

Two men dragged her to her feet, held her up between them. Although she could not understand a word being spoken around her, pride and unsquelched curiosity forced her head up. She stuck her chin in the air and glared at the man who seemed to be giving the orders. Richly dressed, from the broad turban above his bearded face to his heavily embroidered gold satin robe, he lounged on a brocaded divan set on a raised dais. His dark eyes assessed her with a gleam Penny had never before seen in a man's eyes. Part hard-headed business, she guessed. And the other? She suspected it was that unknown—lust.

Hands—all-too-willing hands—ripped at her gown. Penny screamed and fought. Laughing, the men brushed aside her feeble efforts with insulting ease, quickly finishing their task. Chemise, garters, stockings, half boots. Most horribly humiliated, Penny stood before her captors, with one arm clutched over her breasts, and one small hand splayed over her most private part. She could feel a flush rushing up from her toes to stain her cheeks and dizzy her mind. This could not be happening. It simply could not. She was not here. She must have sampled one of the hookahs in the bazaar, and this was all a mad hallucination.

By some miracle, her degradation was brief. After having his two henchmen turn her slowly around so he could inspect every inch, the man on the dais gave a nod of satisfaction and barked a command. An older woman scurried forward and threw a linen robe around Penny's shoulders. The man on the dais waved his hand and two guards, armed with long curved swords dangling from their belts, seized her arms. Penny found herself trailing after the older woman, her feet skimming the floor of the audience chamber. Behind her, she heard the chink of coins. No doubt the sound of her captors being well rewarded for their efforts.

As they followed the older woman across a courtyard, the guards slowed their pace, allowing Penny's feet to touch the tiles, an intricate mosaic so hot she was thankful for the drops of moisture spilling onto the walk from the central fountain. As they continued on in the shadows of a colonnaded loggia, Penny was actually grateful for the strong hands holding her up, for pride dictated she not fall to her knees, and she very much feared she could not stand by herself. The sun spots, which had danced before her eyes as they crossed the open courtyard, had not gone away. They flitted before her, like a legion of fireflies.

She must bear up! But despair shook her. This afternoon had been the worst of her life, and she greatly feared it would only grow worse.

The older woman swept aside heavy velvet draperies hanging over an archway, then seized Penny's arm in a grip almost as strong as the guards' before waving the men to positions on either side of the arch. Inside, the steaming, moisture-laden air hit Penny like a blow. Head swirling, she staggered. More hands clamped down on her arms, and, suddenly, Penny found herself seated on a surprisingly plain wooden stool in a setting so exotic she could not quite take it in. Scattered about the room were women with skins of every shade, from midnight black to brown to warm tan. There was even one with skin almost as pale as her own. Some of the women were sitting on stools exactly like her own. Others perched on a stone dais near the center of the room, a few with small children at their feet. Others lounged on stone benches along the walls. Some of the women wore thin robes of fine white linen, transparent from the dampness. Others wore nothing at all.

Thoroughly shocked, Penny ducked her head . . . until, at last, simple curiosity triumphed over her innate English modesty. She raised her eyes, blinked, and took another look. The misty vapors filling the room originated from four huge sinks set against the walls. Above each one, a large pipe poured out what was most certainly hot water. *Merciful heavens!* This was a bathing chamber! Perhaps not so very different from the olden days in Bath, Penny reasoned, for Aunt Cass had told her that bathing in the nude, even mixed sexes, had once been the custom in Bath's warm sulphurous springs. And had not the Romans spread their intricate plumbing designs to the East, as well as to the West? Constantinople was, after all, the final capital of the Roman Empire.

For a few moments Penny was so fascinated she almost forgot the seriousness of her situation. Until a bevy of hands stripped off her robe and a bucket of startlingly hot water sluiced over her head. She screamed. And was instantly mortified that she had let these women see her fear.

It wasn't fear! Truly, it wasn't. She was simply startled.

Penny only had time for one swift glance, reassuring herself that the male guards had truly stopped outside the velvet draperies, before three women, clad only in linen towels wrapped round their waists, attacked her with sponges so rough they reminded her of the time she had fallen into a clump of raspberry bushes. Penny squirmed, protested, was ignored. Another bucket of hot water poured over her. Once again, the loofahs attacked. Her skin was beginning to turn the shade of a cooked lobster. Tears filled her eyes. This could not possibly be happening. Not to Miss Penelope Blayne, of Sussex, England. Not to Penelope Blayne, who had traveled the world, inviolate behind the protection of wealth and privilege.

At last—after Penny suffered the humiliation of having every square inch of her body scrubbed by strangers—the ignominy of the bath was over. No, not quite. For the drying process was nearly as intimate. When she was finally offered a dry white linen robe, she was so grateful, her tears spilled over. To her surprise, many of the women gathered round, making soothing sympathetic sounds. A huge brass tray, piled high with fruit and pastries, appeared, as if the slave who brought it had been waiting for the pale foreigner to finish her bath. Several of the women continued to hover, offering Penny tidbits from their own fingers, their faces anxious, hopeful, urging her to eat.

Lacking a mutual language, was this the only way the women could say, "Courage, take heart"? Touched, in spite of her fear and despair, Penny accepted a sweet pastry, which melted in her mouth and sent an instant surge of energy to her flagging spirits. By the time she had nibbled a date and sampled two more pastries and a cluster of grapes, her mind was beginning to return from the pit into which it had plunged.

Aunt Cass must be frantic. To whom would she turn for help? Lord Elgin, Viscount Lyndon? Would Faik have any idea how to find her?

Would she ever see family or friends again? Or was she destined to live out her life like the other women in this room, cut off from any society but their own?

Except, of course, for occasional intimate encounters with their lord and master?

Penny had no illusions. She was not that naive. She was in a harem. And it was very likely she was there to stay.

In all of his twenty-one years Jason Lisbourne had encountered few true challenges. He had moved serenely through a life filled with more love and understanding than most young aristocrats of his time. His entrance into Eton and Oxford had been assured from birth; he enjoyed women without suffering any of the pangs experienced by some of his friends. Everyone around him knew he would one day be the eighth Earl of Rocksley, possessor of an old and venerable title, and treated him accordingly. A long line of ancestors, noted for not frittering away their funds on frivolous women or even more frivolous pastimes such as games of chance, had increased the Lisbourne fortune until it was one of the greatest in the land. In short, from the moment the expensive London doctor had handed him to the maid standing by with lace-edged linen towels, a silver bowl of warm water, and finely embroidered swaddling cloths, life had flowed remarkably smoothly for Viscount Lyndon.

Now, for the very first time, he was faced with a challenge worthy of a knight of old. There was a fair maiden in distress, and he, Jason Victor Granville Lisbourne, Viscount Lyndon, was going to rescue her. Though, at the moment, the how of it quite escaped him.

When Lord Elgin had, at last, been granted an audience with the sultan's vizier, he readily agreed to the viscount's presence at his side. Lord Lyndon was, the two men reasoned, a connection of Cassandra Pemberton and, in an effort to impress the totally male society in which they found themselves, would be presented to the Grand Vizier as head of her family. But the vizier, the Ottoman equivalent of prime minister, had merely looked askance at the two noble

British petitioners and barked words that had been translated as: he was distressed to hear of the young lady's disappearance, but even more distressed that Lord Elgin should think he or his magnificence, Sultan Selim the Third, could possibly have knowledge of such an outrage.

So now Jason sat alone, slumped on a divan in the main salon of the villa he and his friends had leased. He had sent the others off on their evening adventures without him. How odd to discover, after twenty-one years, that he had more substance than he had thought, for somehow he could not enjoy himself while God alone knew what was happening to little Penelope Blayne. Why she had become his responsibility, he was not certain. His connection to Cassandra Pemberton was tenuous, at best. But thoughts of the lost girl haunted his days and his nights. He had to get her back. It was his duty.

And, yes, he groaned to himself, his self-esteem demanded it as well. No foreign bastard was going to steal a woman under the protection of Jason Lisbourne! And if his noble fervor was increased by the young lady's sheer beauty, as well as the lively spark in her eye, was that not a requisite ingredient for a knight rescuing a fair maiden?

"My lord, you have a visitor," the majordomo announced, a bit dubiously. "The man Faik."

"My lord." Faik, hard on the majordomo's heels, salaamed, then crossed the room to stand before the viscount. He stood tall and proud, his dark skin highlighted by the room's flickering oil lamps, augmented by a single brace of wax candles. "There is a new rumor, lord. A mere thread, but it is spreading through the bazaar quarter like fire or a plague."

Jason sat up straight, all attention. "Quick, man, tell me!"

"It is said that Mustafa Rasim, a merchant of great wealth, has long wished control of all the poppy fields in the eastern provinces. Such a gift would grant him riches and power beyond all but the greatest men at court."

"Yes, yes, get on with it, man!"

"It is said that Mustafa Rasim has just given a gift of

great price to the sultan, a foreign virgin so fair her hair could be spun from moonlight. A very young woman of great beauty."

"By God, that lying vizier vowed they did not have her!" Jason cried, bounding to his feet.

"He did not, lord. The girl was only given to the sultan today."

"Today? She has been gone for nearly a fortnight!"

"Yes, lord, but it would have been necessary to prepare her—"

"*Prepare her?* What does that mean?" the viscount barked.

"She must be properly bathed and dressed, lord. Her—ah, body hair must be removed. She must be taught how to give obeisance . . ." At the horrified look on Viscount Lyndon's face, Faik's voice faded to a halt.

"Body hair?" Jason inquired faintly.

"Hair is allowed only the head, my lord," Faik murmured, fixing his gaze on a point over the viscount's left shoulder.

"Good God," the viscount breathed.

"Is not so bad, my lord. The women use a paste of *rusma* and lime, which they apply to—"

Jason held up his hand. "That is quite enough, Faik. More, in fact, than I wish to know. Pray tell, what else must Miss Blayne learn?" he added in a tone that could only be termed ominous.

"To crawl up from the foot of the sultan's bed, how to bring him pleasure—"

"Stop!" Jason pounded a fist into his palm. "Dammit, Faik, there has to be some way to get her out. Tell me how!"

The stalwart guide shook his head. "First, my lord, we must know she is truly there. I can think of only one way to be sure."

"And that is?"

"The only women from the outside who may go into the harem and come out again are merchants, those who sell their wares to the sultan's women. They are mostly Jews, my lord. They are called ‘bundle women,’ because they carry great bundles of goods.”

“Tell me where to find one, Faik,” was the viscount’s eager reply. “Just tell me where to find one of these ‘bundle women.’ ”

Chapter Seven

Miss Penelope Blayne had indeed learned a great many things in her twelve days as an odalisque in the harem of Mustafa Rasim. A brisk swat on her bottom and a hard shove to her back had soon taught her the wisdom of mastering the art of prostrating herself. Sharp raps on her knuckles taught her to use only the fingers of her right hand when attempting to eat without knives, forks, or spoons. She learned how to apply kohl around her eyes, how to wash her hair with a special clay mixed with rosewater, lavender and rosebuds. How to apply a beauty mask made from dates and goat's milk. She was, however, still working on mastering the skill of walking on the exceedingly high wooden pattens the women wore when negotiating the slippery floors of the bathing chamber. Most of all, she learned to do as she was "told" by the actions of the women and eunuchs surrounding her.

Her degradation was complete, Penny decided, on the second day of her captivity when two older women applied a paste to all the hair on her body except that on her head. Even her nostrils were not exempt. Nor, to her total mortification, were those parts where no one's hand should go. When the horrid-looking mess was scraped off, to Penny's astonishment, her body hair came with it. She was now as naked as it was possible to be. Surely this was as vulnerable and exposed as a female could get. In the midst of a crowd, she was alone. No one spoke English, French, or Italian. Penny tried them all. And, in spite of the languid luxury of her prison, she might as well have been incarcerated in the deepest dungeon. Like the lost princes in the Tower, she would never be seen again.

Nor was she spared shocks beyond the imagination of her maidenly innocence. Exposing her mind, she discovered, was even more degrading than exposing the full nakedness of her body. Beginning on the fourth day of her captivity, she watched in stunned silence as detailed demonstrations—employing the services of the harem's less mutilated eunuchs—taught Miss Penelope Blayne that hands did, indeed, wander to very intimate places. *Dear God, was this what men and women did together?*

These experiences led to several inevitable conclusions. Penny eyed the scimitars hanging from the guards' belts and did the only thing a sensible sixteen-year-old could do. She submitted. And prayed most heartily that Aunt Cass had not given up hope. That Lord Elgin would help. And Viscount Lyndon. In her dreams the golden-haired Jason Lisbourne became her very own knight-errant, the forlorn hope to which she clung, even knowing, in her heart, how foolish it was to dream of rescue.

There were odd moments, however, that had their attractions, as much as Penny scolded herself for enjoying anything this lavishly appointed and scented prison had to offer. Having her body massaged with scented oils was an astonishingly pleasant experience, once she got over the initial shock. And the food was surprisingly delicious. Small pastries filled with lamb, cheese, or spinach. Rice dishes, vegetables cooked in olive oil, and eggplant served in a variety of tasty ways. And always an assortment of fruits and exotic sweets, including some so chewy they took quite five full minutes to eat.

By the time the day came when there was great excitement in the air—much hustling and bustling in the normally lazily quiet women's quarters, featuring whispers, giggles, and sly looks—Penny was beyond shock. If this great to-do involved herself, it could only mean one thing. And *that* she resolutely shut from her mind. Impossible as it seemed, at that moment she would have chosen to remain a slave in the seraglio for the rest of her life to being thrust once again into the notice of her captor, whom she now knew was called Mustafa Rasim. She could not, positively could not, do *that* with him!

But she would. Most certainly she would.

If she did not wish to be put in a sack and thrown into the Bosphorus or, even worse, be given to a whoremaster in one of the city's brothels, she would do what was expected of her. That had been made perfectly clear by the only words of English, haltingly spoken, she had heard since she had been dumped at the feet of Mustafa Rasim. Though some might say Miss Penelope Blayne suffered from a flaw in her stout English character, Penny discovered she had something in common with the legendary Aimée de Rivery. Sixteen was too young to die.

So after suffering yet another bath, followed by more massage with redolent oils, she allowed herself to be dressed. First, diaphanous azure silk *shalwar,* embroidered in gold, the full drawers revealing more than they concealed. Then a smock of white gauze, with long flowing sleeves, almost medieval in style, followed by a fitted waistcoat of elaborate royal-blue brocade, fringed in gold and fastened with a pearl button. Next came a robe of the same diaphanous azure as the *shalwar,* followed by a wide girdle of shimmering gold, with gems set among the elaborate blue-and-red embroidery. Penny was quite certain that even two layers of the fine silk did not constitute sufficient covering to maintain her modesty.

One of the women threw a nearly transparent veil of white silk over Penny's head, while another placed a *kalpock,* a small raised cap of white satin covered in pearls and diamonds, on top of it. A third woman stepped forward to tweak her veil in place, fastening it with a loop to one of the pearls on the satin cap. All three women stood back, nodding and smiling, plainly pleased with their handiwork. Penny, filled with misery, could only follow blindly as the women led her toward the draperies covering the archway onto the loggia.

She was the virgin sacrifice, going to her doom.

But not quite yet.

Mustafa Rasim, resplendent in a robe of heavy scarlet silk embroidered in gold and silver and studded with pearls, and an immense turban from which glittered a ruby almost large enough to be called a third eye, merely frowned as he examined Miss Penelope Blayne from head to foot before giving a sharp nod of satisfaction. A pink *feradge* was suddenly dropped over Penny's head, enveloping her completely, leaving only a tiny slit for her eyes. And then she was whisked into a litter, the women who had accompanied her from the harem demonstrating, with gestures, how she should recline among the cushions. Curtains swished shut around her, cutting off light, air, but not all hope. She was going *outside*? *She had been found.* Ransom paid, she was going home!

The litter jerked, rose off the floor, began to move. Surely, surely, this meant she was being freed. Oh, dear. Poor Aunt Cass was going to be so shocked by her costume!

After days inside the seraglio, the heat, the smells, the noise of the streets assaulted Penny's senses. Oh to be once more in her beloved Sussex, in that quiet, gentle green countryside. She would never venture away from home again.

It finally occurred to Penny's numbed mind that she was alone in the litter. There was no one to scold if she peeked out to see where she was. A few moments later, she gasped and let the curtain fall, for what she had seen was familiar. Not the harbor and a ferry, as she had hoped, but the Blue Mosque in Sultanahmet Square, with the walls of the Topkapi Palace rising behind it. Her heart plummeted. What a foolish child she was to believe, even for a moment, that this tale would have a happy ending. Too appalled to cry, Penny sat, stiffly quiet, while her bearers—eunuchs from the harem of Mustafa Rasim—passed through the well-guarded gates of the Topkapi Palace, home of Sultan Selim the Third, ruler of the Ottoman Empire.

When the litter came to a rest, the curtains were thrust back and two pairs of hands reached in to help her up. Penny did not care where she was, or why. All that pounded through her head was that this was not home. There was no

Aunt Cass, no Jason. No rescue from the nightmare into which she had fallen.

She was aware she was in an audience chamber, that someone of great importance sat on a great divan of gold, set on a raised dais. A someone with a long black beard, dressed more magnificently than Mustafa Rasim, his sleeveless outer robe edged in sable and an aigrette of diamonds sparkling in his white turban. Even the dais on which his gold throne rested was higher and more ornately decorated than the one her captor had sat on the day she was stripped naked before him. Was that to be her fate once again? Barely visible through the slit in her *feradge* was Mustafa Rasim, making his obeisance to the Great Man on the broad gold throne. Her captor stood upright and began to speak. Penny, fearing the worst, retreated inside herself, seeing nothing, hearing no one.

Suddenly, the *feradge* disappeared in a rustle of silk. Exposed to the view of the fifty or more men in the audience room, Penny stood frozen. Truthfully, garbed as she was, she felt almost as naked as if she were indeed wearing nothing at all. A sharp shove on her back brought her momentarily to life. Automatically, as she had learned over her near fortnight in captivity, Penny prostrated herself before the Great Man, palms flat on the floor, forehead touching the tiles, backside up, knees tucked under. A ridiculous position. She hated it.

And then, with the aid of the eunuchs, she was on her feet, being motioned forward to the foot of the dais. The Great Man—the sultan himself?— waved his hand, one of the eunuchs unfastened her veil. The Great One nodded, the veil was replaced. A giant black man paced forward. Even in her near stupor Penny recognized that his garments were even finer than Mustafa Rasim's. She also noted that her captor was looking exceedingly pleased with himself. Whatever had just happened must have gone the way he had planned.

Numbly, Penny followed the magnificently dressed black man, with two eunuchs close behind—not the same men who had accompanied her litter. Once again, she was alone amid complete strangers. Their route, along yet another arched colonnade, was short. Penny was ushered into a relatively small chamber comfortably furnished with a divan and many large colorful cushions. The giant black man, wearing a white headdress even taller than a shako, reclined upon the plumply upholstered divan. Penny stood. The eunuch guards remained outside the open archway, which was covered by a curtain of rose-red damask.

"Parles-tu français?" the giant inquired, speaking the familiar French one might use to a child.

Penny was so delighted to hear words she understood, she nearly fell to her knees and kissed the hem of the giant's elaborately embroidered robe. And recognized on the same instant that her mind had been shockingly affected by her twelve days in captivity. The proud, independent, carefree Miss Penelope Blayne was already fading into a person from another lifetime. Horrified at her weakness, Penny thrust out her chin, straightened her shoulders, and informed this man that she did indeed speak French.

"You are in the Topkapi Palace," he told her. "A gift from the merchant Mustafa Rasim to his magnificence, Selim, sultan of all lands of the Ottomans. You are an odalisque. Do you understand this word?"

"A slave?" Penny ventured.

"More than a slave," the black giant replied, with a look that indicated he questioned her intelligence, or decried the ignorance of foolish foreign females. "I am the Kizlar Agha, the Chief Black Eunuch," he announced. "I am master of the Sultan Selim's seraglio. A man of great power. A man to be obeyed. A man to be feared. Do you understand?"

Penny nodded, for the moment, too intimidated to speak.

"You are now part of the sultan's harem. You will learn to serve the wives of the sultan and the women who are his favorites. You will also learn how to please the sultan, if it should ever come to pass that he wishes to honor you with his presence. Do you understand?"

"Yes, Excellency," Penny managed. There was nothing in his words she had not come to understand during her time with the women of Mustafa Rasim. Events there, even without a mutual language, had been made all too clear.

"Your name is now Gulbeyaz. Rose White. You will answer to it at all times. *Gulbeyaz,*" he repeated. "You will do as you are told, not only by me, but by the other eunuchs, by the sultan's wives and favorites, and by the more experienced odalisques. A golden treasure you may be, but you have much to learn. Anyone here may command you. Is that understood?"

"Yes, Excellency."

"The Valide Sultana, the sultan's mother, is the great lady here. You will kiss her hand, you will prostrate yourself before her. The wife of our former sultan, Nakshedil Sultana, is also of great importance. It is she who has taught us to speak French."

Aimée de Rivery! Penny's hopes soared. Surely—

"To Nakshedil Sultana, you will not prostrate yourself. She does not care for such formalities. You may, if she indicates she wishes it, kiss her hand."

She would kiss her feet, Penny thought, if only the French sultana would help her get out of this place! But what a slim hope. If Aimée de Rivery had not been able to get herself out, how could she help anyone else? But, then, perhaps after . . . after she had borne a child, there was no going back. Perhaps after even one night there was no return to the Western world, to the green meadows of Sussex, to the cold and haughty eyes of the *ton.*

"You are now the property of his magnificence, the Sultan Selim," declared the Kizlar Agha, rising to his feet. "You will put away all childish thoughts of the world you have known. You are the odalisque, Gulbeyaz. You are here to stay until life leaves your body." He waved her toward the door in a gesture not dissimilar to a farmer shooing chickens. "Go now. The guards will take you to the seraglio, where you will do as you are told. Do not forget!"

Penny nodded and, almost sightlessly, pushed her way through the damask curtain. There was no hope. At sixteen, her life had come to an end. Silently, forlornly, she allowed the eunuch guards to lead her away.

* * *

Miss Cassandra Pemberton's temper, usually well contained by the certainty of her power to control the world around her, grew progressively more uncertain as the length of her niece's disappearance approached one month. Assaulted by guilt, her confidence shattered, she was reduced to taking out her frustration on the two gentlemen who were making the greatest effort to help, Lord Elgin and Viscount Lyndon.

"Your reliance on something called 'bundle women' is absurd," she cried, brandishing her plain tan parasol as she paced the exquisitely knotted carpet in the ambassador's reception room. "You must send another petition to the Grand Vizier, demand an audience with the sultan. If you will not, then I must go myself!"

"No!" "That you will not!" Both men spoke at once.

"Miss Pemberton," the viscount said, containing his youthful anger with some difficulty, "you will only succeed in doing more harm than good. We are trying to conciliate the Grand Vizier, not incite his fury. We must wait until one of the bundle women reports that she has actually seen Miss Blayne in the sultan's harem. Only then do we dare challenge the vizier."

"Believe me, Miss Pemberton," Lord Elgin added, "we are very much on sufferance in this empire so much larger than our own. The sultan may have welcomed our help in driving Bonaparte out of Egypt, but, partly thanks to the dratted Aimée de Rivery, he is, at the moment, more inclined to favor the French than the English."

"But you tell me women have no power," Miss Pemberton shot back, glaring.

The ambassador, wearied by Miss Pemberton's constant nagging, minced no words. "Aimée de Rivery gained her power in a manner I doubt you would wish to emulate, ma'am."

Cassandra Pemberton gasped. Viscount Lyndon turned sharply away to hide his face. And then, because he had grown considerably older and wiser during the anguish of the past month, Lord Lyndon mastered his emotions and managed to address Penny's Aunt Cass with both sympathy and sincerity. "I promise you, ma'am, the moment we hear Miss Blayne is definitely inside the sultan's seraglio, Lord Elgin and I will be on our way to the palace." Though how they would pry young Penny loose from her imprisonment the viscount could not yet imagine.

Hastily, Lord Elgin rang the bell for his majordomo. Miss Pemberton found herself ushered to her carriage with the ambassador's assurances—undoubtedly insincere, she grumbled to herself—still ringing in her ears. But Lyndon was showing far more bottom than she had expected in a gentleman so young. Yes, if anyone could rescue her dear Penny, it was Jason Lisbourne.

A tear coursed down Miss Pemberton's cheek. She, who had vowed never to cry like a silly girl, was once again on the verge of being awash in saltwater. *Oh, Penny, dearest child, is there any hope left? For I fear the men do not think so.*

For Gulbeyaz, the White Rose, newest odalisque in the seraglio of Sultan Selim—ruler of an empire that stretched from Russia through Arabia to North Africa, and from Greece to the Caspian Sea—there were more lessons. She learned to walk more daintily, with steps that seemed to float above the tiles. She prepared coffee over and over again until she earned a nod of approval from the Kizlar Agha himself. She continued her lessons in the other skills necessary to an odalisque, not all of them to do with lotions, potions, and scenting her clothes. In short, Miss Penelope Blayne studied humility and the acceptance that women are placed on earth solely for the pleasure of men.

Blessed with intelligence and the resiliency of youth, Penny conquered her shock, and as one day passed into the next, she raised her eyes and attempted to make sense of this exotic, indolent life, as walled off from the Ottoman Empire as it was from her beautiful countryside so far away in England. She even acquired two new friends, Ayshe and Leyla, dark-haired, dark-eyed beauties of about her own age, who took her in hand and introduced her, by way of gestures, giggles, grimaces, and groans, to the ways of the seraglio outside the hours of their "training."

Yet, in spite of being in the midst of the restricted life of the harem, Penny still found it difficult to imagine that these women would never see the outside world except through a latticed window. They would never go shopping in the Grand Bazaar, never see a play they did not perform themselves. They would not know the thrill of riding a ship under full sail, the wind blowing their hair. They would not dance and flirt or have the opportunity to choose a mate. They would never be seen by any male other than the sultan and their eunuch guards.

With no society but their own, the sultan's women were forced to improvise. Their amusements ranged from fortunetelling to childish games. Some told stories, others wrote poetry. Almost all enjoyed the lush gardens with gilded gazebos, ponds with colorful fish, the sounds of nightingales, canaries, and doves overlaid by the cries and squawks of parrots, macaws, and peacocks. And many liked to peer out the latticed windows facing the Bosphorus, watching ships come and go, the only sign there was a life outside the seraglio. Still others, having long since given up hope of becoming a wife or even a favorite of the sultan, settled onto their cushions, a hookah their only comfort, dreaming away the days of their confinement. Still others, Penny discovered, even more thoroughly shocked than by her lessons in how to please the sultan, found pleasure with the eunuchs or with each other.

She would never adapt, Penny vowed. Never accept this was to be her home for the rest of her life. There had to be something more for her. There simply had to be.

Jason. Dearest Jason. Somehow, during her time of trial, this young man Penny scarcely knew became an intimate friend. Her dream lover, who would surely rescue her from her terrible fate.

He would, he would. She knew he would.

Chapter Eight

The bundle woman was quite certain. She had seen the English miss in the Grand Bazaar. How could she not notice such a fair young virgin? And, yes, young master, the new odalisque in the sultan's seraglio was the same girl, there was no doubt. The Jewish woman, obviously sympathetic, also imparted a second bit of helpful information—a custom that, to his credit, took Jason Lisbourne aback only for a moment. If what the woman told him was true, there might yet be a way out of this coil. Both the bundle woman and Faik left the villa of Lord Lyndon much pleased by the gold in their purses, with promise of far more to come if the woman's information proved true.

But even for the British ambassador who had managed to get approval from the Ottoman Empire for removal of marble friezes from the Parthenon in Greece, an appointment with the Grand Vizier was not easily granted. Particularly when neither the Grand Vizier nor His Magnificence, Sultan Selim, wished to hear what Lord Elgin undoubtedly wished to say. But the day came when excuses waned and the matter could no longer be postponed. Lord Elgin and Lord Lyndon were granted an audience in the royal throne room.

Jason noticed, with interest, that the sultan was wearing what was likely his most impressive sleeveless robe, heavy scarlet silk edged in ermine, worn over a garment of gold brocade. Lord Lyndon also noted that in a room full of men with colorful robes and full black beards, he and Lord Elgin appeared oddly bare in their shaven faces and tight English jackets and fitted breeches. But there was no way they could blend in, after all. They were here to ask the unthinkable—the removal of a female from the sultan's seraglio.

Lord Elgin stepped forward and bowed low before the sultan, the only man seated in this vast room of Ottoman dignitaries and guards. The Scottish lord's petition was simple. He desired the return of Miss Penelope Blayne, a young Englishwoman who had, quite by accident, he was certain, become part of the sultan's harem. Miss Blayne's relatives, represented by Viscount Lyndon—Lord Elgin gestured toward his companion—were most distressed and wished to have her returned to them immediately. If His Magnificence would be so kind—

"You must be aware this is not possible," the Grand Vizier interjected, the dragoman interpreter precisely imitating the official's sharp tone. "No woman leaves the seraglio."

Thomas Bruce, Lord Elgin, squared his shoulders, summoning all his stubborn Scots ancestry to aid him. He spoke slowly and clearly so the translator would be certain to interpret his words correctly. "Lord Lyndon is the eldest son of an earl, the heir. In England an earl is a great pasha. It is known that, on occasion, His Magnificence, the sultan, may give one of his women—if she is untouched—as a gift to a great lord. I therefore assure you that Jason Victor Granville Lisbourne, Lord Lyndon, is such a lord, and I humbly request that he be granted this gift, a token of respect between our countries."

The Grand Vizier began to speak, his words fading into silence at a wave of the sultan's hand. "If such a gift is made," Sultan Selim intoned, "it is required that the pasha marry the girl immediately." His dark eyes regarded the viscount with considerable interest, as if certain the young man would refuse.

Jason bowed so low his head nearly touched his knees. Ever since the bundle woman had told them of this ancient custom, there had been little doubt it was the only hope for Penelope's rescue. He was reconciled to the inevitable.

"Your Magnificence, I would be honored to take Miss Blayne to wife."

"You may return in two days time with whatever man of your religion you choose," the sultan decreed. "You will be married here. You will spend your wedding night in the palace so we may know the matter is properly accomplished. And then you may take your woman and go."

Jason had thought himself prepared for almost anything, but a wedding night in the palace . . . with a hundred eyes watching. *Impossible!*

While Viscount Lyndon suffered from speechlessness, Lord Elgin made a sincere, and properly flowery, speech of thanks. He bowed. Lord Lyndon, recovering his outward aplomb, also bowed, and the two men backed their way out of the presence of His Magnificence, Sultan Selim the Third, ruler of the Ottoman Empire.

Good God, Jason groaned, *how will I manage?*

On a day a little over a month after Miss Penelope Blayne's kidnapping at the Grand Bazaar, events seemed to be repeating themselves. Penny was bathed, oiled, massaged, scented, and dressed in the fine garments she had worn at her presentation to the sultan. The Kizlar Agha escorted her back down the shaded passage that ran between the seraglio and the throne room. Two eunuch guards brought up the rear.

Penny's heartbeat quickened. She was *out.* Though still in the palace, she was out of the harem, which was very odd indeed, for the sultan came to his women, not the other way round. But there was no time to think why. Their small procession entered the throne room, Penny following demurely behind the Kizlar Agha, eyes cast down, as she had been painfully taught. She did not see the Sultan Selim, the Grand Vizier, the Grand Mufti, the Sultan's Sword Bearer, the Chief Executioner, the bodyguards, or the many other men surrounding them. She kept her eyes fixed on the tips of her soft kid slippers and wondered if she was to be given away yet again because she had failed to live up to the standards demanded of an odalisque in the royal palace.

Suddenly, the Kizlar Agha gripped her arm and drew her forward. "Is this the woman you seek, my lord?" the giant black man inquired in French.

Penny's eyes snapped up to follow the Chief Black Eunuch's gaze. *Jason! And Lord Elgin!* And a third man in English garb. But a month's training was enough to keep her in her place. She did not cry out, she did not attempt to run. But her heart soared, as did her prayers.

"I cannot know, Excellency," the viscount returned calmly, "unless I may see her face."

The Kizlar Agha turned to Penny. "You may not remove your veil, but you may speak."

" 'Tis I, Lord Lyndon, Penelope Blayne." Dear heaven, she did not sound at all like herself! Her voice was husky from disuse, strangled by a rush of emotion. In truth, she could barely hear herself over the pounding of her heart. Penny stumbled on, for this, she knew, was the moment, her only opportunity to save herself. "The night we met you took Aunt Cass and me to the roof of the Embassy, so we might view the city and the waters below. You . . . you are related to my Aunt Cass, Cassandra Pemberton of Pemberton Priory in Sussex, England."

"Enough," the viscount declared. "I accept this woman is Miss Blayne."

And there, in the throne room of Sultan Selim, with the Reverend Philip Hunt, chaplain to the British Embassy, officiating and Lord Elgin and the Kizlar Agha as witnesses, Miss Penelope Blayne, age sixteen, became Lady Penelope Blayne Lisbourne, Viscountess Lyndon.

The wedding feast went on for what seemed like hours. Penny, attempting to recline gracefully, and patiently, on a bank of tasseled cushions in a modest-sized private chamber not far from the sounds of revelry, jumped to her feet and began to pace the thick colorful carpet. She had had a month's training in humility, in effacing herself, in living only to serve. But to be excluded from her own wedding feast—that was definitely the outside of enough! She had peeked out the curtains and seen the trays pass by, held aloft by a veritable stream of stalwart servants and piled high with every sort of tempting morsel. She had heard the soft whispers and giggles of the odalisques who excelled at dancing as they rustled by and then the enticing drift of music as the girls performed for the male wedding guests, who were undoubtedly enjoying themselves hugely while she waited, alone and forgotten.

Was she truly married? Or was all this just another entertainment for the sultan's amusement? Would she and Jason go home in the morning, or would they disappear, their bodies joining the others who had displeased the Ottoman sultans, resting forever on the bottom of the Bosphorus?

Penny broke into a tremulous smile as the heavy scarlet velvet curtains parted, and Ayshe and Leyla appeared, bearing food and drink. As the girls released their veils, the sight of these two familiar faces brought tears to Penny's eyes. She allowed herself to be coaxed into eating, for, surely, the girls would not appear so happy and excited if they did not believe Gulbeyaz was well and truly married and on her way out of the seraglio.

If only she had been able to learn more than a few words of their language . . .

When all three girls had eaten as much as they could hold, Ayshe and Leyla, eyes shining with excitement, settled themselves more comfortably onto the cushions beside Penny and proceeded with graphic gestures to remind her how a woman treated her master, particularly on her wedding night. One month as an odalisque in the harems of Mustafa Rasim and Sultan Selim the Third had not made Miss Penelope Blayne immune to blushes. Unshockable, perhaps, by what she might see, but the girls' reminders of what was expected of her when face to face with Jason Lisbourne was almost enough to send her scampering back to the seraglio.

With sad smiles and soft kisses on her cheek, the two young odalisques bade farewell. Tears fell. The girls replaced their veils, picked up the tray and the ewer that had contained fruit juice, and departed, leaving only the inevitable eunuchs standing guard outside the curtained archway. Once again, Penny was alone. Carefully avoiding so much as a glance at the huge divan-style bed set against one wall, she slumped against the bank of cushions and indulged in dire thoughts. She acquitted Ayshe and Leyla of being part of any conspiracy. Undoubtedly, they were as deluded as she herself. At the end of the wedding feast, attended only by men, with dancing girls for entertainment, the Sultan Selim's Chief Executioner would step forward and lop off Jason's head.

And that unsatisfactory odalisque, Gulbeyaz, would be next.

Penny shivered, crossed her arms over her royal-blue brocaded waistcoat, and waited for her fate.

Jason Lisbourne thought himself a man of the world, though, truthfully, his experience with women was not great. In the environs around Rockbourne Crest he had learned a thing or two from a willing tavern wench and had expanded on these interludes of exploration during his years at Oxford. Yet, although his rank kept all but his best friends from mentioning it, Lord Lyndon tended toward the bookish. Indeed, his friends frequently groaned as they struggled to learn what Jason Lisbourne absorbed not only easily, but with relish. The two who accompanied him on the Grand Tour had had private, and somewhat crusty, instructions from the Earl of Rocksley to make sure that his son enjoyed foreign attractions other than all that demmed art and architecture. And they had gleefully complied, until the young viscount's attention was wholly caught up in the rescue of Miss Penelope Blayne. If anyone had thought to ask, each of Jason Lisbourne's friends would have said the viscount was the last man on earth to become a rake. That his interest in women was appreciative, but bordered on the academic. A fine piece of sculpture or an illuminated manuscript brought a far greater gleam of interest than the most enticing female. His friends shook their heads. Odd, very odd indeed.

So on the night the Sultan Selim, the Grand Vizier, and

selected members of the court finally rose from their cushions and indicated that the newly married man might go, Jason Lisbourne was inclined to fancy he knew how Mary, Queen of Scots, felt while walking toward the axeman. He had married a schoolgirl, a perfect stranger. A hundred lascivious eyes would be watching, yet he could not touch her. Bedding Penelope Blayne was not only against his own inclinations but against every code of honor he had ever been taught. She was little more than a child. A family connection under his protection.

Yet they were married. The marriage lines were tucked inside his jacket. The efficient Mr. Hunt had even provided a register for them to sign.

Married. A life sentence.

Jason's guide pushed velvet draperies aside, motioned for him to enter. She was there, his schoolgirl bride, kohl-rimmed blue eyes wide above her veil. She straightened abruptly, then, going to her knees, bowed low. Hell and damnation, what was this nonsense? They were alone . . .

But, of course, they were not. He had never thought they would be. Faik, the bundle woman, even Lord Elgin, had warned him that a palace, particularly an Ottoman palace, had a thousand eyes.

"A salaam is not necessary. We are alone," Jason said carelessly, as if he truly believed it. He folded himself down beside her, staring, tongue-tied, as he realized even more fully that neither his knowledge of the classics, his limited knowledge of women, nor his total lack of knowledge about schoolroom misses was going to come to his aid. They were well and truly in the suds.

She knew. She knew about the watching eyes and ears. Otherwise he was quite certain she would have thrown herself into his arms and wept for joy. Or did she, perhaps, know something he did not? Would neither of them leave the palace alive?

Jason leaned forward, unfastened his bride's veil. And swore—a sharp exclamation he managed to swallow before it left his lips. The female before him was not a child. From her high forehead, plucked brows and kohl-enhanced eyes to her softly painted cheeks and lips, she was a woman of infinite beauty. About her clung the scent of roses, possibly cloves, and other mysterious odors that enticed his senses and dizzied his mind.

Heaven help him!

"They are watching," he whispered, "I am certain of it. The mosaic over the bed, the intricate designs on the walls—all could hide peepholes."

Gulbeyaz, the well-trained odalisque, merely nodded, her eyes properly lowered to her lap.

"The lanterns are deliberately placed too high for me to reach," Jason continued. "There will be no darkness. Do you understand? We will have to pretend." He paused, silently cursing all Ottomans and foolish Englishwomen who dragged innocent virgins into danger. "Penelope," he sighed, "do you have any idea what I'm talking about? Can you possibly know what it is we must pretend?"

Penny's chin came up and her eyes flashed in a most un-odalisque temper. "You are so *English,*" she hissed. "So blind. I have been in a harem for more than a month, and you think I might *not* know! Do not be absurd."

He'd married a shrew, by God! All he had sacrificed for this little chit, and she was mocking him.

"There is no need to pretend," she told him grandly, if still very softly. "I have been well trained. I am ready to do what is expected of me."

Jason ducked his head, fist to his mouth, finally remembering to cover his shock by a fit of coughing. *Good God, what was she doing?*

Gulbeyaz removed her jeweled *kalpock* and long trailing veil, tossing them aside. She ran her hands through her long silver-blond hair, which shimmered like a waterfall in the torchlight. Jason drew in his breath, even as his arousal, already quickened, strengthened very much against his will. "You must go to the divan," she said. "I may not come to you until after you are settled."

"Wha-at?" Lord Lyndon murmured, all too aware the situation was slipping out of his control.

"The woman enters the bed after the man," Penny stated

patiently. "They will be watching to see that I remember my training. Do you not understand? It is not only that they wish to be sure we are together as man and wife. I fear if I do not do everything in the manner in which I have been taught, they may not let us go."

Jason swallowed his protest. She might well be right. Yet he must not touch her.

But he had never seen a woman so beautiful, a woman with skin so soft, so sweetly smelling that he wanted only to lose himself in her. And her eyes . . . he had seen many practiced looks of enticement, but never anything like those of his bride. Penelope's eyes glowed with lustrous and inviting warmth. Was it possible she cared for him, or was she merely grateful for her rescue? Whatever the cause, there was no doubting her sincerity. She was magnificently beautiful, warm, willing. She was his wife.

And he was bloody well old enough to know better! He was the elder by five years and would have to keep his head, even if little Penny could not.

Penny, ha! This was not Penelope Blayne. The Ottomans were right. This was—what did they call her—Gulbeyaz? This was an odalisque bent on making a blithering idiot of him. He would show the blasted little chit that he was a man of the world. Somehow they would get through this night with Penny still a virgin, yet with the Sultan and his court convinced that he had properly consummated his marriage. Whether or not he could do this and still have his wife's eyes glow with adoration was another matter entirely.

Abruptly, Jason stood and found his way to a corner of the room, sheltered by an intricately carved wooden screen. There he washed and relieved himself and abandoned his English clothing, putting on the thin white linen robe that was waiting for him and concealing in his hand the tiny vial of blood Faik had procured for him at the bazaar. Lord Lyndon had not asked what kind of blood; he did not wish to know.

Gulbeyaz, the White Rose, torn between the knowledge she had become an actress on an Ottoman stage and the thrill of thinking how surprised her new husband would be when he discovered all she had learned in the art of pleasing a man, could barely contain her excitement. While Jason, her dearest rescuer Jason, her dream lover, was occupied behind the screen, the White Rose sat in the welter of cushions with her legs crossed, eyes cast down, hands folded demurely in her lap—all for the benefit of watching eyes. But she could not help peeping from under her lashes, waiting for the grand moment when Jason Lisbourne, her husband, the most wonderful sight in all the world, would reappear. When he did, golden head high, one hand clutching the white linen robe for which there was no belt, the eyes of Gulbeyaz followed him as he strode across the room, whipped back the top of the sea-green duvet, dropped the linen robe in a puddle at his feet, and settled himself on one side of the great divan.

The White Rose caught her breath. Her husband was as beautiful as she had imagined. She was the most fortunate of women.

Rising to her feet with nimble grace, she put aside her diaphanous azure silk robe. She removed her waistcoat of blue brocade and her gem-studded gold girdle. Then, ever conscious of the multitude of eyes applied to peepholes in the walls, perhaps even the ceiling, she moved toward the foot of the bed, still clad in her wide-sleeved white gauze tunic and the transparent azure silk trousers tightly gathered to her ankles. For a moment, Miss Penelope Blayne of Pemberton Priory, Sussex, England, came to the fore. She was parading in transparent garments before what could be half the sultan's court!

She was doing what she must to go home.

And then she was at the foot of the great bed, and she saw her husband's eyes upon her and knew that he had watched her every step of the way, just as she had watched him. Inwardly, Gulbeyaz smiled. Then she lifted the duvet and climbed into the bed at her husband's feet, sending the plump sea-green cover into a series of undulations like that of the rolling sea.

"Penelope . . . Penny!" Jason choked. "What do you think you're doing?"

"Only what I have been taught, my lord," came the muffled reply from Gulbeyaz, the White Rose, former odalisque of His Magnificence, Sultan Selim the Third, ruler of the Ottoman Empire. "Only what I have been taught."

Chapter Nine

Morning came, as mornings inevitably do. Jason Lisbourne could scarcely look at his child bride. That she was still a virgin was a miracle. No one would ever know what it had cost him, just as he was quite determined no one would ever know he had failed to maintain his much-vaunted English fortitude, spilling his seed like a puling boy with his first woman. Thoroughly mortified, he was unprepared for his bride's good humor as she playfully slapped his fingers when, after delivery of a breakfast tray of fruit and cheese, he reached for a cluster of grapes with his left hand. Evidently, the little minx was well pleased with the night they had spent together. Truthfully, why should she not be pleased? There had been enough activity under the covers to satisfy the most lascivious peeping Tom. And there would be blood on the sheets, of that he had made certain, though Penelope's eyes had widened when she saw it, and he had been further embarrassed by being forced to whisper an explanation in her ear.

Jason looked up, to discover his wife's eyes fixed on his face. Huge blue eyes, solemn, questioning, no longer playful. "Time to get dressed," the viscount said, feigning a confidence he did not feel. Wordlessly, she nodded, adjusting her golden girdle before donning her *kalpock,* her veil, and the all-encompassing pink *feradge.* The viscount called a guard to help him with his boots.

This was it, then. The moment when they would discover if they would exit the Topkapi Palace via the gate or—having provided an evening's entertainment for the court—

would they exit the grounds through the gardens, fastened into sacks, unwanted flotsam to be tossed into the waiting Bosphorus?

Jason took Penny's arm. Together, they stepped forward, following the two guards who had spent the night outside their room. The walk seemed endless. Neither saw a thing around them. *Eyes forward, keep walking. Pray.*

At the moment the cone-shaped towers and crenellated archway of the Gate of Salutations came in sight, both thought them the most wonderful sight they had ever seen. The guards stood back, salaamed. Lord and Lady Lyndon passed through.

And before them was an open carriage, with Faik beside the driver and Miss Cassandra Pemberton sitting, regally straight-backed and shaded by her utilitarian tan parasol.

They drove straight to the docks, where Lord Elgin had arranged passage on a Portuguese vessel bound for Lisbon. The sooner the young couple were out of reach of the Ottoman Empire, the better. Theoretically, this invisible line of empire began in the waters off Italy. More realistically, the Ottoman influence extended the length of the Mediterranean, a very long distance indeed. No one, from Lord Lyndon to the stalwart ship's captain, would feel completely safe until they passed through the straits of Gibraltar.

Miss Penelope Blayne, totally oblivious to the nuances flying around her, was enveloped in a cloak of euphoria. Within minutes of their ship hoisting sail and getting under way, she had slipped out of the cabin she was to share with her Aunt Cass and raced to the deck, looking back at the receding skyline of Constantinople, most particularly on the domes and turrets of the Topkapi Palace, as if she could scarce believe the miracle of her escape. She was *free.* She was back with Aunt Cass and Noreen. She was married to dearest Jason. Wonderful, darling Jason who had risked his life to save her. Surely theirs was a romance worthy of an epic poem, to be recounted by troubadours in feast halls throughout the Western world . . .

Penny, leaning on the ship's rail, turned her face into the wind and heaved a great sigh. There might still be feast halls in the Ottoman Empire, but in the world to which she was returning those days were long gone. For the first time it occurred to her that the story of her captivity, the tale of her marriage and wedding night with Jason Lisbourne would not be considered an epic love story in London. Far from it. Her experiences in Constantinople were enough to ruin her forever, no matter how finely the tale might be tuned.

And where was he? she wondered. Jason, accompanied by his two companions and their servants, had disappeared as soon as they boarded, as if he were a chance-met acquaintance who simply happened to be traveling on the same ship. By the time Noreen came to tell Penny her presence was required by Miss Pemberton, the high spirits of the former Gulbeyaz had plummeted considerably. Only a few minutes earlier, she had expected her private reunion with Aunt Cass to be filled with pure joy. Now, she was not so sure. It was possible—nay, likely—there would be some very awkward questions.

Oh, dear God, what had she done?

As free as Penny now felt herself to be, while on deck she had remained shrouded in the pink *feradge,* well aware that the brilliant sunlight sparkling off the Sea of Marmara would turn her azure silk robe and *shalwar* almost wholly transparent. Now, as she entered her cabin, she realized how very strange she must appear to an aunt whose eccentricities had never extended to anything more daring than a split skirt for riding on a camel. Penny threw off the *feradge,* tossed her *kalpock* and veil onto the bed, and fell to her knees, burying her face in her aunt's lap. Tears burst from both ladies, and it was some time before any coherent words could be distinguished.

First came Penny's apology, over and over, "I'm sorry, so very sorry, Aunt Cass. Forgive me for wandering off, for causing you so much grief." To this, Miss Pemberton made the expected denials of any guilt on Penny's part. A strong woman, who seldom displayed emotion of any kind, Cassandra Pemberton was on shaky ground, wandering in a slough of sentiment to which she was totally unaccustomed. The child was safely returned. She should be content. But she was Penny's guardian, as well as her aunt. She had a responsibility . . .

Miss Pemberton forced herself to the inevitable question. "You are married to Lyndon, my dear?"

Penny raised her huge blue eyes, shimmering with tears, yet glowing with love. "Oh, yes, Aunt. He was quite, quite wonderful. Like a knight rescuing a maiden in a fairy tale."

Miss Pemberton paused, flicking a glance out the porthole, as if she might find there a solution to this uncomfortable moment. "And you spent the night with him?" she inquired carefully.

"Yes, of course." Frowning, Penny searched her aunt's face.

Miss Pemberton made a small sound that sounded suspiciously as if she were strangling. "And may I assume that young devil had sense enough not to touch you?"

"He is my husband!" Penny protested, reverting quite suddenly to the White Rose of the seraglio.

"Penelope!" cried Miss Pemberton, much shocked. "Never say—"

"They were all watching, you see," Penny burbled. "We were actors on a stage. Our performance had to be perfect. Even the blood—"

"Blood! What blood?" Cassandra Pemberton cried.

"The blood on the sheets. Jason laid the coverlet back so they would be certain to see—"

"Oh, dear God," Miss Pemberton groaned, hugging Penny tight. "Say no more. Men are an untrustworthy lot. We are far better off without them."

Penny, who had suffered through far too much in the past few weeks, did not attempt to analyze what had just happened. She was simply glad to be back where she belonged. Later, she would wonder if Aunt Cass had misinterpreted her remarks. Did her aunt believe she had lost her virginity? And what if she had? She was, after all, married to dearest Jason. And there would be time enough to mend matters when they were all back in England. At the moment, Penny wished only to put the days in Constantinople behind her.

Except, of course, for the moments with Jason, which she would treasure forever and ever. And ever.

While she looked forward to the many more to come.

But in Lisbon, Penny, her Aunt Cass, and the ever-faithful Noreen O'Donnell transferred to a ship bound for the fledgling United States of America. The young Viscount Lyndon, reviled by Miss Cassandra Pemberton and shattered by what he felt to be his personal failure on his wedding night, returned to England a changed man. He had tried so hard. He had, in fact, risked his life, and look at the result. He had tied himself to a schoolgirl, who had caused him to make a great ass of himself. Miss Pemberton was accusing him of rape . . . and what else could one call it when an experienced man of one and twenty allowed himself to be seduced by . . .

By Gulbeyaz, the White Rose.

Never, never again, he vowed, would he be so vulnerable. If he lived to be a hundred, no woman would ever again be allowed to touch his soul as had the silver-haired, blue-eyed girl with whom he had spent one night in the seraglio.

Chapter Ten

Shropshire, 1812

Miss Penelope Blayne threw the book she had been attempting to read halfway across the room, where it fell to the carpet with a most unsatisfactory thud. "How dare he?" she fumed. "I might as well be back in the seraglio. A guard, Noreen. A guard at our door. *Infamous!* I cannot credit it."

"Lord Brawley says it's for your protection, miss. Until his lordship's guests have all departed."

"And what does that say to the nature of his guests?" Penny sniffed. "More like he does not care for me to see his array of Cyprians."

"Nor would you wish to, miss," the Irish maid reminded her, a bit tartly.

With an indeterminate noise that sounded suspiciously like a snort, Penny leaned back into the blue-brocaded chaise longue and glowered. "Do you think I will be allowed out for supper?" she mocked, "or is it to be another tray in my room? I swear to you, Noreen, if I had had any idea what awaited me here, I would rather have starved in the street—"

"You would not, miss," declared the Irishwoman who had, through the years, become far more than Penny's maid. "Indeed you would not. I've known you since your aunt found me teetering on the edge of being cast into the streets of Florence. Thirteen you were, and already a wily old lady who'd seen more of the world than a poor girl from Dingle ever thought on. And one thing I know is the grand stiffness of your backbone. Like m'self, miss, y'r a survivor. You'll manage his lordship as you have all else, whether it be traipsin' 'round the world, a month in a harem, or the long days of poor Miss Pemberton's last illness. You've no cause to be discouraged, child. If his lordship cared not what you thought, he'd parade his doxies before you instead of make sure your eyes were not sullied by their presence."

"He knew I was coming. He needn't have had them here at all."

For a moment Noreen O'Donnell looked out the window where darkness was already settling over the winter landscape, though the hour was little past four o'clock. "I think, miss," she said slowly, "that your aunt hurt the boy's feelings when she was so harsh with him. Hurt him enough that her accusations were not forgotten when the boy grew into a man. She herself was sorry, was she not, when you finally spoke of the matter?"

Dumbly, Penny nodded. "So many years of misunderstanding," she murmured at last. "By silent agreement we tucked the matter away, never to be spoken of. With each mile our ship sailed from the Levant, I became more and more aware of just how far I had strayed from what was expected of a young Englishwoman. I had been . . . *ecstatic* about being Jason's wife. And, gradually—oh so gradually, as he clung to his friends and made nothing but polite conversation when we dined with the other passengers—I realized I was a mere incident to him, nothing more.

"And then I would tell myself he could not talk to me, show any preference, for if his friends knew the whole, I would be ruined. And that fairy tale kept me quite propped up for years, as you recall, until Aunt Cass pointed out how gloriously my so-called husband was enjoying himself without me."

"Aye," Noreen interjected with a spark in her eye, "she went so far as to tell you she assumed an annulment had been arranged."

"Yes . . . and I was young enough, and ignorant enough, to believe her," Penny sighed. "I did, in fact, believe it right up until today when Jason—Lord Rocksley—told me we were still man and wife."

Noreen O'Donnell placed her hands on her sturdy hips and regarded her charge with stern eye. "And have you thought about what changed your aunt's mind, child? About why, in her final days, she did her best to throw you into his lordship's arms?"

"Oh, yes," Penny said. "I've had plenty of time to think about that since the will was read. It was the talks we had while she was ill, when, for the very first time, we discussed what actually happened in Constantinople. When she was willing to listen to how truly noble Jason was. How he spared my virginity . . . in spite of great provocation."

"Aye, that was it," the Irishwoman agreed. "It was a blow, miss, indeed it was. To learn how wrongly she had judged him. I could see how sorely she took it. Within a week she'd sent for Mr. Farley."

"And never said a word to me," Penny whispered. "Not a word of warning about what she planned."

"She was ill, miss, her head not as wise as it should have been. But she did try to make things right."

"How can it ever be right?" Penny asked, her voice little above a whisper. "It's too late, Noreen. Far too late."

A soft scratching at the door proved to be Hutton with word that all the guests, except for Lord Brawley, had departed, and his lordship would be pleased if her ladyship would join him for dinner at seven.

"Ask him if the guard is to be taken from our door," Penny called to Noreen, who was standing face to face with the butler.

A jerk of Hutton's head and the poor footman who had spent the day outside the door of the Countess of Rocksley was seen to lope off down the corridor as fast as his long legs could carry him.

Penny, still speaking only to Noreen O'Donnell, said: "You may inform that sorry excuse for a butler that the *countess* is so overcome by his lordship's generosity in allowing her out of her prison that she is even willing to dine with him."

After the door was firmly closed in Hutton's face, Noreen turned on her mistress. "Ah, child, it's a fool you are if you toss this opportunity away. He was a stout lad who didn't shirk his duty, and he's grown into a fine man, for all his rakish ways. Lord Lyndon offered his life for you once. Don't let the sad mistakes made since that terrible time keep you from seeing what's right under your nose."

Penny hung her head, feeling once again the thirteen years she was when she first met Noreen O'Donnell. Was she childish—or at the best, mistaken—to think her hurt greater than Jason's? Was she a hopeless romantic to wish it were possible to recapture those moments of joy when she had truly thought he cared for her?

She was a few months short of six and twenty. Long past the age to put away childish things.

With great dignity, Penny raised her head and said, "I have not been a child for a very long time, O'Donnell. I survived the seraglio, I survived abandonment by my husband. I will do what I must to survive this very strange reunion. Though . . . in truth, I am not at all certain what that will be. Come," she added briskly, "let us see if there is a gown suitable for the Countess of Rocksley to wear while dining with a lord of the realm."

The Earl of Rocksley sampled a slice of roast beef, his thoughts wandering from the conversation Gant Deveny was attempting to have with Penelope Blayne. Penelope *Lisbourne,* Countess of Rocksley. *His* countess. He was getting old, Jason decided. He must be, or he would not be reveling in the quiet serenity of a table set for three. With his wife on his right, his most trusted friend to his left, what more could a man want? Only a day earlier he had thought he was enjoying himself to the tune of shrieks of laughter, raucous guffaws, and vulgar behavior from those who had spent days sampling his wine cellar and each other. In the twinkling of an eye that reality now seemed as distant as those long-ago days in the Levant. More so. For here was little Penny, his wife, all grown up . . . and looking as if she faced the hangman on the morrow instead of the vicar.

But of course she did not know about the vicar, so it must be the awkwardness of their situation that made her look so dour. As if she were Hannah More, by God, passing judgment on his household. Miss Prim and Proper, portrayed by a female who once crawled into his bed wearing nothing but two transparent pieces of silk, while he was arrayed only in the skin the good Lord had given him.

Unfortunately, very little of his lordship's sense of misuse had dissipated by the time he was finally closeted alone with his wife in the small intimate study adjacent to Rockbourne Crest's impressive bookroom. The gentlemen had not lingered over port, and Gant Deveny had been quick to heed his friend's scowl, taking himself off to the billiard room with alacrity, almost as if he were a gleeful conspirator in giving the earl and his countess ample time to spar with each other.

The earl stood, hands behind his back, while his wife took her time arranging the skirt of her lavender gown over the buff leather of the bergère chair. When she had composed herself, folding her hands in her lap like some innocent child—which annoyed him still further—Jason announced, "I fear matters have not proceeded as I had planned." Ah, that caused a flicker in those cold blue eyes. "I had thought we might be married, as if we were bound by a long-standing betrothal, without reference to our—ah—past association. Unfortunately, my incautious words in the hall last night—"

"Incautious?" Penny huffed. "You were foxed!"

"Regrettably." Jason spun round, poured out a dollop of brandy. Then, after staring at the snifter for some time, he left it lying atop the marquetry cabinet. "Even then," he said as he paced back to his wife, "I thought we might carry it off, but one of my—ah—guests came upon Mr. Deveny and myself while we were discussing the matter. I fear she is not a woman noted for her discretion. There has been considerable talk, below stairs as well as above. I have sent for the vicar. To avoid further questions about where we married or how it came about, he will renew the ceremony here tomorrow. Hopefully, that will put an end to any rampant speculations. My guests have gone, undoubtedly to spread news of my marriage throughout the *ton.* But at least I control my own servants. They will be content to witness our marriage and attest the matter is properly settled. And they will not dare ask about the past."

"Others will," declared his wife, unhelpfully.

Jason eyed her sharply. "You are saying we must be in agreement about what we tell of our past."

"*If* we go through with this," Penny said. "Although I concede you have a legal right to decide my fate, my lord, I do not grant you the moral right to do so. Earlier today, you asked me to consider making our marriage a reality. Now, without a moment's discussion, you are telling me we are to be wed tomorrow. Surely, you cannot expect me to approve this abrupt manipulation."

Jason strode back to the marquetry cabinet, downed the brandy in one swallow. He stood with his back to her, looking toward the crackling fire, avoiding his wife's penetrating gaze. "I should have emulated the sultans and dropped you overboard on that long trip through the Mediterranean," he pronounced, still gazing at the flames licking upward from the glowing red logs. "But, no, I was King Arthur, Lancelot, and all the knights of the Round Table rolled into one. I had rescued the fair maiden, and she was mine. I had only to wait for her to grow up."

So it was true, Penny thought. It was not only she who thought him a hero. He had been as bedazzled as herself. Of course, she reminded herself sternly, it had not been personal. It was the romance of it all that had tickled his boyish fancy.

"I have been full grown a long time, Jason."

Wearily, as if well aware of his guilt, the earl walked back across the room and finally sat in the matching chair opposite Penny. "You were the child, Penelope; Cassandra Pemberton and I the adults. Therefore, the fault is ours. I acknowledge it. I was young and foolish, and all too easily put off. I cannot blame you for being hurt and angry. But what I am making such a mull of saying is that matters have gone even more awry since we spoke earlier today. We must renew our vows and make a marriage of it—"

"Or we must apply to the court for a formal separation," Penny interjected.

The earl, his cobalt eyes gone to winter ice, leaned in close. "Penelope, you cannot possibly wish to live alone for the rest of your life. I knew a girl in the seraglio one night, and I am absolutely certain that girl was never destined to live her life without love."

"Love? You dare to speak to me of love when I wasted so many years adoring you, waiting for you—"

"Enough!" the earl roared. "I'll not have a woman like you wither away on the vine. Look at you! You're already nothing but a shadow of that glorious child. Is she gone, Penelope? Have I lost her? If so, then it must be a divorce, for I wish to have a real wife, children—all that posterity implies. A separation will not do at all. Is that what you want then? Divorce? To be ruined forever, while I make a wholly new life for myself? For that is the way of the world. No matter who is at fault, the wife is ruined, shunned, forever damned in the eyes of the *ton.*" Abruptly, the earl straightened, leaned back in his chair, regarding her with piercing, patently angry, eyes. "Well, tell me, my dear countess, which is it to be?"

She hated, absolutely hated to allow him his triumph, but she had discovered the meaning of *ruined* nine and a half years earlier when she had strayed away from Aunt Cass and her bodyguards in the Grand Bazaar. She had spent the intervening years striving to become a pattern card of the proper young English gentlewoman. A life of ostracism, as was guaranteed by the dread decree of divorce, was not to be borne. She would not, however, give him the satisfaction of actually voicing her capitulation.

"I believe," said the Countess of Rocksley to her husband, outwardly perfectly composed, "you spoke of creating a past upon which we could agree."

Only by the slightest curl of his lips did Jason Lisbourne indicate the surge of satisfaction that swept through him at his wife's oblique reply. His sangfroid was not, alas, as much to spare his wife's feelings as his own. After all, he too had his pride.

On the morrow—Penelope's second wedding day—she woke to the sound of sniffles interspersed with outright sobs. It took her several moments to identify these most unusual noises, and another moment or two to discover the source, a young housemaid who was in the process of stoking up the fire.

Penny, after shoving the heavy velvet bed hangings further aside, stared in consternation at the sobbing maid. "Whatever is the matter?" she asked.

Eyes wide, the young maid clapped a hand over her mouth, stifling a wail of surprise. She was, in fact, so startled, she teetered on her heels, then sat down hard upon the wooden floorboards.

"Well?" Penny persisted, as the housemaid sat before the fire, mobcap askew, her black skirt tumbled up to reveal the white petticoat beneath and the tall black stockings on the thin legs stretched out in front of her.

"Oo-o, miss—m'lady," the girl gasped, "I never meant to wake ye. Mrs. Wilton be having my head, she will."

Since the little housemaid, who couldn't be a day over fifteen, now had a streak of charcoal across half her face, Penny's lips twitched before she once again asked the girl to tell her what was wrong. It took a bit more persuasion, but in the end the chambermaid's tale came tumbling out.

After wiping her tears with her apron, the girl sobbed, "I be in the family way, m'lady, and Mrs. Wilton, she says I has to go, and my pa won't have me back, and it's the workhouse for sure—"

"Merciful heavens, how old are you?" Penny asked.

"Sixteen, m'lady. Sixteen on All Saint's Day, I was. I'm fully growed."

Sixteen. And looked a babe. No wonder Jason had once thought her a child.

"And your young man? Will he not help you?" Penny asked.

"Oh, m'lady, poor as a church mouse, he is. And his pa'll skin 'im alive if'n he finds out."

Oh, dear. "Is he gentry?" Penny inquired carefully.

"Ah, no, ma'am, a farmer he is, but his pa wants him to marry sumthin' better'n me. Says he'll cut my Ned off without a penny if'n he marries me."

"And your—ah—Ned will marry you if a way can be found for him to make a living?"

The young housemaid left off wringing her apron, her eyes taking on a glow of hope. "Oh, yes, my lady. In a minute, he would." She clasped her hands in front of her, as if in prayer. "My lady, if you could help, I'd be grateful fer all of me life."

"And what is your name?"

"Blossom, ma'am—miss—m'lady."

Penny had been handling crises for so many years that it was only now that the oddity of the situation struck her. "Blossom," she inquired carefully, "may I ask why you seem to think I might be able to help?"

"But you're the mistress, m'lady. Everyone says so. And you're in the mistress's rooms, now ain't you? And that Mrs. Coleraine, she threw one of them fancy China vases against the wall o' her room yesterday. Smashed to smithereens, it was. Kept screamin', *'Married!'*, she did. Tossed the basin and pitcher too, m'lady. Took two o' us an hour just to brush up all the pieces. And she put a silver candlestick through a window too. His lordship wasn't half pleased, I can tell you."

"Mrs. Coleraine?" Penny echoed faintly.

"Mrs. Daphne Coleraine, his lordship's—" Once again, Blossom clapped her sooty hands over her mouth. "Y'r fire's workin' fine now, m'lady. I'd best be off. And thanks ever so fer askin' about me problem." Poor Blossom was out the door before Penny could form a question from the disastrous thoughts suddenly flitting through her head.

Mrs. Daphne Coleraine. But of course Jason would have a Daphne Coleraine in his life. Perhaps two or three at once, if all that she had heard were correct. Honesty forced her to admit he had sent the woman away. None too kindly, from the sound of it. At the moment Penny was more inclined to sympathize with the unknown Mrs. Coleraine than with her errant husband.

She was about to be tied to an insensitive rake.

She had been tied to an insensitive rake for nine and a half years. The only difference now was . . .

Her second wedding night would not leave her a virgin.

As it turned out, she was, once again, mistaken.

Chapter Eleven

The breakfast room was a surprisingly cheerful spot, with a roaring fire in a redbrick fireplace adorned with an intricately carved oak surround. Through two floor-to-ceiling windows, obviously added at a more recent date, sun could be seen sparkling off the snow outside. And delicious odors wafted from beneath the round silver covers set upon the sideboard, mixing with the pungent smell of coffee. Praise be Jason had not lost his preference for coffee in the morning, Penny thought, even as she noticed she had the room all to herself.

Relief flooded through her. She had never cared to chat before breaking her fast, and on this particular morning—her wedding day—she could well do without the presence of her erstwhile husband, the Earl of Rocksley, or his companion, Lord Brawley, who seemed to see the world as one vast source of cynical amusement. Penny allowed Hutton to bring her two shirred eggs, bacon, and toast. She took a sip of coffee, sat straighter in her chair, and decided that perhaps she would, after all, survive her wedding day.

As Penny was finishing her meal, Mrs. Wilton entered the room. A woman of middle years, the housekeeper might have looked less strained, Penny speculated, if she had not had to cope with what was likely a veritable parade of dubious houseguests. Yet this morning Mrs. Wilton seemed to have made a special effort, not so much as a wisp escaping her severe dark coil of hair, her white cap starched to perfection, her keys dangling over black bombazine so stiff the gown looked as if it might well stand on its own. Her lips, however, hinted at a tremble and her tone, when she spoke, was quite altered from the previous night. "I beg your pardon, my lady," she said, standing stiffly erect, "but did you wish to look over the menus for today?"

Penny finished chewing a bite of toast, swallowed, then regarded Mrs. Wilton with curious eyes. "May I ask why you think I might wish to do that, Mrs. Wilton?" she inquired.

"I—ah—as his lordship's wife, it is your right, m'lady," Henrietta Wilton managed, telltale white knuckles showing on the hands that were clasped in front of her. "I'm that sorry, my lady, I did not know who you were when you arrived. I fear I did not . . . that is, when his lordship said you were to have the countess's suite, I never dreamed— Ah, my lady, if you'll forgive my impertinence . . ."

"It is scarcely your fault, Mrs. Wilton, if the earl did not tell you," Penny assured the stricken housekeeper, "but I admit I am curious about why you are now so certain the earl and I are married."

Henrietta Wilton turned pale, then under Penny's continued stare flushed to an alarming shade of strawberry puce. "Hutton heard his lordship say so, my lady, and then, of course, we realized the earl would never put anyone but his wife in the countess's rooms."

"And were all the earl's guests privy to this information as well?" Penny asked softly.

Mrs. Wilton struggled visibly between the flat truth, the necessity of being loyal to her master, and the certain knowledge that from this time forth her life would be governed by the lady sitting in front of her. "I believe, my lady, some of the guests left before the facts became generally known. Those who left later in the day, however, could not fail to have been aware . . ."

"Yes, Mrs. Wilton?"

The housekeeper pressed her lips together, disapproval radiating from every pore. "There was talk, my lady, some of it rather loud. In the end, there was not a soul in the household who had not heard of his lordship's marriage."

Rather loud. Mrs. Daphne Coleraine screaming, "Married!" and tossing things about. A China vase? Idly, Penny wondered if it had been Ming. Poor Jason. As much as his negligence hurt her, she could never forget the sacrifice he had made. If he had not married her under such strange circumstances, would he have become a rake? Or would he have made a conformable marriage to a proper young lady and been the father of a hopeful family by now?

Penny looked up to find the housekeeper still standing stiffly in front of the door that led to the kitchen regions. "By all means, let us begin as we mean to go on, Mrs. Wilton. Is there a room where we may confer in comfort?"

The housekeeper must have anticipated her agreement, Penny thought, for the morning parlor at the rear of Rockbourne Crest was as warm and cozy as the breakfast room. And more colorful, as its furnishings were a cheerful blend of bright yellow and gold, accented with cherry. It was, in short, an inviting parlor any lady would welcome as the ideal place to speak with her housekeeper, write letters, or indulge in the latest novel. Penny's decidedly mixed emotions about Rockbourne Crest tilted more strongly toward the favorable.

When she had approved the menus, including a rather sumptuous evening meal Mrs. Wilton termed a wedding feast—a gesture Penny found oddly touching—the Countess of Rocksley realized the moment had arrived when she must try out the story she and Jason had concocted the night before. The housekeeper was a good woman, and efficient. A proper, respectable messenger for what the Earl of Rocksley and his countess wished the world to know.

Penny smiled as she returned the neatly written menus to Mrs. Wilton across a pedestal table placed only a few feet away from the steady glow of the fireplace. "Mrs. Wilton," she began, "I am sure you must be curious . . ."

Several hours later, in the earl's study, Penny joined her husband in recounting the same remarkable tale to the vicar. He was young, Mr. Adrian Stanmore—as the Reverend Philip Hunt had been young. And Mr. Stanmore was almost uncomfortably handsome. Somehow she had hoped for the comfort of a fatherly vicar, even a grandfatherly one. At least Mr. Stanmore did not appear as dour as Mr. Hunt. Nor did he indicate one whit of disapproval as the earl explained the awkwardness of their situation.

"I was doing the Grand Tour with some friends," the Earl of Rocksley said. "And, to my surprise, whom should I meet in Constantinople but a connection of my family, Miss Cassandra Pemberton, and her niece, Miss Penelope Blayne. Several weeks were spent by our various parties enjoying the sights, and then Miss Pemberton fell ill." Jason leaned forward, confidingly. "I am certain, Mr. Stanmore, you have heard of the many diseases prevalent in the East, most particularly of Lord Elgin's unfortunate disfigurement."

"Indeed, my lord," said Adrian Stanmore, his handsome face wreathed in genuine concern, "a tragedy. As was his divorce and the current contretemps over the marbles."

So, the earl thought, the young whelp had two thoughts to rub together. An improvement over certain vicars he had known. He had appointed Stanmore to the living, as he recalled, because a friend had asked it as a favor. Perhaps the boy had more possibilities than he had expected.

"Miss Pemberton," the earl continued, "was thought to be on her deathbed. She and Miss Blayne, who was little more than a child, were thousands of miles from home. She begged me, as a representative of the family, to look after Miss Blayne. When the doctor told us Miss Pemberton would not live through the night, I acquiesced to her pleading that I wed her niece so that all would be proper for me to escort her back to England. I was one and twenty, Mr. Stanmore; Penelope, a scant sixteen." The earl's voice dropped to nearly sepulchral tones.

"But then my aunt made a miraculous recovery," Penny contributed. "Aunt Cass and I eventually sailed off to the Americas, while Jason—Lord Lyndon then—returned to England. My aunt and I continued to travel until we were forced out of Lisbon in the great evacuation just before Marshal Junot's invasion."

"Unfortunately," the earl continued, "Miss Pemberton had formed an—ah—rather poor opinion of my character by that time and discouraged both my wife and myself from revealing our marriage."

"And then my aunt fell ill . . . again," Penny said, "a lingering deterioration of nearly three years."

"I wrote to Miss Pemberton," the earl said, "attempting to reconcile the situation with my wife, but when Miss Pemberton informed me she was truly dying this time, if by inches rather than from a virulent fever, I could not, of course, take Penelope from her side."

"Most proper, I'm sure," Mr. Stanmore nodded, though Penny could see that the vicar's intelligent eyes harbored a few doubts about the earl's laggardness as a lover.

The Earl of Rocksley removed a worn and much-folded document from his inner jacket pocket. "Here are our marriage lines, Mr. Stanmore, signed by the Reverend Philip Hunt with Lord Elgin as one of the witnesses."

"But since so many years have passed," Penny said, "and because the marriage was in such a distant land, we would be pleased if you would allow us to renew our vows."

The young vicar's slightly puzzled frown dissolved into a pleased smile. "Splendid. The very thing," he declared.

"Today," declared the earl. "Now, in fact, for we do not wish to give the appearance that we are living under the same roof without being husband and wife." Jason Lisbourne raised one inquiring brow. "I trust you brought the necessary items with you?"

"Yes, my lord, though when I read your letter, I was not expecting to perform the service for such an illustrious couple. May I say I am honored, truly honored—"

"Yes, yes, shall we get on with it?" Jason interrupted, rising to his feet. When the butler answered his tug on the bellpull, the Earl of Rocksley ordered, "Assemble the servants in the drawing room, Hutton. Tell them to step lively. We are about to have a wedding."

Turning, he offered his arm to his wife. "My lady, if you will come with me to the drawing room . . ."

Had she been this frightened the first time? Penny doubted it. For her marriage to Jason had meant release from the seraglio. Going home. Returning to the life she had learned to treasure as the best of all possible worlds.

But this time . . . this time was a plunge into an unknown almost as great as the harem of Sultan Selim the Third, a man of more kindness than she had appreciated at the time. A man who had since been assassinated by his own janissaries, and all because he had become too modern, too westernized by his Francophile ways. Indeed, Penny would forever believe it was Aimée de Rivery who had influenced the sultan on her behalf.

Oddly enough, the French schoolgirl had triumphed in the end. The janissaries' revolt had been short-lived, and Aimée de Rivery's son now ruled the Ottoman Empire and was proving to be the most enlightened sultan yet.

And now . . . ? Now, she would remember that no matter what she thought of Jason Lisbourne, she owed him her life. And her right to live the life of an Englishwoman in her own land. For that, she would renew her vows. For that, she might even forgive some of his neglect.

More importantly, she would do it for selfish reasons. Because she did not truly wish to live out her life alone. Because she fervently wished to have some of those wonderful children who had run through the rooms and gardens of the seraglio, shrieking with joy and laughter, whose tears she had dried on occasion. Those charming, willful, loving little creatures, wide-eyed over their limited world and too young to understand the severe confinement to come, for even royal princes could not run free after a certain age. In a world where sultans enjoyed multiple wives and primogeniture was not the norm, the life of princes was almost as hazardous as the life of princesses was boring.

So now she would allow Noreen and Mrs. Wilton to fuss over her while the household assembled in the drawing room. The oddity of it struck her. The guests at her first wedding had been the highest authorities in the Ottoman Empire. This time, everyone except Lord Brawley was a servant. But she had Noreen at her side, and Mr. Stanmore appeared considerably less formidable than Mr. Hunt, who had said the words of her first marriage service in the sultan's throne room as if he were committing an act of blasphemy.

In an unusual attack of feminine vanity, Penny glanced down at her gown. A relic from the years before Miss Pemberton's illness and no longer in the first stare of elegance, its soft blush silk was, nonetheless, the perfect foil for Penny's golden-brown hair, from whose modest coil Noreen had tweaked soft curls to frame her mistress's pale but lovely face. Mrs. Wilton offered a Book of Common Prayer with white leather cover, to which she had added long white ribbons that trailed nearly to the floor. Tears sprang to Penny's eyes as she accepted the housekeeper's gift. And then she gasped as a veil dropped over her head.

"Not a word," Noreen hissed in her ear. "I've kept that piece of silk tucked away all these years. Why not make use of it?"

But Noreen did not understand. Could not understand what that transparent white silk meant to her. It was her shroud. A manacle binding her to that horrible time. A symbol of all that had gone wrong in her life. She could not be *married* in it!

How exceedingly foolish. She *had been* married in it. She had repeated her vows from under its silken folds once before, and she would now do so again. Marriage or loneliness forever. Which did she prefer?

Clutching her prayer book, Penelope Blayne Lisbourne took her place at her husband's side. Noreen stood to her left, Gant Deveny to Jason Lisbourne's right. Mr. Adrian Stanmore regarded them all with a benign smile, and then he began the service.

That night Penny regarded with considerable resignation the serviceable cotton nightdress Noreen was holding up. "I wish I might have had some inkling of the earl's intentions," she grumbled, "so I might at least have acquired a few bride clothes."

" 'Tis the best I could find, m'lady. I fear you've had little thought for yourself these past few years."

Penny allowed Noreen to slip the plain cotton garment

over her head. There was, at least, a bit of lace trim around the high neck and on the edges of the long sleeves. Not that it mattered in the dark. Ignoring Noreen's protest, Penny ordered her to extinguish all candles before she left the room.

And then she waited . . . her mind inevitably filling with visions of her first wedding night. The transparency of the azure *shalwar* and tunic. Her simple joy that rescue was at hand. Her eagerness to show Jason how well she had learned her lessons. Heat stained Penny's cheeks. She could not have been that foolish child who actually thought Jason loved her. She could not have been Gulbeyaz, who crawled up from the foot of her lord and master's bed and . . .

O-o-o-h! In anguish, Penny groaned and buried her face in the pillow. Now, in her wisdom, she knew she had thoroughly shocked him. He had turned away from her in revulsion, running back to the safety of his friends as soon as it was possible. And staying away for nine and a half years . . . until, driven by the necessity for an heir, he had finally acknowledged her existence.

Heirs were good, Penny conceded, shutting out those mortifying images from the seraglio. To children she could give love and receive it in return. And, if she were very careful not to further offend Jason, possibly they would go on very well. Certainly as well as the many other couples who had marriages of convenience. Yes, she would be exactly what he wanted, a proper English wife who would bear his children, ignore his occasional peccadillos . . .

Well, possibly not. She would consider that another day. For the moment she must remember to be everything she was not on her first wedding night. Cool, calm, resigned to her fate. A true Englishwoman of noble birth.

Men of thirty did not approach their brides with pounding hearts. It was absurd. He had quite happily dragged his feet for ten years. He had fallen into the habit of addressing all thoughts of his wife with reluctance. But now, memories of that first wedding night surged across Jason's vision, sending his blood pulsing in a way he had forgotten was possible. And tonight . . . tonight he was no longer under restraints. Tonight he could enjoy his bride to the fullest. Ah, he hoped . . . surely she had not forgotten all those delicious things she had learned in the seraglio. No, of course she had not. Together, they would rediscover each and every one of them.

Jason fumbled as he tied his soft wool robe about his waist. Why knot it at all? He would not be wearing it long. Just a few steps through the adjoining dressing rooms, and then . . . Lord, he was practically salivating, though his bride wasn't half the beauty Gulbeyaz had been. Perhaps he might procure some kohl, some of the exotic scents that had wafted from his child bride's skin and clothing. Yes, Penelope would like that, he thought. What harm in indulging their fantasy with a few items from the East?

As he started toward his wife's bedchamber, Jason's knees were weak. The flood of memories! His first wedding night had been the most agonizing moment of his life. And the most glorious. Truthfully, he could hardly wait to repeat it. With a more satisfying ending.

His wife was sitting straight up in her bed, the covers clutched beneath her chin. Only slightly taken aback, Jason accepted that it was a chilly night, the fire already beginning to turn to embers. In spite of his eagerness, he took the time to add more logs, using the bellows to encourage them to burn. Then he turned back to his bride.

As Jason approached the bed, he succumbed to his unexpected eagerness, allowing his robe to drop to the floor. His wife's eyes went wide, then instantly shifted away.

"I want you to know," she announced in clipped tones, "that I am perfectly reconciled to doing my duty." Chin up, eyes fixed on the heavy draperies at the foot of the bed rather than on the sight of her naked husband, she more closely resembled a Christian martyr about to be thrown to the lions than Gulbeyaz welcoming her long-lost husband.

"You are *reconciled,*" Jason repeated, standing with his backside roasting from the newly stoked fire and his once eager front side frozen by the fullness of his disappointment. "That is how you approach our marriage bed?"

"Is that not what you wish?" Penny asked, thoroughly confused.

"Hell and damnation, woman," the Earl of Rocksley roared. "I want a flesh and blood woman, not a sacrificial virgin!" And with that he swept up his robe and stalked, naked, from the room, trailing the green wool behind him. When it caught in the slamming door to the dressing room, he left it there. Let the redoubtable Noreen O'Donnell puzzle that one out!

Behind him, Penny slid down and buried herself beneath the covers. What had she done? What went wrong? Just when . . .

What had happened to that glorious hero she once knew?

What had happened to her dreams of loving, bright-eyed children?

And where did their lives go from here?

Chapter Twelve

Lord Brawley, graciously pleading his lack of desire to play gooseberry to newlyweds, fled Rockbourne Crest directly after nuncheon. No one could blame him, for the atmosphere inside the early-seventeenth-century seat of the Earls of Rocksley vied with the windswept chill of winter without. And, of course, good manners dictated that no matter how bleak Jason Lisbourne might look . . . no matter how pale and bristling his wife, it was time for friends to take themselves off, even when it meant leaving the unhappy pair to find their way out of whatever quagmire they had stumbled into.

But the pit between them had had nearly ten years to grow into a well of despond, the depth of their misunderstandings far beyond any single misconception or overly sensitive reaction. The earl, in the fullness of his pride, would not chance his manhood again to his wife's obvious distaste. Penny, now certain that her behavior on their first wedding night had given her husband a revulsion of her from which he could never recover, threw herself into her household duties. Only in the dark loneliness of her bed did she allow herself to wonder about a solution to their impasse. Jason wanted children, he had told her so. So why his abrupt departure on their wedding night? Why had he not come to her since? She had told him she was willing, had she not?

Yet now she questioned even her memories. What was real? What a mere fantasy she had indulged in during her long days in the harem and in the years that followed? Even now, reality was elusive. Jason had said he wanted a true wife. Then he had taken one look, turned on his heel, and stalked out. It was as if she had been transported to a moor and set down in the midst of a quaking bog. The ground trembled beneath her feet, and she could see no way out. She was being pulled under and would surely drown, while Jason stood, unmoving, on the bank and watched, this time lifting not so much as a finger to help.

The days dragged on, the earl and his countess meeting occasionally in the breakfast room, dining each evening in stiff and solitary formality at a table designed for twenty. Penny did her duty, as she had for so many years at Pemberton Priory. She continued to confer with Mrs. Wilton about the menus. She inspected every room, making notes where refurbishment was necessary. She began an inventory of the linens. Each evening she played the piano (with modest skill) while the earl listened with some attention, thanking her each time with words so stiff and formal that further conversation died unborn. Until one evening, more than a fortnight after their wedding, when the icicles had disappeared from the eaves, the snow had melted into a sea of mud, and the spike-like leaves of snowdrops and crocuses could be seen poking through the earth.

Perhaps it was this tiny waft of spring, Penny thought—even if she had not ventured farther than halfway through the dormant gardens spread between the rear of Rockbourne Crest and the slope of the rugged hill that rose behind it—but, certainly, some imp of change spurred her on. She might not have the courage to initiate a discussion of their obvious problem—for if she did, it seemed most likely Jason would reveal his change of mind by sending her away—but she recalled she had a legitimate topic of conversation, one which might elicit more response than the state of the weather or the roads, or even the state of the realm.

After playing a group of English country songs, mostly in a minor key, Penny embarked on a Scarlatti piece, equally sad and soulful. She did not sing, but echoed the words in her head as the song begged an unknown lover to cease to torment and wound. And if he could not, then the singer begged him to kill her. Penny found comfort in this mute protest, though she doubted the earl had the slightest idea of the song's lyrics.

"O, lasciatemi morire!" The last vibrating strings died away. Penny's hands rested on the pianoforte's keys. Head bent, she remained silent, summoning her courage to speak to her husband.

"Good God, woman, don't you know anything lively?" the earl barked. "*Oh, let me die,* indeed! Oh, yes, I daresay I am as familiar with Italian songs as you. Did we not both make the Grand Tour?" he taunted.

How much more could he hurt her? Penny wondered, as her stomach churned. Yet anger was good, for it loosened her tongue, which had been woefully stuck to the roof of her mouth these past few weeks. She stood, with dignity, and crossed the room to sit across from him in an elegant giltwood armchair upholstered in gold brocade. The warmth of the fire was welcome after the chill of the air around the piano, which was situated on the far side of the room. "I promise I shall not stay exclusively in the minor key, my lord," Penny said carefully. "Tonight, I was perhaps influenced by something I wished to discuss with you."

The earl's face, already unwelcoming, grew more saturnine.

"I am concerned about the maid, Blossom," Penny said.

The earl gawked. "I beg your pardon," he murmured. What was the woman up to? Who the devil was Blossom?

"Blossom Early," his wife said, as if he should know and recognize the name of every servant in his employ.

"You do not speak to me for days," the earl intoned, "and now you wish to make a May game of me."

"I have so spoken to you," Penny protested indignantly.

"There is speaking, and then there is speaking," Jason grumbled. "You cannot possibly claim that wishing to speak to me about someone with the outlandish name of Blossom Early can be anything but nonsense."

"Oh," said Penny, much struck, for in the stress of her days at Rockbourne Crest, the absurdity of Blossom Early's name had not occurred to her. "You are quite right," she conceded," it does sound contrived, but that is the name she gave me, truly it is. The child is but sixteen, you see, the same age I was when—" Penny broke off, blindly crumpling a handful of her rose silk gown in her fist. "Blossom," she began again, knowing she must go on or she would never forgive herself, "Blossom is in the family way, and I fear Mrs. Wilton and I are in grave disagreement about the solution to her problem—"

"Disagreement?" Jason interjected. "You are mistress here, not Mrs. Wilton."

"I do thank you for that," Penny breathed, shooting him a truly grateful glance, which he felt all the way down to his nether regions. "But the problem is that even if she is not thrown out of the house without a thought for her future, as Mrs. Wilton wishes, she is still *enceinte* and unwed."

"And you wish me to do what?" Jason inquired silkily. "Keep her on and raise up the brat as a stable boy?"

"You need not be difficult," his wife snapped. "Her lover is quite willing to marry her, if only his father had not threatened to throw him off the land if he does so. For the father, you see, wishes him to marry someone a bit above a chambermaid."

And now her summer-sky eyes were truly fixed on his face, glowing with entreaty. An odd emotion poured through him. Even though the breathtaking child had become a thorny martyr, he actually wished to please her. "I take it the father is one of my tenants," Jason said. At Penny's affirmation, he mused, "Then I believe he forgets from whose land he threatens to eject his son."

His wife laughed aloud and clapped her hands, a childish gesture that delighted him, reminding him of the young girl he had first known.

But her joy did not last, a frown wiping her smile away. "Surely, if you coerce the father, Blossom and Ned cannot be comfortable living in his household."

Jason leaned back in his chair, stretching out one of his long legs until it came close to touching his wife's toe. Ah, yes, he rather liked the sensation of being so close. "You may leave the matter to me," he assured his countess. "I promise you I handle my estate affairs with greater skill than I have handled my marriage."

Merciful heavens . . . a concession, Penny thought. Surely as close to an apology as she would ever hear from her laggard husband. A crack, the veriest chink in the solid wall built up between them. But was it a new beginning, or merely a brief flash of rapport, as swift to fade as it had burst upon them following a surfeit of doleful music?

It was enough, Penny decided. Enough to hint it would not take another ten years to mend the damage of the past. Drifting for a moment into the flights of fancy of her youth, the Countess of Rocksley wondered what would happen if she threw herself into her husband's lap and put her arms about his neck.

But she would not, of course she would not. Pride was a terrible thing. Penny stood, sank into a respectful curtsey, and said, "My lord, I am most grateful. I am sure you will not regret any help you may give to Blossom and her Ned. Goodnight."

Hastily, Jason pulled back his foot so she would not trip on it. Stubborn chit. She had given him nothing to go on. Not the slightest hint she was ready to declare a truce in their silent war. Blossom and Ned, indeed. Surely the way to his wife's heart did not lie in the fate of two country bumpkins.

He had only one way to move in his marriage, Jason reminded himself, and that was up, for how could things be worse than the "reconciled" icicle he had found in his countess's bed?

So Blossom and Ned it was. Even if he found the entire affair ludicrous.

For a considerable time the earl scowled at the pianoforte where his wife persisted in playing music so mournful it set his teeth on edge. Impossible woman! If he'd had the slightest idea what was to come, he would have joined a caravan to Persia the moment Cassandra Pemberton had turned to him for help. Damn and blast the gentler sex. They were a good deal of trouble. Grabbing up the candelabrum from a table beside him, Jason headed for his study, where a full bottle of brandy awaited him.

Penelope Blayne Lisbourne. His wife. Hell and the Devil confound it!

Rockbourne Crest, built in an era when life was still uncertain in the Marches, the sometimes rugged hill country between England and Wales, was situated on a plateau about a third of the way up a hill that looked like a mountain to someone accustomed to the softly rolling terrain of Sussex. Nor did the small but sparkling lakes Penny could see from the windows of her bedchamber bear any resemblance to the flat water marshes and choppy seas of the county she had called home for so many years. Feeling almost as trapped as the young girl who had once gazed longingly from behind the lattices of the seraglio at the ships plying the Bosphorus, Penny could scarcely wait to explore the Shropshire countryside.

Therefore, when the sea of mud that passed for roads finally firmed under occasional bursts of sun that penetrated winter's low-lying clouds, Lady Rocksley ordered up a carriage and escaped the silent but contentious atmosphere that permeated the seventeenth-century stone fortress, which had been renovated and enlarged over the years in an attempt to turn it into something more closely resembling a nobleman's manor house. The attempts had been only partially successful. There was no outer wall, no moat, and the ashlars of red stone glowed warmly against the dark winter earth and barren trees. Yet its partially crenellated roofline, its towers and turrets, never let anyone forget it had been built for safety, rather than for beauty.

Penny, accustomed to the bright and airy feel of Palladian architecture, based on classic Greco-Roman lines, or the graceful red brick and columned façades so popular in the previous century, was taking her time adapting her notion of beauty to accommodate the uncompromising solidity of Rockbourne Crest. Shut in, as she had been by the weather, she tended to think of it more as a prison than a home. And of her husband as her jailer. Unfair, perhaps, but when had she ever known freedom? As a child, her every action had been controlled by her Aunt Cass. During the past years, when she had had the running of the household and the care of her aunt during her final illness, she had a modicum of independence but, certainly, nothing that could be called freedom. And now she was a possession of the Earl of Rocksley, his to do with as he pleased.

And it would seem he pleased very little.

As the carriage made its cautious descent toward the valley below, Penny gulped a lungful of crisp air and scolded herself for her foolishness. She was tired, tired, tired. No one could know . . . no one could even imagine what the care of an invalid entailed. Even with a houseful of willing servants . . .

In time, she would recover. Life would not seem an insurmountable obstacle dropped square in front of her by a vengeful God who did not think her fit to be a proper English lady. Penny slumped against the squabs, and for the next half-mile felt quite sorry for herself, until her natural stubbornness and resiliency reasserted itself, even through the exhaustion that seemed to penetrate all the way to her bones. She was the Countess of Rocksley. She was about to make the acquaintance of the people in the village below. A village to which she should have been introduced by her husband—if she had bothered to inform him she was going. She would carry off this excursion as she had every other challenge in her life. If not always with triumph, she could at least manage panache.

The village of Cranmere was a pleasant surprise. The carriage crossed a stone bridge over a rushing stream that tumbled down a series of granite ledges before plunging over a fall marked by the huge wooden wheel of a mill and then racing off down a slope toward a small lake, or mere, that gave the village its name. A few of the houses were of red brick, but the majority of the homes and shops showed the distinctive half-timbered construction of the sixteenth and early seventeenth centuries. The church, however, appeared to have been built of the same sturdy red granite as Rockbourne Crest. It was a fine edifice, with an impressive bell tower. Penny speculated that the first Earl of Rocksley, undoubtedly more devout than the present holder of the title, had ordered the church built of the same materials as his castle.

Since one of Penny's errands was to make sure Blossom Early and her Ned had arranged for the reading of their banns, she went first to the church, where she admired the stained-glass windows and the intricate carving on the pulpit before she finally discovered Mr. Adrian Stanmore in the vicarage, hard at work on his Sunday sermon. Instead of resenting the interruption, the vicar beamed at her and urged her to take tea with him. The embers of Penny's self-esteem, severely damaged by her husband's disgust of her, flickered, settled into a soft glow ready to be snuffed out by the slightest hint of disdain.

Ah yes, Adrian Stanmore told her, his handsome face wreathed in smiles, Blossom Early and Ned Jenks would be wed in ten days' time. The earl had been kind, most kind. For Sam Jenks was a difficult man. Without Rocksley's aid, the two young people could not have managed.

The young vicar raised his cup of tea in salute. "Blossom Early tells me they owe it all to you, Lady Rocksley. Scarce three weeks at Rockbourne Crest, and already you are a true lady of the manor."

"Not at all," Penny demurred, though the small compliment touched her injured spirit like a warm rush of summer sunlight.

"Pray allow me the honor of introducing you to the village," Mr. Stanmore offered. "I assure you they have been all agog since they heard of the wedding."

"But you are working on your sermon, sir," Penny protested feebly, making a valiant effort not to show how gratified she was by the vicar's offer.

Adrian Stanmore rose, a tall blond Viking who had somehow managed to fit into a village where the residents tended to be smaller, darker, and more similar to their Welsh neighbors than to their Saxon ancestors. "My sermon, my dear lady, will keep," he pronounced. "After all, 'tis but Thursday. Come, let us set the village about its ears." He proffered his arm. "Mrs. Hensley," he called to his housekeeper, "Lady Rocksley's cloak, if you please."

Laughing, Penny stood and allowed him to place her fur-lined cloak about her shoulders. Indeed, it was quite wonderful to see good humor in a man's eyes. And admiration.

Without so much as a thought for the husband who had been a ghost through all but her first wedding night, Penelope Blayne Lisbourne, Countess of Rocksley, began her tour of the village of Cranmere, happily ensconced on the arm of Mr. Adrian Stanmore.

Chapter Thirteen

Jason Lisbourne leaned against the gray marble mantel in a salon adjacent to the dining room and examined his wife from beneath lowered lashes as she entered the room, sweeping toward him as if she had no other care but procuring a glass of sherry for herself. Her evening gown was one of her more cheerful ones, he noted sourly, made of some shade of green that did not look as if it were the darkest hue she could find. And she was actually wearing a bit of jewelry, an emerald of fine cut and color dangling from a chain of gold. For once, she looked a step above the drab creature any member of the *ton* would dismiss as a governess, companion, or poor relation upon first glance. In addition, her trip to the village must have improved her temper as well as her looks, for her cheeks were pink, her step more lively, her eyes more aglow than he had seen since . . . since that first wedding night, which he had so disastrously failed to recreate on the occasion of his second.

Abruptly, Jason stopped fingering his glass of aperitif and moved to pour some sherry for his wife. "Your drive to the village was a success, my lady?" he inquired.

"Indeed," she confirmed, with what appeared to be a genuine smile, "I have met the butcher, the baker, the candlestick maker, wives, children, and cousins. I have encountered a formidable dame, who, I am told, is wife to the squire, and her exceedingly meek daughter—"

"Ah, yes, Mrs. Matthew Houghton and Miss Mary."

"Poor child. On occasion, I thought Aunt Cass domineering, but she could not hold a candle to Mrs. Houghton. Neither Miss Mary nor I could get a word in edgeways."

Jason chuckled, finding himself more in charity with his wife than he had been since the night he had demonstrated his idiocy by fleeing his marriage bed as if he were the veriest greenling. How could a man marry the same woman twice and make a fool of himself on two different wedding nights? On the first occasion, by enjoying himself too well and, on the second, by running like the hounds of hell were on his heels, and all because reality had been so much less than his eager anticipation?

Like a small boy denied a treat, he had thrown a tantrum and, quite literally, slammed the door on what should have been a new beginning for them both. In a trice, his failure to consummate his marriage, compounded by the previous years of neglect, assumed the proportions of an insurmountable object. Now, he could only stand back and hope that time would erode their differences, but at the moment—

"And then there was a quite delightful young woman I met at the linen draper's," his wife was saying. "A Miss Helen Seagrave. An impoverished gentlewoman, Mr. Stanmore tells me. She teaches harp and the pianoforte. Do you know her?"

"Stanmore?" Jason echoed, dismissing his shadowy recollection of Miss Seagrave in an odd surge of alarm that his wife had spent time with Cranmere's overly handsome vicar. "You spoke with the vicar?"

"Yes, of course. I spoke with him about Blossom's and Ned's wedding, and then he was kind enough to escort me about the village, introducing me to absolutely everyone."

A task he should have undertaken himself—as he very well should have known. Inwardly, Jason groaned. He and his wife were finally living under the same roof, and still he could not adapt his ways to being married. He did not *feel* married.

And whose fault was that? Who had gone into a snit because matters had not gone as he had thought? Who had filled his head full of dreams of a golden child in nearly transparent silk garments mincing across their bedchamber and burrowing beneath the covers? Who had let his bitter disappointment send him scurrying off like a whipped cur instead of asserting his rights as a proper husband should?

Little wonder he did not feel married. What gentleman would under such inauspicious circumstances? Indeed, what *man* would?

And what man would be inspired by the lackluster spinster before him? Oh, she might be a bit more spirited tonight, her gown a trifle finer, but with the exception of occasional bursts of shrewish temper, he could see little life in her at all. This was not the glorious girl he had hoped would share his life. She had vanished, as if by black magic, to be replaced by this dull, proper pattern card of womanhood, sunk so low as to be nearly drowned in the middle-class morality propounded by the ever-growing clamor of the Evangelists.

He had made a dreadful mistake. If he had told his father about his little escapade in Constantinople, Rocksley would have managed to find a way to an annulment with few repercussions for either Penelope or himself. And yet he had clung to the vision of his night in the seraglio . . . to memories so gloriously erotic they would never go away . . .

Hutton announced dinner in a tone designed to carry above the clamor of a crowd of fifty. (For since his lapse the night of the countess's arrival, he had striven mightily to repair his tarnished image as a man fit to be butler in a nobleman's country home.)

Jason, startled from his reverie, proffered an arm to his countess.

This *was* the same girl, he told himself as they walked toward the dining room. Gulbeyaz, the White Rose, was in there somewhere, and he would find her. Although his own behavior, to be perfectly truthful, had caused him to lose so much ground, that he did not know how many times he would have to chance the course before he crossed the finish line in triumph.

But he would. He most certainly would. Though the track he was on might have devious turns and twists . . . even pits where a man might lose himself, trodden down by his wife's cold bed and cold heart. The news he had received from Brawley in today's post was certainly a complication he could have done without. Perhaps, however . . . yes, perhaps he could make this new complication work for him. If he made his wife angry enough to strike sparks . . . If he could but goad her out of her icy indifference . . .

Jason sighed. He had taken his life in his hands when he went into the Topkapi Palace to rescue young Penelope Blayne. No risk he might take now could equal that.

The earl pared a slice of apple for his wife, then cut a square of cheese. The covers had been removed, and he had poured port for both of them. His wife had not demurred. Ah, yes, the spirited child still lurked inside there somewhere.

"I am leaving for London tomorrow," he announced.

"You might have given me some notice!" Penelope gasped.

"I am," Jason returned calmly.

"Surely you must realize I do not like to ask Noreen to scramble around so. It is many years since we spent our time travel—"

"I believe," Jason interjected, "I said *I* was going to London. "I do not expect you to accompany me."

Alas, his wife's reaction was far from the expected. She simply froze, the wedge of Stilton dangling from her cheese fork. The pink faded from her cheeks. She lowered the fork to her plate, folded her hands in her lap. The only sound from her was a faint, "Oh."

"It is Lord Elgin," he heard himself say. "In spite of astronomical debts, he continues to refuse an offer of thirty thousand pounds for the marbles, a situation not at all aided by that idiot Richard Payne Knight, who maintains the marbles are Roman copies. And now Brawley informs me, some young Scottish whelp with literary pretensions has turned Elgin into a monster."

"But how—"

"It seems the lad inherited an English baronetcy, made a grand tour, and now considers himself the God-given authority on antiquities. He has written an epic which has made him the lion of London. And in it, he has excoriated Elgin as despoiler and thief of the marbles."

"*Childe Harold!*" his wife exclaimed. "That must be what Mrs. Houghton was nattering on about, asking me if I had yet seen a copy, though, truthfully, I felt forced to let her stream of words go in one ear, then out the other, or else I would have been quite swept off my feet."

"*Childe Harold,*" the earl confirmed glumly. "That's the scurrilous tale. I fear the blasted boy will do more harm than all of Knight's ignorant posturings. And since we are both indebted to Elgin, I feel I must support him, both in society and in Parliament, even though that may mean advising him to settle for what he can get before Byron's rants force the price lower yet."

"But Aunt Cass and I saw them cutting the metopes from the Parthenon," Penny cried. "And, surely, Lord Elgin has paid out twice that sum—"

"At the very least," Jason agreed, pleased the mention of Lord Elgin had diverted his wife's fury from himself. "And, yes, the work has cost Elgin a fortune, one he did not possess. At this point it would seem he owes half the world back wages and outstanding loans. But, believe me, he would be wise to settle."

"I can sympathize with Byron's horror," his wife said after some deliberation, "since Aunt Cass and I felt the same when we watched the destruction. But calm reason states that if Elgin had not taken them, the French would have."

"Precisely."

"Evidently, from what Mrs. Houghton has told me," Penelope said, "*Childe Harold* is a phenomenon, a success difficult to counter. But Knight is dog in the manger, claiming the marbles are Roman copies. I can only think he is jealous that he, the so-called expert, did not procure the marbles himself. All the more reason," she added shrewdly, "why I should go to London with you, for although I may not be able to argue convincingly on Elgin's right to take the marbles, I can most certainly attest to their authenticity."

"As can I, and all Elgin's staff who accomplished the deed," Jason said, "but they were never paid, you know, and

I fear their endorsements of Elgin are less than ringing. Nor," he added gently, "do I think Parliament would be impressed by the recollections of a young lady barely turned sixteen."

A flash of anger lit his wife's eyes, and then she sighed. "It is all so sad," she said. "Lord Elgin has spent his fortune acquiring the marbles, yet he cannot get another diplomatic post because of his poor face. Knight has cast grave doubts about the marbles' authenticity, while Byron rants on about their theft. And to crown his sorrows, Lady Elgin disgraced herself with another man. It seems most frightfully unfair. I do not believe Elgin deserves such calumny heaped upon him. Without his help, I fear I should still be in the seraglio. Not that your actions were not heroic, my lord, but—"

"You are quite right," Jason agreed. "Without Lord Elgin, I never would have had access to the sultan. You know," he added on a suddenly whimsical note, "until this moment I had almost begun to wonder if you were truly the girl I once knew, the Gulbeyaz of the seraglio."

His countess gasped. "My lord, I have done my best to forget those days—"

"A pity," the earl murmured provocatively. "I rather thought she was enchanting."

And because he feared he might take his stiffly correct wife in his arms, thus spoiling his devious plans by putting the cart before the horse, the Earl of Rocksley rose and, after helping his wife to her feet, bid her an abrupt goodnight.

Penny, her mind in a whirl, stood perfectly still, gazing blindly at the doorway through which he had passed. He could not possibly have meant . . . She must have misheard.

Gulbeyaz? Enchanting?

The Countess of Rocksley did not play the piano that evening. She did not read a book or search out her embroidery. She went straight to her bedchamber, where she threw herself on her bed and burst into tears. She was *not* Gulbeyaz. She had never been Gulbeyaz. The White Rose of the seraglio was a long-ago dream, a fantasy. That alluring, knowledgeable girl could not be resurrected.

Even if she wished to.

Which, of course, she did not.

Enchanting. Jason did not mean it, of course. It was all a hum. Her husband's way of torturing her for the scandal of her past. He was seizing the excuse of Lord Elgin to run off to London without her, because he was ashamed of her. She was a woman who had covered a scandalous past by becoming as dull as the wife of an Evangelical parson. She was neither fish, nor fowl, nor rare roast beef. A lost soul masquerading as a proper lady.

No wonder, after a scant month of marriage, Jason was bored. Running off to the company of his friends, to the cynical humor of Lord Brawley and the voluptuous charms of Mrs. Daphne Coleraine. Penny uttered a few highly satisfying words she had picked up from sailors on board the many ships on which she had traveled. Yes, she could quite understand why men used such awful terms. There were times when ordinary English simply would not do.

So . . . how was she to manage?

Lady Rocksley sat up, found a handkerchief large enough to accommodate her dripping face. When she could breathe again, she sat on the edge of her bed and considered her husband's enigmatic remark. Was that a challenge she had heard? Had he truly found Gulbeyaz enchanting? Did he actually remember the skills of the White Rose with fondness, perhaps eagerness, instead of disgust?

But even if he did, there was no way to go back. She could not be that girl again. She was overcome by mortification at the very thought of what she had done that night. She could *never* . . .

Could she?

Impossible! She was nearly six and twenty. So far past her prime it was a wonder Jason had allowed her back into his life.

Undoubtedly, a gesture he now regretted.

But if he did not regret Gulbeyaz . . .

Penny stood and, holding a candelabrum high, walked to the tall cheval glass in one corner of her room. Carefully keeping the light away from her reddened eyes, she examined her image. From her simply dressed hair to her emerald pendant, from her finely fringed and embroidered wool shawl to the soft green silk of her gown and matching slippers, her appearance was acceptable, suitable for dinner at home in any nobleman's household in the land.

Suitable. Which translated to dull, uninteresting, drab, lackluster, lifeless, colorless, prosaic, lacking in imagination or spirit of any kind. She had had nearly ten years in which to develop her disguise, and she had done it very well. So well she had almost fooled herself.

In short, Penelope Lisbourne, Countess of Rocksley, needed to reinvent herself.

It was just as well Jason was going to London. She was sorely in need of time to think. To plan. And discover if there were any modicum left, not of Gulbeyaz, but of the young and sometimes willful Penelope Blayne, who had wavered between eager child and charmingly independent young woman, the true-blue product of her Aunt Cass's upbringing. Yes, it was the beautiful young girl, fresh from the schoolroom, who had first caused Jason Lisbourne's eyes to glow with interest that night they met in Lord Elgin's courtyard.

She would need new clothes, head to toe! For whose purchase she had not so much as a ha'penny, Penny amended, her spirits plummeting.

Yet the finest garments in all the world would not, Penny reminded herself sternly, do the trick alone. The woman she could be was not in her clothes, but inside her head. In her attitude, in the way she walked, the tilt of her head, the tone of her voice, the confidence that shone from her eyes, the certainty that she was worthy.

Ah, but was she?

And when had she started to question her purity? Penny wondered. Was it on board ship when Aunt Cass looked at her in shock, then clamped her teeth over questions to which she obviously had not wished to learn the answers? Was it Jason's indifference, his almost . . . *embarrassed* indifference? Or was it the oddly assessing, and sometimes overly bold, looks from Jason's traveling companions, Mr. Yardley and Mr. Timmons, during the long days of their voyage back to Lisbon? Or perhaps it was Aunt Cass's determined effort to travel incessantly, keeping her out of England until, at long last, the threat of Marshal Junot's troops had sent the Portuguese court scurrying all the way to Brazil and forced a mass exodus of foreigners from Lisbon?

Was it possible she had been laboring under a misapprehension all these years? Had she spent nearly ten years erasing a personality her husband found enchanting?

He was leaving her.

He was leaving the dull stick she had become. Nor could she blame him. She, too, was heartily bored with this shadow creature. Yet what could she do to mend the matter when Jason was in London and she was in Shropshire?

She could think on it, Penny realized. She could renovate her outlook, if not her wardrobe. She could rest and recover from three years of caring for an invalid. She could learn to smile more readily, perhaps to laugh. She could unbend her spine far enough to be something a bit more lively than a pattern card of propriety.

In the early summer she would be six and twenty. Most women her age had given their husbands an heir, a spare, and one or more fine girls as well. Yet here she was, twice married to the same man, yet still at virgin. An intolerable situation!

Yes, she must think on it. There had to be some way to solve this ridiculous imbroglio.

Chapter Fourteen

London

Gant Deveny settled back into a brown leather wing chair, stretched his long legs onto a matching footstool, and eyed his friend and host, Jason Lisbourne, over the rim of his brandy snifter. "Word's come Old Boney's invested Badajoz. Surely that's enough to oust your own small contretemps from everyone's tongues."

The Earl of Rocksley, seated across from his friend, did not even lift his well-sculpted chin from his chest. "As we all know, a scandal is of far more interest to the *ton* than Wellington's campaign in the Peninsula. Therefore, I doubt Badajoz will cause so much as a ripple in the tale of how I have married a cast-off from the sultan's harem."

"If only Yardley . . ." Deciding that even the mention of the earl's former traveling companion was painful, Lord Brawley clamped his jaws shut.

"Yardley!" Jason snorted. "Ten years he held his tongue. Yet no sooner does he hear the tales brought back to town by my dear departed guests, than he must begin with, *Oh, if only I might tell . . . if only you knew what I know . . . ah, what I could tell if I would.*" The earl's mimicry had a lethal cutting edge. It was a wonder, Lord Brawley thought, that Rock had not called Yardley out.

"It was inevitable someone would contrive to ply him with wine," the earl continued through bared teeth. "Inevitable the idiot would babble the whole sordid tale. And make it sound as if I pried the child from the sultan's bed."

Jason downed the last of his brandy and flung the fine crystal snifter onto the hearth, where it shattered in a satisfying crash of flying glass.

When the last tinkle had come to rest, Gant Deveny said, with more care than he usually took about his remarks, "Yardley, overcome by a fit of conscience, has retracted." For a moment the two men's eyes caught and held. Mr. Yardley's decision not to dine out on his story, as they both knew, had been more due to fear of serious bodily injury than the result of a belated attack of conscience. "The other friend who was with you in Constantinople is with Wellington," Lord Brawley continued. "Lord Elgin, Hunt, the others at the embassy at that time, are too much the gentlemen and too well trained in diplomacy ever to reveal the truth. And in the past few days you and I have put about the story of Miss Pemberton's illness, resulting in your hasty marriage to her niece. By next Season, Rock, you should have no difficulty presenting your bride to the *ton.* There will have been a dozen worse *on dits* by then."

The earl was still slumped in his chair, glowering at the tips of his toes. The brandy decanter on the table beside him was nearly empty. "Once again, I am grateful for the warning, Gant. If I had brought Penelope into the midst of this . . ."

"At the rate Caroline Lamb is making a fool of herself over Byron, the tale of the Countess of Rocksley as a harem girl should be short-lived. Some say the Lamb had herself delivered to Byron on a silver platter. Without a stitch, Rock, without a stitch."

That caught the earl's attention. He lifted his head, raised a questioning brow.

"Apocryphal, perhaps," Lord Brawley shrugged, his hair shining even redder than usual in the flickering firelight, "but that's how the tale goes. She was curled up, naked as a jay, under a great silver lid. When the cover came off, *voilà,* there she was, a dish to tempt a king."

"Or the snottiest young lord in the realm," the earl growled. "He deserves to be haunted by Caroline Lamb and every other foolish female who sighs over that blasted

Childe Harold. What he and Knight have done to Lord Elgin is a bloody sin. The man saved some of the world's finest works of art. Sculptures going to rack and ruin by weather, war, and every passing thief, including Napoleon Bonaparte." And long before our time, the Greeks themselves destroyed part of the Parthenon by converting it to a church. Then the demmed Turks turned it into a mosque."

The earl leaned forward, his cobalt eyes alight with indignation. "It's a high point, the Acropolis, a perfect site for a fortress. So, naturally, the Turks stored gunpowder there, which was blown sky high by lightning, taking the Propylaea with it. And in the seventeenth century the Venetians had the temerity to shell the place, with the Parthenon taking a direct hit. Think on it, my friend. Can you imagine anyone so mad as to shell the Acropolis? And then Bonaparte's agents came along and were bent on stealing what was left. So what was poor Elgin to do? And yet, between them, Knight and Byron have succeeded in making him such a villain that I fear he may be reviled down the years of history, instead of praised for what he has done."

Slowly, Jason hauled himself to his feet and went in search of another brandy glass. "Even my dear wife," he said over his shoulder, "tells how she cringed when she watched the workers chipping out the metopes." As he poured more brandy, the earl shook his head. "Some of the greatest archeological treasures of the world now rest in the Duke of Devonshire's courtyard, and no one but poor Elgin and his voluble detractors even seems to care."

Lord Brawley, in an attempt to divert his friend from descending from morose into melancholia, chose an abrupt change of subject. "And what of the fair Daphne?" he inquired. "Have you seen her since your return?"

For a moment Gant Deveny feared a second snifter would follow the first into the fireplace.

"She has seen me," Jason mumbled into his brandy. "At the Havershams' rout and the St. Aubyns' ball. She initiated two conversations, to which I responded briefly. That is the sum of it."

"Yet you have not formally broken with her?"

"Should I?"

"Should you not?"

The Earl of Rocksley's shoulders stiffened as he teetered on the brink of grabbing his best friend by the crisp white linen of his cravat, hauling him to the door, and booting him down the front steps. Fortunately, the earl's mind was not so fogged by brandy fumes that he had totally forgotten his friend spoke nothing but the truth. Instead, Jason decided to take umbrage with Lord Brawley's uncharacteristic sensibilities. "I was under the impression, my friend," said the earl, "that you prided yourself on being a man of the world, a sophisticate of the first order. And do I now hear recommendations of marital fidelity? Turned Evangelist, have you, dear boy? My wife is a cast-off of Sultan Selim the Third, yet I am expected to eschew my delightful mistress of two full years—"

"Damnation, Rock! Are you saying that scurrilous tale is true?"

The Earl of Rocksley set his brandy glass on the side table with a thud. "Not that it's any of your bloody business, but my wife—" Jason bit off his words, a horrifying thought rushing through his mind. He could not truly attest to his wife's virginity. The Grand Vizier had assured him that only a virgin could be given to a pasha as a wife, but he did not actually *know* . . . Therefore, his intended hot-headed response that his wife was most certainly a virgin might not be true. Nor could he attest that his wife was still as virginal as the day she was born, as he had had a grand total of two wedding nights with her and a series of nights to follow in ice-bound Shropshire, and yet he had done nothing. Nothing at all. A lack of action to which he could not possibly admit.

So he would lie—or at least pretend a conviction he did not have. "My wife's purity has never been in doubt," declared the Earl of Rocksley, a trifle too pugnaciously. "She was a virgin on our wedding night and, unlike poor Charles Lamb with his Caroline, I have no reason to doubt her fidelity. And damn and blast you, Brawley, for having the temerity to ask."

Jason pushed himself to his feet. "And now, if you would

be so good as to find your own way out, I'm for my bed. Rescuing my wife's reputation is demanding work. I find myself quite fatigued."

As the butler bolted the front door of Rocksley House behind him, Gant Deveny stood motionless on the front landing, his pale face reflecting more sorrow than cynicism. Never had he seen a woman who appeared less like a harem girl than Penelope Lisbourne. He would have helped squelch the scandalous tales about her, even if Jason were not his best friend. And yet, there was something else gone wrong, something he could not put his finger on. Something deeper than the *ton*'s latest *on dit.*

He thought of the gallant manner in which the ice-encrusted Lady Rocksley had dealt with a drunken butler and a hostile housekeeper while sounds of raucous revelry drifted down from the gallery above. Ah, yes, there was more to Penelope Lisbourne than met the eye.

Suddenly, Lord Brawley gave a great bark of laughter. He—tall to the point of gangly, red-haired, pale-skinned, freckled, and afflicted by a terminal case of cynicism—was actually considering playing Cupid. With a jaunty whistle, and swinging his cane as if he didn't have a care in the world, Gant Deveny set off toward his rooms at the Albany.

Half a block away, he broke off in mid-whistle, his cane freezing in mid-swing. What if Lady Rocksley followed her husband to town? What if she stepped straight into the harem scandal, exacerbated by the earl's unresolved relationship with Daphne Coleraine?

Oh, devil it! He'd think about it in the morning. Lord Brawley's whistle was not heard during the remainder of his walk to Oxford Street, where he hailed a hackney to take him back to his rooms near St. James.

"Your pardon, my lady," Hutton said, interrupting Penny's frowning perusal of the linen inventory in the cozy morning room at the rear of the house, "but Mr. Thomas Tickwell has come to call." In response to his mistress's blank look, the butler added, "Mr. Tickwell is the earl's solicitor, my lady. Handles all county legal matters for his lordship. Though, naturally," Hutton added in what he fancied was the tone of a most superior household majordomo, "Lord Rocksley also has a legal gentleman in London."

For the Countess of Rocksley, a haze seemed to pass over the sun outside; the room dimmed most alarmingly. For what possible reason . . . ? Jason had made it quite clear he wanted an heir, so a legal separation was out of the question. Dear God, did he mean to divorce her? That must be it. Having discovered he could not bear to bed her, he was going to petition Parliament for a divorce. *That* was why he had gone to London. Leaving his local solicitor the sorry task of imparting the dire news.

Coward! Truthfully, Penny was unsure if her epithet was aimed at her husband or herself, for her feet refused to obey her command to move. "Hutton," she murmured, "perhaps you would be kind enough to show the gentlemen in here?"

"Of course, my lady." The butler bowed himself out, returning shortly with a man of such medium age, medium height, and innocuous appearance that Penny's spirits rose a notch, in spite of her conviction that his business with her must be quite shocking. Mr. Thomas Tickwell simply did not look like an ogre bent on destroying her life. To top off the contrast with what Penny had expected, his hazel eyes were twinkling and his full lips curved into a broad smile.

"Lady Rocksley," her husband's solicitor said, with a neatly executed bow, "may I offer my congratulations on your marriage? You are a most welcome addition to Cranmere and the county."

Murmuring an automatic response, Penny asked him to be seated. She folded her shaking hands on top of the linen inventory and regarded the solicitor inquiringly. Inside herself, she felt as icy cold as the night of her arrival at Rockbourne Crest. Her mind was in tumult, yet her heart seemed to have stopped.

"Ah, yes, here we are." Mr. Tickwell drew a stack of papers from the leather case at his side. "Lord Rocksley deeply regrets that urgent business took him to London before he settled the matter of your allowance. He has asked me to rectify the situation. He did not, of course, intend to go off and leave you without a feather to fly with." Mr. Tickwell beamed at his own mild humor, adjusted his gold-rimmed spectacles, then once again dipped his head to the papers in front of him. "The earl wishes you to have an allowance of a five hundred pounds per quarter, my lady, with the stipulation that any extraordinary expenses, such as a court dress, will be paid from his funds." Stiff parchment rustled as the solicitor turned to a different page. "And the earl further acknowledges that you have a right to access the income from the monies left to you by your father, the late Lord Christopher Blayne. Lord Rocksley's solicitor in London—and indeed I concur—believes that Mr. Hector Farley erred in cutting you off from these funds as your father's will stipulates the monies should come to you on reaching your majority."

Penny's manners deserted her. "W-what?" she stammered.

Mr. Tickwell favored the countess with a look of avuncular indulgence. Obviously, he was most pleased to be the bearer of such good tidings. "Your parents were not enormously wealthy, my lady, but the younger son of a marquess does not go unshod into the world. "Your inheritance was some twenty thousand in the funds that has grown quite nicely over the past seventeen years. I am most happy to tell you, Lady Rocksley, that the earl is placing the accumulated interest of these funds under your control." The solicitor's cheerful everyman face was dimmed for a moment by a frown. "A most unusual action, I assure you, but he was adamant. The money is yours, he said, to do with as you wish. Miss Pemberton's monies," he added carefully, "will also come to you directly, as stipulated in her will. But for those, I fear you must wait until your thirtieth birthday."

Mr. Thomas Tickwell sat back in his chair, looking quite pleased with himself, while Penelope Lisbourne, Countess of Rocksley, continued to stare at the sheaf of papers in his hand as if they were a snake that might come alive and strike at any moment.

The papers did not move. They did not suddenly burst into flame.

"I am independently wealthy," Penny murmured at last. "Truly?"

"Most truly, my lady. I have been in direct correspondence with both Lord Rocksley and his London solicitor." He held out two sheets of parchment. "You have merely to sign here and here, and I shall be on my way. After, of course"—he rummaged through the contents of his leather case, reaching all the way to the bottom—"I am to give you this," he said, triumphantly producing a leather pouch obviously filled with coins. "Your first quarter's allowance, my lady." He jingled the bag, his smile close to mischievous.

Penny knew she should say something, but the reality of this meeting was so far from her dire imaginings that her tongue seemed turned into one of Lord Elgin's forever-frozen marbles. Wordlessly, she laid the two legal documents on top of the linen inventory and signed her name where indicated, recalling in the nick of time to add *Lisbourne* at the end.

Somehow she also remembered to say *thank you* as she handed the pages back, remembered to shake hands and offer the usual polite phrases of farewell. But never afterward would she recollect exactly what she said. *Jason did not want a divorce!* He had made her independently wealthy. He had, in fact, given her her freedom.

Freedom to run away to that cottage in the country. To bury herself somewhere so far from civilization that no one would ever know . . .

Oh, no, that was not the case at all. More like, Jason was mindful of the story about the little bird released from its cage that came flying back, of its own free will, to its master.

Master. Unfortunate thought. *Master* was not a word she cared for. Not a whit. It reminded her of Mustafa Rasim and the sultan.

For days now her mind had been preoccupied with just one thought—how to make her marriage viable. And it would appear Jason had thoughts of a similar nature. He did not want a divorce. He wanted a wife . . . and children.

A pity, the earl had said when she rejected all memories of Gulbeyaz, *I rather thought she was enchanting.* Had he really?

Very well, she was now free to go to London and find out. She would acquire a wardrobe fit to dazzle a prince, let alone an earl from the wild marches of Shropshire. She would captivate the *ton* with stories of her world travels. She would even help defend Lord Elgin and his marbles, attesting to seeing them torn from the buildings on the heights of the Acropolis in Athens with her very own eyes. She would urge Jason to speak on the subject in Parliament. She would become a grand political hostess . . . or perhaps she would have a salon, featuring the finest poets, musicians, artists, and thinkers.

The schoolgirl Penelope Blayne clapped her hands for sheer joy. Yes, she would burst upon the *ton* in the come-out she should have had long years ago when they were still traveling the Americas. And it would all be a surprise. Yes, that was it. She would not again arrive on Jason Lisbourne's doorstep the poor bedraggled woman she had been the night of the sleet storm. She would burst upon his vision a new woman, done up to the nines in the latest fashions, from the hair on her head to the tips of her toes. From the set of her shoulders and the jauntiness of her walk to the confident smile on her face. She would be . . . *beautiful* again.

Beware, Jason, your wife is on the attack. Like Wellington at Badajoz, she would besiege her husband's heart. And conquer. He would find her too dazzling, too tantalizing, to turn from her in disgust.

Penny raised her eyes to stare out the window at the fresh shoots of green now decorating the trees and bushes. Hope springs eternal, was that not the ancient adage? And she believed, because she wanted to believe. She had a marriage to resurrect, and somehow she must manage it. For if Jason wished to be rid of her, granting her all this money was surely not the way he would have gone about it.

So now, all she had to do was find a way to slip into London quite anonymously . . . Penny bounded to her feet, her energy suddenly shooting up to a level not seen since before Cassandra Pemberton's last illness. She must find Noreen. The Irish had a talent for survival. Together, they would contrive. Ah, yes, Noreen O'Donnell was the very one to aid and abet the Countess of Rocksley's last desperate bid for love.

Chapter Fifteen

Ten days later, a modest hotel on the edge of Mayfair was honored with the patronage of the Widow Galworthy. Eschewing the elegancies of the Pulteney, the Clarendon, or Grillon's, Mrs. Edmund Galworthy, clad head to toe in unrelieved black, her face obscured by a black silk veil that fell in graceful folds from the rim of her bonnet all the way to her elbows, stood wilting to one side of the hotel desk while her most superior maid demanded a suite of the Ashley Arms' finest rooms. Mrs. Galworthy maintained her silence, with grand stoicism, until the porters had deposited the ladies' baggage in their rooms, acknowledged their generous vails with salutes and a grin, and bowed their way out.

The so-called Winifred Galworthy then stripped off her veil—with all its hated recollections—and, with a cry of triumph, threw herself into a great overstuffed chair placed near their third-floor window. "We've done it," Penny cried. "We've actually done it. We are in London, and no one has the slightest idea who we are or how to find us. It's—" The Countess of Rocksley broke off, searching for some way to express the unexpected surge of emotion that had overtaken her the moment the door closed behind the porters. "In my whole life, Noreen," she said at last, "in my whole life I've never really been free. Everyone in Shropshire assumes I am at Rocksley House, and my lord is happily certain I am safely stashed away in Shropshire."

"And does it not occur to you freedom could be a mite lonely?" the Irish maid cautioned.

Penny stretched her arms high above her head, as if

reaching for the sky, holding them there for a moment before allowing them to fall back into her lap. "You are, of course, quite right," she admitted. "Aunt Cass was free, was she not? And though she loved roaming the world and discovering new things, I cannot believe it brought her much happiness in the end."

Noreen paused, her hand on the first buckle of her mistress's trunk. "I don't believe I've ever told you," she said slowly, "but your Aunt Pemberton contrived to be in Constantinople when Lord Lyndon was there. It was all they could talk of below stairs in the weeks before we left for Greece. She was writing letters to all her cronies, she was, asking what fine young gentlemen were making the Grand Tour. Chose Lyndon for you, she did. And was overjoyed when he had to marry you."

"Then why—"

" 'Tis as we've said before, m'lady. Miss Pemberton thought Lyndon had violated you—though what would have been so bad about taking your virginity, I'm sure I never saw. You were married, and sixteen is not a child, no matter how your aunt thought on the matter."

"So when she discovered Jason was positively heroic in his defense of my virtue . . ." Penny's voice trailed into a drawn-out sigh. "I cannot think about that time without my spirit curling into a knot of anguish. I *was* a child, Noreen. And acted most foolishly."

"And now," Noreen declared briskly, "you are both ten years older, yet discovering neither of you is ten years wiser. This journey to London is merely the beginning, the entry to the path that will heal the breach. *If* you tread lightly, my girl, and remember that fine gentlemen expect to give orders and have others jump to their tune. Even wives."

"Merciful heavens, Noreen, are you saying we should not have come?"

The Irish maid considered. "Ah, no, my lady. With you in Shropshire and his lordship in London, there was no path to peace at all, now was there? I'm just saying you might tread careful around the thought of freedom, for it's not a word goes hand in hand with marriage."

By this time Penny's chin had sunk into her hands, her *joie de vivre* vanished as if it had never been.

"Ah, miss—my lady! I'd no call to damp your spirits. I'm that sorry, truly I am."

"No, you are quite right, Noreen. Although I shall always treasure these few days of freedom, I cannot imagine living this way forever. I am here to bring an end to my brief freedom and to my husband's, which has gone on far too long. I am here to bedazzle him so well that he will willingly accept the concept of two people, long separated, becoming one. And overlook my rather shocking transgressions," Penny added softly.

In a sudden change of mood, Lady Rocksley flashed her maid a brilliant smile. "Leave the unpacking, Noreen. Go down straightway and inquire the names of the finest modistes and milliners on Bond Street. Tomorrow, we start our campaign. And may it not take as long as it has for Wellington to triumph over the French!"

The Widow Galworthy, with the aid of well-placed golden guineas and Noreen O'Donnell, who combined the arrogant command of the most superior butler with the organizational skills of a duke's housekeeper, was granted after-hours appointments at the best establishments on Bond Street. Long accustomed to serving a noble clientele who paid their bills in a manner that ranged from snail's-pace to never, the Widow Galworthy's advances upon her bills produced gleeful smiles on the faces of tradesmen hovering behind the fine storefront façades of Mayfair.

The midnight oil burned, and generous vails went to the many assistants who also worked late, for, as Mrs. Galworthy informed those who labored on her behalf, she had traveled the world and well knew the value of good service. Though it's true the various shopkeepers, including the vastly superior modiste, Madame Madelaine (of Chelsea), who garbed some of the finest ladies of the *ton,* thought the Widow Galworthy an odd duck indeed, they were scrupulous in their attendance upon her. For they were all agreed that, no matter how strange her ways, the Widow Galworthy was a lady of the first stare. Knew her way around the world, she did. Yet never failed to thank those who gave her service, not even the lowliest maid who brought her tea. Yes, a right fine lady was Mrs. Galworthy. And if some of those coins were paid out for privacy, then they were glad enough to give it. Lady knew what she wanted, she did. And who were they to say her nay?

Yet the mystery deepened, along with the head-to-toe finery now piled into two new trunks in the widow's suite of rooms. Who was the heavily veiled lady garbed all in black? Where had she come from? And why must her obvious intention of putting off her mourning be a mystery? Other widows did not require such secrecy when going back into colors. And another oddity, that was, for widows usually went from black into half-mourning, garments of gray or lavender, worn with black gloves. None of Mrs. Galworthy's garments boasted these dull colors, nor, stated the glover quite firmly, was there a black glove among the array of finely stitched kid the widow had accumulated over the course of two weeks.

Miss Wiley, the milliner, not only boasted of selling an astonishing number of bonnets to the widow, but declared every one of them in the height of good taste, as well as fashion. No vulgar poppies or surfeit of feathers for the Widow Galworthy. A lady she was, through and through. The merchants shook their heads. In the end—though some did not wish to think it of so fine and generous a lady as Mrs. Galworthy—it was decided she was either on the lookout for a titled gentleman or was setting herself up as queen of the muslin company. There was something about her, was there not? A certain gleam in the eye as she appraised herself in the glass. A determined set to her chin. A look of . . . calculation—yes, that was the word. The Widow Galworthy had *plans.*

But the buzz in the back rooms of Bond Street was as soft as it was avid, for coins jingled in the pockets of those who served the veiled widow, and proffered bills were promptly paid. Everyone smiled and bowed and put the Widow Galworthy's orders before all others. Walking dresses, carriage dresses, afternoon gowns, ball gowns, riding habits, spencers, pelisses, shawls, bonnets, gloves, half-boots, and slippers of every matching color.

And lingerie. The so-called Mrs. Edmund Galworthy's sky-blue eyes shone with delight when she examined the pile of chemises, petticoats, and, most particularly, nightwear Noreen had laid out for her inspection before the delicate garments were packed away. The finest muslins and linens, all embroidered to perfection and trimmed with inserts or hems of lace, some almost as transparent as the *shalwar* and tunic she had once worn before her husband in the Topkapi Palace.

Penny's soft smile faded. The Countess of Rocksley, in her guise as the Widow Galworthy, had had time for serious thought while she accumulated a wardrobe fit for a princess. *I rather thought she was enchanting.* Jason's brief comment haunted her night and day. And had he found Penny Blayne attractive as well? She had seen it that first night at Lord Elgin's party. So, surely, if she tried very hard to remember what young Penny was like . . . her wit, her charm, her enthusiasm for life.

If she dressed even more magnificently than the sixteen-year-old Penny . . .

If she could convince herself that the lessons learned in the seraglio were not a horror to be buried forever in the depths of her memory . . .

Yet the new clothes were nothing more than a symbol, she knew that. They were a reminder, a crutch, if you will. They could do little for a woman who did not believe herself beautiful, within as well as without.

That evening, as Penny was undressing for bed, she waved Noreen away, turning to study herself in the room's full-length mirror, as she had once surveyed her dull self in Shropshire. She proffered a tentative smile to the woman who stared back, flickeringly illuminated by candles on each side of the mirror. This was not the lifeless, defeated woman she had seen in the cheval glass at Rockbourne Crest. This woman's skin and hair glowed with health; the depths of her blue eyes reflected hope. Though she was clad only in the simplest of her new white chemises, this evening's reflection was remarkably lovely. Indeed, she bore no resemblance to the poor sad creature who had stumbled, ice-coated, into Jason Lisbourne's entrance hall on a nasty night near the end of February. The girl in the glass was . . . *beautiful.* After trying so hard to hide it all those years, Penny found it difficult to admit, but even at the advanced age of five and twenty she was strikingly attractive.

Would Jason find her enchanting? Or was an English rose no substitute for Gulbeyaz, the kohl-eyed, scented White Rose of the seraglio?

The Countess of Rocksley reaffixed her smile. The girl in the glass smiled back. Softly, secretively. Hopefully. *Oh, yes, surely he must.*

On the following morning, the staff of the Ashley Arms stared in awe as a fine lady, dressed in the dernier cri of fashion, swept down the front staircase. If it had not been for the stalwart Irish maid following close on her heels, none of them could have guessed the lady's identity. Her carriage dress was a shade of blue only slightly darker than the azure silk she had worn on her wedding night. Over it she sported a cloak of textured wool, deep teal in color and trimmed in sable. Her high-poke bonnet, which matched her gown, was lined in finely pleated white silk and decorated with a single understated white silk rose, shining against the rich blue of the bonnet's brim. Behold, the reborn Penelope Lisbourne—on her way to dazzle her lord and master, the Earl of Rocksley.

The hotel manager was so astonished at the transformation—at the hotel's dark chrysalis burst open to reveal a brilliant beauty—that he failed to reprimand his staff, who drifted along behind what had once been the Widow Galworthy and heard, quite distinctly, her order to have all her baggage sent to Rocksley House on Cavendish Square. They then trailed her to the front of the hotel and watched with avid interest as the lady and her maid climbed into a hackney. Afterward, all agreed the women had ordered the jarvey to take them to Rocksley House as well.

Speculation was rampant. Had the Ashley Arms been hosting the notorious Lady Rocksley? Or did that rakehell

Rocksley have yet another string to his bow? In the end, the manager was forced to line up his entire staff and remind them, forcefully, that discretion was the prime rule of hotel management. Whoever the Widow Galworthy was, or had been, was none of their business. This tale was not to be repeated.

With many sighs and disgruntled groans, the staff of the Ashley Arms returned to work. But in their memories the lady's transformation would glow for years to come.

"M'lord, m'lord." Kirby, Lord Rocksley's valet, hovered over his lordship, who was clinging to sleep as if he were indeed the Rock his close friends dared call him. "M'lord," Kirby hissed a bit louder, "Lady Rocksley has arrived. Stackpole has shown her into the drawing room. M'lord!" Kirby came close to losing his customary suavity. "M'lord, you must wake up, truly you must."

"Wha-at?" Jason peered at his pesky valet from under half-opened lids.

"Lady Rocksley, m'lord. Here. Now."

"The devil you say," Jason muttered. "Come up from Bath, has she?" He started to sit up, groaned, and fell back on his pillow, one arm over his eyes. "I suppose she's heard the rumors, though what mama is doing here at this hour I cannot imagine."

"Perhaps she spent the night with one of her friends here in town, m'lord," Kirby suggested, as unaware as the earl that the butler, in his surprise, had failed to indicate their visitor was the younger Lady Rocksley. "If you will allow me to prop up these pillows a bit, m'lord, I believe we can have you sitting well enough to swallow my restorative. As always, you will soon feel much more the thing, ready to greet Lady Rocksley in no time at all."

But it was nearly forty-five minutes before the Earl of Rocksley was presentable enough to be seen by his mama, Eulalia Lisbourne, the Dowager Countess of Rocksley. And even then his lordship trod the stairs quite gingerly, unsure if his vision was perfectly sound. Nor was his mind sharp enough to deal with what would undoubtedly be questions far more penetrating than he could wish. *Damn and blast!* He was truly fond of his mama, but he wished most fervently she had stayed in Bath.

"Lord Rocksley, my lady," declared Stackpole, the butler, in stentorian tones, as a footman hastened to throw open the door to the drawing room.

Jason affixed what he hoped was a welcoming smile to facial muscles that were so stiff they positively creaked. "Mama!" he cried. "To what do we owe the pleasure of—" His voice broke off. He gaped at the vision of loveliness rising to greet him. "Oh, my God," he moaned.

Penelope? Was this gorgeous creature his Penelope? Little Penny Lisbourne—Gulbeyaz—grown into the full promise of her beauty?

But, unfortunately, a muddled head combined with the shock of stark reality kept the earl's admiration bottled up inside. Jason Lisbourne stalked across the room, for all the world as if he had not been struck dumb by his first glimpse of his wife's transformation. "Are you mad?" he roared. "The town is rife with rumors. To show your face here now is to be torn limb from limb. Tell your coachman he may turn around and return to Rockbourne Crest this moment!"

Penny had set out from the Ashley Arms suffused with confidence, determination, eagerness, even optimism, but during each of the forty-five minutes she had waited in the earl's drawing room, these emotions had eroded until, as her husband strode through the door, only a faint and wavering hope was left. Now, even that was gone. Shocked beyond tears, she could only stare at him. Never, in her worst nightmare, had she dreamed he would cast but one quick glance over his beauteous wife and instantly send her back to Shropshire.

"Perhaps you would care to hear the latest rumor?" Jason snapped, without so much as asking his wife to be seated. "It seems I have married a half-French trollop—undoubtedly someone has heard a garbled version of the tale of Aimée de Rivery. This half-French, half-Turkish harem girl was cast off by the sultan for having a roving eye and was foisted on the young Viscount Lyndon when, to hear the tabbies, he was scarce out of leading strings. A shocking misalliance his family succeeded in concealing for many years until the scheming creature arrived on his doorstep demanding all the rights due a noblewoman in England."

Penny, whose stomach now felt as queasy as the earl's, took a step back and sat down abruptly on a sofa upholstered in cinnamon brocade.

"The bastards!" declared Noreen O'Donnell roundly. "Begging your pardon, my lord." The countess's long-time companion slapped her hand over her mouth and kept it there.

Chapter Sixteen

Stackpole," Lord Rocksley called, "bring tea and brandy at once." Then, becoming aware how thoroughly he had once again mishandled the situation with his wife, Jason sat down beside her and spent a few thoughtful moments staring at the white rose on the bonnet that completely obscured her face.

"Penelope . . . Penny," he said at last, "you are looking very fine. Wherever did you find such elegant garments in Shropshire?"

His wife did not turn her head, but she did deign to answer him. "I have been in London more than two weeks, my lord, acquiring a fine new set of clothes. I—I had wished to surprise you." She paused, still with her face turned from him. "It would seem that I did," she added softly.

"You have been in London and did not tell me," Jason returned ominously. "And where did you stay, may I ask?"

"At the Ashley Arms, a most respectable place, I assure you. I registered as the Widow Galworthy and wore a black veil at all times. No one saw me. Until this morning, that is." Penny, recalling that everyone in the lobby and on the street outside had heard her order the jarvey to take her to Rocksley House in Cavendish Square, tightened the clasp of her hands in her lap until her grip was painful. That was all the explanation the Earl of Rocksley was entitled to hear. She would not chronicle her hopes and dreams, nor lay bare her puny efforts to impress him. All she had done . . . and she had failed. Once again.

The earl opened his mouth for a scold, then snapped it

closed. Good God, however had he developed a reputation as a rake, a ladies' man of no little skill, when he could not manage aught but a hostile relationship with his wife?

Stackpole delivered a tray with a silver tea service, placing it on a table directly in front of the countess. As a footman followed with a tray holding a decanter of brandy and sparkling glasses, the earl said to his butler, "I presume Lady Rocksley's rooms are being prepared, Stackpole?"

"Yes, my lord, the maids have been hard at work ever since her ladyship's arrival." The butler glanced at Noreen O'Donnell. "And if my lady's maid will come with me, a dray has arrived with a number of trunks. There is a good deal of unpacking to be done."

"Leave the trunks as they are," countermanded the earl.

Stackpole, the footman, and Noreen O'Donnell all stared. The Countess of Rocksley's bonnet came to attention. A small gasp escaped from beneath it.

During the previous colloquy, Penny, who was quite familiar with having her finely laid plans overset, had begun to recover from what was merely one more shock among many. "You cannot still insist on my returning to Shropshire, my lord. It is perfectly obvious only my presence at your side can put an end to the gossip."

With a sharp wave of his hand, the earl sent everyone scampering from the room, leaving him alone with his countess. Still glowering, he snapped, "If you think for one moment I would allow you to be ripped to shreds by those tabbies or leered at by their husbands—"

"As bad as that?" Penny asked, turning at last to look directly at him.

"Take that foolish bonnet off," the earl ordered, a trifle irrelevantly. "Let me have a look at you. A nice touch, the white rose," he added more softly.

Ah, yes! he thought as his wife removed her bonnet. Here was the woman he had secretly hoped would exit the post chaise that winter night in Shropshire. What, he wondered, had inspired this transformation . . . could it possibly have been himself? "Penelope . . ." he began and then, most unfortunately, thought better of displaying his sudden surge of youthful eagerness.

"Penelope," he said in a tone amended to a calm reasonableness he was far from feeling, "I know you have lived in isolation for far too long, and you are most certainly entitled to spend the Season in town, but I must tell you this is not the year to do so. By next year this nasty *on dit* instigated by Yardley—you recall young Yardley, the idiot, do you not?—will be old news. My close friends are already helping to combat the rumors, and I see now I shall have to enlist the aid of my mother. She is a formidable dowager, I assure you. By next year we will have come about, and you and I shall do the Season in style. I promise you, Penelope, truly we will."

"But surely if they see me—"

"They will see what they want to see," Jason responded grimly. "You must recall even the truth is not all that exonerating. Your Aunt Cass was always considered an eccentric, and there's no way around the fact you *were* part of the Sultan Selim's harem. If Yardley had kept his mouth shut . . . but that's of no account now. I cannot call him out without making the—"

"Call him out!" Penny cried. "Surely you would not. You could be killed."

Light gleamed in his lordship's eyes. "Would you mind, Penelope? Would you truly mind?"

"Idiot," Penny murmured, lowering her sky-blue eyes before they could give away all her secrets. "You must know that once was quite enough for you to risk your life for me." Abruptly, she turned her attention to pouring out the tea.

Absently, the earl accepted his cup, fixed just the way he liked it. "Very well," he said at last, "I suggest a compromise. But do not say I did not warn you. You may stay in town tonight. This afternoon we will drive in the park at the hour when at least half the *ton* takes to Rotten Row in an effort to see and be seen. You may be roundly snubbed, but you *will* be seen in a setting where we may move on if anyone is rude. And . . . yes, tonight I shall take you to the opera. We will invite Brawley and perhaps one or two others, for there, too, you may be seen for the lady you are in a situation where we can control who enters my box."

"I trust Mrs. Coleraine will not be one of the party."

The earl's temper flared . . . and died, as he noticed his wife's lips twitch in an effort to keep her countenance. *The minx!* "She will not," he said shortly. "And, after that, it is back to Shropshire for the both of us, I think, for, truthfully, I have not the heart to send you back alone."

At this, Lady Rocksley's lips trembled with another emotion entirely. "Will you truly come with me? That is all I ever wanted, you know. For you to—" Horrified by what she had nearly let slip, Penny broke off, fixing her concentration on her tea and a tasty almond macaroon.

Lord Rocksley promptly took advantage of this opportunity to study his wife. Her light golden-brown hair gleamed in the sunlight illuminating the drawing room through a series of floor-to-ceiling windows overlooking a fine garden. Her enticing figure was perfectly accented by the cut of the blue gown, so similar in color to the garments once worn by Gulbeyaz. Her lips were full and marvelously pink, though it was plain to see she wore no paint, as had the child-woman in the seraglio. Her lashes dusted cheeks flushed with color not brought on by the heat from the nearby fireplace. And her chin . . . ah, yes, that was as set and determined as ever. Or was it? Was that a quiver he detected?

It occurred to Jason that he had, perhaps, a motive other than compassion for treating his wife with kindness. Possibly even a reason beyond his vague urge to settle down and set up his nursery. Here before him was the woman of dreams, the one he had feared he had lost forever. And, surely, she had not come all the way to London and bought trunksful of new clothes merely to please herself?

Tonight, he and the White Rose—he and his *wife*, he amended—would be alone together in their adjoining suites of rooms upstairs. The perfect opportunity to accomplish what had been so long delayed. Jason's mind flooded with exotic images. Dancing girls, diaphanous silks, his wife crawling beneath the undulating quilt . . .

"Do you think we might visit Lord Elgin's marbles?" his

countess inquired, eyes shining with an eagerness she had never turned on him. Not even in the seraglio, dammit, where her "acting" had never gone beyond a charming shyness and a startling display of skill.

His married life was doomed. There could be no other interpretation of the cross-purposes that dogged their steps.

With considerable effort, the Earl of Rocksley took himself in hand. "Of course, my dear," he responded coolly. "I believe they are at Burlington House now. I will send round a note to ascertain if we might view them before our drive in Hyde Park."

Marbles! He had as good as offered his wife a reconciliation, and all she could talk of was Elgin's blasted marbles.

What, after all, did it matter? He would see she gave him a houseful of children, as Lady Elgin had done before her lord cast her aside. See if he wouldn't, by God!

"A sad spectacle, was it not?" the Earl of Rocksley asked his wife, who sat glum beside him as he tooled his way up Piccadilly toward Hyde Park. "I, too, was shocked."

"Such beauty reduced to a ramshackle shed without so much as a single window," his countess sighed. "To be forced to peer at the greatest sculptures in the world by lantern-light! Yet at least those in the shed are protected," Penny conceded, "while the large pieces outside are fully exposed to England's iniquitous climate. It is a tragedy, my lord. You *must* urge Lord Elgin to sell."

"You did not see the marbles when they were in Park Lane? I assure you the shed there was a veritable palace compared to what we have just seen."

"No." Penny shook her head. "We made a brief visit to London in the spring of 1808, but Aunt Cass adamantly refused to look at the marbles. I even slipped away one afternoon, with only Noreen at my side, and attempted to get in, but the young men guarding the place were quite fierce. Only serious students of antiquities might view the marbles. They turned me away as if I were a mere fly buzzing about their treasure."

"Good God, did they really?" the earl murmured. "No

doubt you should have gone armed with Miss Pemberton's lethal parasol."

"Jason!" Penny chortled. "If only you . . ."

"Yes?"

The Countess of Rocksley squirmed a bit, went so far as to bite a knuckle on one properly gloved finger. "If only," she said at last, "you showed your humor to me more frequently. You can be so charming to others, you see, but . . ."

"But to my wife I am an ogre." The earl's tone was flat, bereft of any hint of humor.

"Here, and in Shropshire as well, you . . . you tend to look at me as if you cannot imagine who I am or what I am doing here. It is very lowering, I assure you."

Once again, all Jason could see was that blasted white rose! Why the devil were women allowed to hide behind huge bonnet brims while men had their every expression constantly on display? Glumly, the earl decided that that was why most men solved the problem by learning never to display any emotion at all.

"I shall endeavor to improve my attitude," Jason returned stiffly as he skimmed his pair of perfectly matched grays through a gate into the park at a pace that could be matched only by the most skilled whips. In the process he brought to a halt the progress of a portly gentleman on a bay stallion, two stylishly dressed couples strolling toward the gate, and a landau containing two elderly ladies, whose coachman forgot himself enough to toss an outraged epithet at the earl's rapidly retreating back.

"I do not believe," said Lady Rocksley, "that scattering members of the *ton* like chaff before the wind is the way to go about improving your attitude."

"You have turned into a sour Methodist shrew, my dear," the earl returned cordially. "Dress as finely as you will, there's a starched-up Evangelist beneath that bonnet."

The countess's fuming reply was cut off, unspoken, as the earl deftly maneuvered his way into the line of fashionable carriages slowly circling the park. They were now much too public for a quarrel, particularly as the eyes of every last soul taking the air that afternoon widened at the sight of the unknown woman sitting up beside the Earl of Rocksley. From those on the bridle path to those taking a leisurely stroll, from the occupants of sporting curricles and high-perch phaetons to the elegant passengers of barouches and landaus, the earl and his companion were the cynosure of every gaze. Was that . . . ? Could it be . . . ? Surely not. The woman was much too civilized to be the notorious Countess of Rocksley.

Meticulously, Jason nodded to every person with whom he was acquainted—a rather high percentage of those they passed—but he did not chance an introduction until they were more than halfway round the vast park. Deliberately choosing a lady of impeccable social standing augmented by a kind heart, Lord Rocksley made her known to his bride. Though visibly startled, the middle-aged matron recovered quickly, welcoming the countess to London with becoming enthusiasm. The earl drove off, well pleased, as the lady was also known for her ability to chatter nineteen to the dozen, and the identity of his mysterious passenger would soon be known throughout Hyde Park and, within a day or two, the entire *ton* as well.

Another round of the park, a second well-chosen introduction, and Jason was beginning to be pleased with himself. Perhaps he had been drowning his sorrows prematurely. Perhaps matters were not as bad as he had feared.

And then the atmosphere within the park changed. Nods became perceptibly cooler. Some carriages speeded up as they passed by, the occupants keeping their eyes straight front. Full half the riders on horseback kept their chins in the air, certain ladies going so far as to whisk their full skirts aside, as if they might be contaminated by the proximity of the sultan's whore. Even those the earl recognized as Fair Cyprians out on the strut seemed to shrink from his wife, as if she were a leper. And then, as if fate were piling disaster upon ignominy, a carriage pulled up beside them and a feminine voice cried out, "Jason, Jason, my dear. Do hold! I wish to meet your charming companion."

Penny, by this time grateful for any kindly face, proffered an immediate smile across the distance that separated the carriages, even as her hand closed over the earl's arm in silent appeal, as he seemed about to move on without so much as a glance in the lady's direction.

"Believe me," he muttered, eyes fixed on his grays' ears, "you do not wish to meet the lady."

"Yes, I do," Penny returned stubbornly. "It is not as if there are people waiting in line to meet me."

As it turned out, the decision was taken out of their hands as congestion among the carriages in front of them forced the earl's curricle to a halt directly next to the stylish barouche beside them. Penny eyed the woman who had called out to them with open admiration and a slight quavering of her newfound *amour propre*. In spite of her new clothes and new attitude, this polished gem of the *ton* reduced her to the level of a gawk from the country. The lady, of approximately her own age, was garbed in a striking carriage dress of poppy red kerseymere, sparkling with gold buttons and gold lace in the military style, every inch designed to set off as voluptuously enticing a figure as Penny had ever seen. The plumes on her bonnet were dyed to match, gracefully swirling into the air before curling down to point the way to dark eyes set into a face that seemed to promise a gentleman anything he might desire.

"My lady," the earl declared through gritted teeth, "may I introduce Mrs. Coleraine and her escort, Colonel Gibbons. And this is my wife, Lady Rocksley," he added with cool formality.

Mrs. Coleraine. Daphne *Coleraine?*

But of course. How could she have been such a fool as not to have thought of the possibility of encountering her husband's mistress in the park? No wonder he had not wished to make the introduction!

"But, my dear, how charming you are," beamed the wicked beauty. "So unlike the dastardly rumors. Truly, one would never guess." With a throaty laugh, which added to Penny's envy as well as animosity, Daphne Coleraine addressed the earl. "You must bring her to my soirée on Wednesday next, Jason. Indeed you must. I am certain we will all be great friends."

The congestion eased. With the road in front of him clear, the earl whipped up his horses, leaving the barouche behind with nothing more than an abrupt nod to the woman who had kept him well entertained for the past two years. As he pointed his horses toward the gate nearest Cavendish Square, his inner rage was great. Daphne Coleraine's temerity in forcing an introduction to his wife took second place to the *ton*'s treatment of his countess. *How dare they?* How could they treat the wife of an earl in such a manner?

Yet he had known how cruel the haut monde could be. Though he had not mentioned the matter to Penelope, this was the primary reason he had come to town—to attempt to unravel this mess before she was cast into it, sink or swim. Lord Elgin had dug his own pit with his obsession with Greek marbles, but little Penny Blayne was an innocent, a child wronged, her reputation lost through no fault of her own.

And yet he had taunted her for her propriety. For her obvious efforts to erase the scandal of those few weeks in Constantinople. He was a beast. He should be flayed alive.

Deuce take it, he had, in fact, so successfully avoided the burden of having a wife that he had allowed her to be totally ruined. If he had come back from Constantinople with a bride, nothing more than a raised eyebrow over the age of his wife would have marred their marriage. By now his nursery would be full . . . and his wife looking around for a lover . . .

Hell and damnation! He'd been quite right to attempt to drown his sorrows. There was no proper solution to this impasse.

"We will not go to the opera, I think?" Penny ventured after they turned off busy Oxford Street.

"You would wish to expose yourself to further calumny after what you have just endured?"

Her face was turned toward him, wistfulness plainly written upon it. "I-I have never been to the opera, at least not in London. And I should not care to disappoint Madame Madelaine, who is counting on me to display her fine designs," she added judiciously.

Incredulous, the earl retorted, "You would risk censure so you may be seen in a new gown?"

"Pray do not be ridiculous, my lord. I love the opera, and I promised Madame her garments would be seen everywhere. Then you tell me I must return to the wilds of Shropshire on the instant. And you wonder why I would risk the cut direct from a foolish few in order to be let out of my cage for a single night! You are—"

The earl silenced her with a wave of his palm. "Very well. If you can bear the scrutiny, we will indeed attend the opera," he consented dourly. "If you have an evening gown as fine as your carriage dress," he added on a grudging note of satisfaction, "for I should like the devils to get a good look at a true lady."

"Oh my," Penny murmured, "was that a compliment?"

"I believe it was."

"Thank you."

"You forget," the earl replied coolly. "I am nearly the only person in existence who knows for a surety how false those vicious rumors are."

"Again, I thank you, for truthfully even you do not know the whole of it," his wife responded, most obscurely.

"I beg your pardon?" It was fortunate they had arrived at Rocksley House, for the earl came close to dropping his reins, an error of shocking proportions seldom committed by even a rank beginner.

There was no reply, as his countess was descending from the curricle, with the aid of a footman who had rushed out from the house. Jason sat high on the curricle bench, like the veriest idiot, while his wife swept up the walk, up the shallow steps, and through the door being held open by Stackpole. Grimly, he recalled his vow earlier that day to see that she filled his nursery before he let her turn to another man, as Lady Elgin had done.

He could, of course, divorce her. Marry again, start fresh. As Lord Elgin had done.

But he would not. Because he had no grounds. Because thoughts of young Penny and her innocence and of Gulbeyaz, who had been so eager to please, had come back to haunt him, beginning to fill his days as well as his nights, reminding him of what he had missed by being so hell-bent on his freedom. So satisfied with his gallantry in Constantinople that he had smugly slithered out from under his long-term obligations, leaving his bride to wither on the vine.

In the end, he had grudgingly offered her a position at his side, all for sake of an heir. It was a wonder she had not torn a strip off him. Instead, she had seized the reins in her own capable hands and transformed herself into at least a semblance of the woman she thought he wanted. While he embalmed himself in brandy, even as he assured himself he was making valiant efforts to restore the reputations of both Lady Rocksley and Lord Elgin.

Boiled in oil. That was the punishment Selim the Third might have ordered for the reluctant earl. What a fool he was.

"My lord?" Jason's groom was standing at the horses' heads. Slowly, the earl climbed down. Stackpole's eyebrows twitched as Lord Rocksley walked through the still open door. Today, the earl feared, afternoon tea would have a decidedly bitter flavor.

Chapter Seventeen

The house on Cavendish Square—built outside the bustle of fashionable Mayfair, yet fitted out with every elegancy a noble gentleman's townhouse should command—had been the sole extravagance of Jason Lisbourne's father, the seventh Earl of Rocksley. The sweeping staircase, suspended over the entry in a veritable miracle of design, was, Jason decided, the perfect foil for his wife's quite stunning beauty as she descended the stairs that evening, garbed in full regalia for the opera. Her high-waisted half-dress of white gauze, embroidered in silver and studded with brilliants, opened over a gown of soft peach. Her golden-brown hair was dressed high and entwined with silver cord, one softly unwinding curl falling in front of each ear. As she caught his eyes upon her, she deliberately—or so he hoped—allowed her silver-mesh shawl to droop, revealing the swell of softly mounded flesh whose perfection had been, until now, left to his imagination.

Jason suddenly regretted inviting Brawley and another friend, Mr. Harold Dinsmore, to give them support at the opera. He did, in fact, come close to forgetting the opera altogether.

Enticing feathers do not a willing woman make. He was unsure who had said that, but the words popped into his mind like a canker. This woman had been nothing but trouble from nearly the moment he met her. Tonight was merely one more ordeal to be gotten through as lightly as they could. Both now . . . and later. For, after they returned to the quiet house on the outskirts of the city, the earl had Plans.

His wife, too, had plans. Though Penny was unsure if she could carry them out. The stern discipline by which she had lived the last ten years in an effort to eradicate her past was so ingrained, she feared the best of intentions could not conquer it. So for now—this moment—she would be content with small things, such as riding in a shadowy carriage, hip to hip with her husband, inhaling the scent of him—was it sandalwood or simply essence of Jason? She sat very straight and tried not to touch him, but her efforts were to no avail when he removed a slim velvet case from his inside jacket pocket and said, "I took the liberty of consulting with O'Donnell about your gown, my dear. I trust you will find these a satisfactory complement."

Penny found herself unable to move, gaping at the jewel case as if she had never seen one before. The earl flipped open the lid to reveal a delicate necklace of diamond filagree, nestled in a bed of white satin. "Allow me," he murmured, removing the necklace from its case. He paused expectantly, obviously waiting for her to turn around.

As her husband's fingers touched the back of her neck, Penny was taken by a shiver that rocked her all the way to her toes. As well as a few other nameless places in between. She did not breathe as he pushed her artfully arranged curls aside and affixed the first of the matching earbobs with a skill so deft she could not help but be reminded of his vast years of experience with women.

Not that it mattered. *Nothing* mattered, but that they were together now, tonight, and that he would be returning to Shropshire with her on the morrow. Let the *ton* do its worst. Jason was right. By next Season the *on dits* about Lady Rocksley would have been replaced ten times over by even more shocking scandals.

But as she was frozen in place, holding her breath and thinking of better times to come—while her husband's face hovered nearly as close as his hands—the inevitable occurred. The Earl of Rocksley had no sooner fastened the second diamond earbob in place than he cupped his wife's chin between his palms and bent his lips to hers. Though each had reached the conclusion that their marriage must take the inevitable final step, neither was prepared for the hot flare of emotion that leaped at them the moment their lips touched. Panic-stricken, Penny shoved hard, then, discovering the earl's chest as immovable as a boulder, pounded on him with her fists, finally breaking away to back herself into a corner of the burgundy velvet squabs. The earl, breathing hard, flung himself into the other corner. Across the few feet separating them, they glared at each other, shock vying with anger.

"I beg your pardon," Penny gasped when she finally found her tongue. "That was most improper of me. I—I can only plead that it was most unexpected—"

"After ten years of marriage, you are shocked when your husband kisses you?" The earl's tone was filled with such cool sarcasm his wife was tempted to deliver a good solid yank to the bronze lock of hair that fell so intriguingly across his brow. But that would mean touching him . . . and that, it seems, she could not do without disastrous results.

"I truly beg your pardon, Jason," Penny declared most humbly. "I am aware I leave a great deal to be desired in a wife. I have caused you nothing but trouble—" If only he knew she had lost her way in the bazaar because her mind had been filled with visions of the youthful and oh-so-charming Jason Lisbourne.

"We will discuss this matter later," the earl pronounced austerely as his carriage joined the line of other vehicles outside the Royal Opera House. "Later tonight," he added most ominously, just as the footman opened the door and let down the step.

Dear God, Penny thought, stumbling and being saved from the muddy gutter only by the strong arm of the liveried footman. Surely her night at the opera could not have had a more inauspicious beginning.

Yet, at first, the evening was not the ordeal Penny had feared. Yes, the buzz in the great house increased threefold when she took her seat at the front of the earl's box. Every quizzing glass in the vast tiers of boxes, and in the pit as well, was turned in her direction. But at acting a role Penelope Lisbourne had long since proven her skill. She sat, erect as a queen, and allowed them to look. Thanks to Madame Madelaine and her own rediscovered inner strength, she had never looked better in her life. And at her side was one of the *ton*'s best-known peers—her husband—supported by two friends, whose reputations might be as rakish as the earl's but who were as eagerly sought after by hostesses of the haut monde.

Penny was so enthralled by the spectacle of the vast opera house and its glittering patrons—in spite of their rude perusal of her person—that she ignored the three gentlemen sharing the box until Mr. Dinsmore hissed into the near-silence between the orchestra's tuning-up and the first notes of the overture: "Oh, I say, Rock, look at this!" And proceeded to wave the playbill under the earl's aristocratic nose.

Penny saw Jason's face, already set in stoic lines, visibly pale. Lord Brawley, leaning over his shoulder to read the playbill, uttered a word so frightful the countess gasped. The earl merely dropped the offending playbill to the floor, crossed his arms, and stared at the great gold-fringed velvet curtain as if it were the most fascinating of spectacles. While the orchestra played the lively overture, Penny turned, hiding behind her fan, and took a look at Gant Deveny, who was seated behind her. His face, however, revealed nothing, as it was always pale, though the humor that usually graced the perpetual cynicism of his green-flecked hazel eyes seemed to be missing. Something was wrong, something other than the blatant scrutiny she was receiving, yet she could not imagine what it could be. Annoyed by this phalanx of male secrecy, Penny turned her attention to the stage, where the curtain was going up at last.

Speaking? The characters were speaking, instead of singing? Had they come on the wrong night? Gently, Penny tugged on her husband's arm.

The earl promptly bent his head to hers, his words whispered through inexplicably tight lips. "*Singspiel,*" he said. "Much of the story is in dialogue, like a play. The songs are written simply for pleasure."

Smiling her thanks, Penny returned her attention to the

stage. Caught up in the beauty of the first song, she did not immediately notice the costumes and the setting. But as the applause died away and the next unintelligible bit of gutteral German dialogue rang out, her attention wandered to the painted backdrop, reversed with startled intensity to one of the main characters who was wearing *shalwar* and a turban, and then, with growing horror, back to the domes, minarets, and latticed balconies of the colorful stage set.

Heaven forfend! And then, although her German was not as competent as her French, Italian, and Spanish, the meaning of one oft-repeated phrase finally became clear. *"Is this the Pasha Selim's house?"*

Penny gasped, pushing so far back into her delicate gilt chair that Lord Brawley was forced to reach out a strong arm to keep it from tipping over. Jason seized her hand, leaning over to speak directly into her ear. "I am most sincerely sorry," he said. "I had no idea the opera was to be *Abduction from the Seraglio.* More of the infinitely bad luck that seems to dog our footsteps."

"But the *same name,*" Penny choked out.

"Kindly remember Mozart wrote about *his* Pasha Selim before you were born," Jason told her, a tad sternly. "I assure you he did not have you in mind when he penned this supposed comedy."

Comedy. This travesty on her experience was a comedy? Penny clutched her fan so tightly the ivory sticks snapped.

"Do you wish to leave?" her husband asked.

The old Penny—the girl who had risen from the remains of the once romantical Penelope Blayne, the girl who had shriveled and died on the voyage from Constantinople to Lisbon as reality had replaced her foolish girlish fantasies—would have said yes. The new Penny, who had taken her fate in her hands and set out to dazzle her husband, lifted her eyes to the earl's and shook her head with vigor. She was here at her own personal hero's side, in full view of the *ton*, and here she would stay, and brazen it out. And, in truth, when in the third act the hero raised a ladder to the harem window in order to rescue his beloved, the absurdity struck her full force. *Abduction from the Seraglio* was indeed a comedy, with no relation to the true heroics that had effected her own rescue from the harem of Selim the Third. She could laugh, and applaud Belmonte's rescue of his Constanze, and still hold her head high.

She was here, in this box at the Royal Opera House, instead of sitting forlornly behind a lattice in the Topkapi Palace, because of Jason Lisbourne, a man who had dared everything for her. And never, ever, must she forget it, no matter how difficult matters might become.

During the two intervals, Penny noted, no one was admitted to their box except those whose understandable curiosity was mellowed by long-time friendship. Mrs. Daphne Coleraine was not among them, for which Penny gave hearty thanks. And just before the end of the second interval, Lord Brawley leaned forward and whispered in her ear. "You have done well tonight, my lady. You have faced them all under the most trying conditions, and, shallow as they are, there's none so blind they cannot see you for the fine lady you truly are. They are a strange lot, the *ton.* Give them time to grow accustomed to the fact they have made a mistake, and they will come around. Mercifully, their memories are short."

Penny offered a grateful smile before turning her attention back to the stage, her glow of pleasure shortly turning to a frown. In all the tension of the evening, she had nearly forgotten the earl's ominous promise as she exited the carriage.

Later tonight.

And, inevitably, *later* arrived.

Noreen O'Donnell, sensing an *atmosphere,* blithely laid out her mistress's most elaborate nightwear, a garment whose only relief from transparency came from elaborate white embroidery on the bodice and a panel of white embroidery down the front, which, Penny was certain, tended to draw the eyes *to* her private places rather than cover them up. Over this doubtful garment—the countess could not now imagine why she had selected it—O'Donnell wrapped Penny in a dressing gown of the same white lawn, but this garment featured an abundance of flounces on the sleeves and from knees to hemline. Perhaps that is why she had chosen it, Penny thought frantically. The robe was made of so much fabric, it was like an all-encompassing protective tent. There were even two layers of flounces that came right up under her chin, and those on the sleeves came to the tips of her fingers.

Tent, indeed! She looked like Haymarket ware. A veritable trollop. Good God, she had chosen something Mrs. Daphne Coleraine might wear!

But was that not what men liked?

Penny slumped down onto the edge of the bed, her back to the fateful dressing room door. She still had no idea what Jason wanted in a wife. Every time she thought she had reached a conclusion, something happened to make her wonder. For long years she had convinced herself Jason had taken Gulbeyaz in disgust. Now, he called that naive but well-trained odalisque enchanting. Yet, at the very same time, he was so reluctant to declare her his wife, he had roistered right up to the moment of her arrival. Even after the formal renewal of their vows, he had failed to bed her. He had run off to London. She suspected he was continuing to drink more than was good for him. And yet, he had given in—if ever so slightly—to her desire to view London. He had been kind—yes, that was the correct word. He had gifted her with diamonds.

He had kissed her.

And now he was coming to her. For more than conversation. Surely she had not mistaken his intention. A vivid flash of the powerful emotion that had swept her at Jason's kiss suffused her body, causing her to blush fiery red, in startling contrast to the multiple white flounces. What if she made a mull of it?

Again.

The dressing room door opened so softly she almost did not hear it. Penny simply felt his presence, knew she was no longer alone. She sat up straighter, then recalled the stiff little figure who had told her husband she was perfectly reconciled to doing her duty. And the woman earlier tonight who had fought off her husband with her fists. Truthfully, it was a wonder he had come to her at all. Struggling against her long efforts to forget those weeks in the harem, Penny made a determined effort to resurrect Gulbeyaz, that terrified yet eager child, who had embraced her husband with enthusiasm and wonder.

Would he recognize her playacting, or the anguish that lay beneath it? Penny went through the requisite motions, sliding along the bedcovers, allowing herself to sink, seductively, onto the pillows at the head of the bed.

"You were expecting me, I believe," her husband inquired, sounding so sure of himself her stomach churned.

She could not look at him, she would be lost. That perfectly terrifying emotion that had overwhelmed her in the carriage would take over and claim her life. She must remember that she had, in fact, made a marriage of convenience, both then and now. She must be pragmatic, realistic. Give Jason the children he wanted and never let him see how much more she wanted for herself.

So, clamping her tongue over the fierce urge to tell Jason Lisbourne that she had been expecting him for close on to ten years, the Countess of Rocksley smiled invitingly, welcoming her husband to her bed.

Alas, as seemed to be the usual case between the earl and his countess, the results of her blatant invitation were not as expected. Her smile, her seductive posture, her expensive and alluring dishabille seemed to inspire nothing more than a scowl. The earl's cobalt eyes darkened to mysterious depths in the dim light of one flickering candle. He stood a full ten feet from the bed, enveloped in a robe of dark blue silk that clung to his lithe form like a second skin, looking very much as if he were reviewing every last rancorous word he and his countess had exchanged since they renewed their vows.

Or, Penny wondered, was he thinking of the delightful and excruciatingly embarrassing moments as she had demonstrated her skills before the watching eyes at the Topkapi? Those moments when she had been so full of wonder at the sight of her husband's young and muscular body.

So . . . so *proud* of being able to please him. Those moments when, at last, they had both forgotten the voyeurs peeping at them and had . . .

Penny's thoughts plummeted back to the here and now. Jason was still glowering, and she was lying there, like an overly decorated sweetmeat, hidden behind a mountain of flounces, a smile so fixed to her face she feared she must spend the rest of her life behind the same false façade.

Remove the flounces. Yes, that was it. But if she did, the transparent linen beneath made her *shalwar* and tunic look positively modest.

Was this, her third attempt at a wedding night, a time for modesty?

Most certainly not!

At a speed so laggard Jason was ready to throttle his countess, she wriggled her way off the bed, and, with a shrug of her shoulders, the multitude of flounces fell to the floor. With the candle on the nightstand directly behind her, little was left to the earl's imagination. His mouth went dry, his body came to attention. Rancor faded to a dim dark recess where he might retrieve it at a more propitious moment.

Penelope, moving with the sensuous grace of the odalisque Gulbeyaz, threw back the bedcovers and once again arrayed herself against the pillows. The earl, with considerable interest, noted that she did not pull the covers up to her chin. Indeed, she did not pull them up at all.

And then she stretched her arm to the far side of the bed—displaying, as she did so, a remarkably enticing view into the depths of her exceedingly low neckline—and flicked aside the covers. The earl was not so far gone in lust that he did not recognize that the look his wife cast him at this point was more challenging than seductive. Oh, he granted her a good deal of credit for trying, but at the sticking point she had failed. That enchanting creature, Gulbeyaz, had gone back into hiding, leaving only the Penelope of five and twenty, visibly making an effort to be the wife he wanted her to be. And nearly as grimly determined to lose her virginity as he was to take it.

Hell and the devil! At least now he would know the truth.

In a few short minutes he would know if his wife's bed skills had come from training or from practice.

And if from practice, hissed the mind of the reasoning man behind the earl's rakish façade, *did it truly matter?* For the child had had no control over her life in the harem. Whatever had happened there should be buried forever, not to be touched upon again.

Lose Gulbeyaz? The joy of his life, for whom he had searched through so many women he had long ago lost count?

Dropping his robe as unceremoniously as his wife had dropped hers, the earl stalked toward the bed. Penny's eyes widened. He was more . . . ah—*developed* than she recalled. As was she, of course. She should not be surprised. Goose bumps broke out, including some in very strange places. And then the bed seemed to be engulfed in flames. She was so hot she could not breathe. She clutched a handful of sheet and hung on, even after her husband's body loomed over her, one of his powerful arms entrapping her shoulder, while the other stripped down one side of her gown so he could suckle on her breast.

They had waited too long for finesse, for the gentle maneuverings of a considerate bridegroom on his wedding night. They plunged into passion with that extra intensity, not only of lovers long denied, but of lovers who had known hurt, resentment, guilt, as well as desire. Later, they would be sane. But not tonight. This moment was theirs.

Chapter Eighteen

It was gone eleven before the Countess of Rocksley descended to the breakfast room, wearing a delicious morning gown of pale green muslin sprigged in lavender. She did not look at all like a woman packed and ready to leave for Shropshire. Nor did her husband—who had, in fact, arrived in the breakfast room only minutes before his wife—appear to be a man hastening through a meal so he might be off on a lengthy journey. Dressed in the height of town fashion, from his artfully arranged bronze locks, fresh from Kirby's ministrations, to the tips of his glossily polished boots, the Earl of Rocksley slouched back into his chair after his wife's entrance, looking very much like a man who might be content to stay rooted to that spot all day, so long as he might be entertained by the beguiling sight of his no-longer-virginal bride.

After one swift glance at what she could only term the smug satisfaction on her husband's usually saturnine features, the countess ducked her head, nodding dumbly as Stackpole proffered a variety of selections from under their round silver covers. Blast the man! And what if she had not been a virgin? Would he have rejected her out of hand? Would she now be standing beside her trunks in the foyer, waiting for the coach to be brought round? The coach that would take her into exile, abandonment, and divorce? The world, Penny thought, not for the first time, was vastly unfair to its females.

"Well, sir," she said with more asperity than intended, "are we off to Shropshire, or are we not?"

The earl paused with a bite of beefsteak halfway to his mouth, then laid his fork carefully upon his plate. "I believe we did indeed discuss this matter at some time during the night, my dear. Did you not express a loathing to run away as we did from Constantinople?"

"And did you not counter by reminding me of Wellington's tactics of strategic retreat and live to fight another day?"

"Perhaps I did," the earl murmured, adding provocatively, "I fear I was not completely attending to the debate at the time."

"Jason!" His wife, much shocked, once again bent her head to her gammon, eggs and toast.

The earl, lips twitching, resumed his attack on his beefsteak. After some moments of taut silence, he suggested, in as mild a manner as he was capable of, that he still believed the wisest course was to return to Shropshire and let the entire matter fade of its own accord.

"That is cowardly!" Penny shot back. "All my beautiful clothes . . . I had such plans . . ." The countess, encountering her husband's unwavering stare, choked to a halt.

"Your gowns will be as lovely in Shropshire as they are in London," the earl pointed out with maddening logic.

"And who will see them?" his countess demanded.

"I will."

"Oh." Penny, mortified, fisted a hand to her lips. Hot tears sprang to her eyes. Was that not what she had wanted all along? For Jason to see her as beautiful? Did it truly matter that this was not her year to dance at balls, reign over a salon of artists and authors, or be the so-clever hostess at dinner parties for the influential politicians of the day? Once again, she had been dreaming, constructing castles of glittering crystal when she needed to appreciate the good English earth beneath her feet.

Shropshire. It would be beautiful now, fulfilling the green promise of spring that had begun to decorate the hills, valleys, and gardens just before she left for town. As long as Jason came with her, as he had promised, all would be well. Her disappointments were the silly maunderings of an overgrown girl who had never had a Season. Next year would do as well, of course it would.

"Lady Rocksley," Stackpole intoned, interrupting Penny's penitent thoughts.

"Mama!" The Earl of Rocksley shot to his feet so fast his napkin dropped to the floor. Penny's surprise was so thorough only years of strict training brought her, wavering slightly, to her feet. Unconsciously, she held on to the back of her chair for support.

The lady who had just swept through the doorway examined her daughter-in-law with exacting scrutiny. The dowager countess was not an imposing female, it being instantly obvious the earl had inherited his height from his father. But her garments were precise to a pin, her dark brown hair had only enough streaks of gray to reveal that she did not resort to artifice to cover her age, and her cobalt eyes—so like her son's—were alight with intelligence and worldly wisdom.

"So," she declared a moment before it was perfectly plain the new countess was about to take umbrage at her inspection, "you have gotten yourself into a pickle, have you, Rocksley?"

Her son, ignoring this jibe, said, "Perhaps you would care to join us for breakfast, mama?"

"I broke my fast at Lady Carlyle's, where I spent the night and," she added with a baleful glance at the pair of them, "received the full gist of this disaster. But I might be coaxed into another cup of chocolate."

The footman immediately pulled out a chair for the dowager, and a maid scurried in with all the amenities for a full place setting. After the elder Lady Rocksley had allowed she might also have one of cook's muffins, with butter and a bit of blackberry jam, the earl dismissed the footman and calmly returned to his breakfast. His countess, however, merely stared at her plate, unable to swallow more than a sip or two of coffee.

Eulalia Lisbourne, Dowager Countess of Rocksley, finished her chocolate, placed the cup precisely in its saucer. "I must admit, Rocksley, to being profoundly shocked when you wrote to me of your marriage. And if you think I believed that faradiddle about how you came to marry this woman in the first place, you are fair and far out. Cassandra Pemberton was in her third Season when I made my come-out, and I know full well what an eccentric—"

"Aunt Cass had a Season?" Penny burbled, startled into forgetting her manners, as well as her horror at the dowager's arrival.

"Oh, indeed she did, and quite frightened off every eligible nobleman in London. A shocking bluestocking she was. Matched wits with anyone who would listen, espoused female independence, trod on every masculine feeling of superiority. And quite hoodwinked her papa into leaving her in control of all his money. Most improper! So then she was off on her jaunts, growing more odd by the year, with nothing slowing her pace, not even when she took on your care, my child," said the dowager, looking not unkindly at Penelope.

"But," she declared, drawing breath and fixing her son with a stern eye, "if you wish me to think she did not plan to entrap you, Rocksley, you are much mistaken—"

"No, truly—" the earl interjected.

"Nonsense! I daresay she was fit as a fiddle, laughing into the pillows of her sickbed the moment she discovered she had fooled you into acquiescing to her outrageous scheme—"

"Mama!" the earl roared. "You will listen to what I have to tell you." And the true story came rolling out, occasionally augmented by soft, chagrined additions or corrections from the younger Countess of Rocksley.

"Merciful heavens," the dowager gasped when the earl came at last to his renewal of vows in Shropshire. "I daresay even Monk Lewis never came up with such a tale."

"I am so sorry, my lady," Penny murmured. "But Jason was a hero, truly he was. If not for him, I would, this moment, be a poor soul lost forever in the sultan's harem." Hopefully, she peeped at the dowager countess, looking for a miracle, as she and Jason were certainly at an impasse.

Eulalia Lisbourne contemplated her empty plate, raised her eyes, unseeing, to the colorful hunting scene hanging on the wall. "I believe Rocksley is right," she said at last. "We must do as our dear General Wellington has done. This, like the campaign on the Peninsula, is not going to be an easy task. We must regroup and plan our strategy."

Regarding her daughter-in-law's fallen face with some compassion, the elder Lady Rocksley added, "Yes, yes, I see you wish to stay and fight, but it simply will not do, my child. Though it may be through no fault of your own, you have blotted your copybook most shockingly, you know. There is a most nasty seed of truth at the bottom of Mr. Yardley's lies. We must . . ." The dowager tapped one slender finger against the tablecloth. "Yes, I think we must go to Rockbourne Crest, where we may plan our campaign in privacy, perhaps for a recovery during the less busy season just prior to Christmas." Lady Rocksley folded her napkin, and placed it on the table. "When do you wish to leave?"

"But you have just arrived from Bath, have you not?" her son protested.

"Yes, it is most unfortunate I did not know the whole before," she said in significant tones, "but it cannot be helped. Hopefully, my maid has not yet begun to unpack."

In view of the dowager's stoicism and the impossibility of the younger countess referring to her own exhaustion from a nearly sleepless night, the earl's entourage of two coaches, burdened by a mountainous quantity of luggage, in addition to Kirby, Noreen O'Donnell, and Hitchins, the Dowager Countess's most superior maid, departed in the early afternoon, returning Penelope Lisbourne to the wilds of Shropshire she had left with such high hopes little more than a fortnight earlier.

Shropshire

The Earl of Rocksley was decidedly fond of his mother, who possessed a great deal of good sense for a female, and to whom he would be eternally grateful for not cutting up stiff over his most peculiar marriage. But he did not want her at Rockbourne Crest at this moment. Though, in all fairness, he had to admit that if his mama had any idea she was intruding on the equivalent of a wedding journey, she would scurry back to Bath with all alacrity.

But pride would not allow him to drop so much as a hint of the turtle-like progress of his marriage. Unthinkable his mama should discover him to be such a slow-top! But it was hard, devilish hard, to find himself alone with his bride only in the late evening privacy of their suite of rooms—with the odor of greening earth and early blossoms drifting in through the open windows reminding them of nature's renewal of life—and do anything but what was uppermost in his mind. And what, he very much hoped, was in the mind of his wife as well.

Yet, when daylight came, the passion of the bedchamber seemed part of a separate world, for his mother and his countess had plunged with near frenetic intensity into the world of women, including visits to neighboring families and taking a hand in the affairs of the village, while he was left to attend to estate business, a classic division of duties that did not, at the moment, appeal to him in the least. The Earl of Rocksley truly did not care if Blossom and her Ned had been blessed with a baby boy. Nor that his countess was determined to find a wife for the vicar. (And spending far too much time in that blasted Greek god's company, by Jupiter!) Nor did he wish to sit between his mama and his wife in the high-backed Lisbourne family pew while Stanmore flashed his benign gaze, perfect white teeth, and overly friendly smile upon his captive audience of a Sunday morning. But there he had been the past two Sundays—with visions of endless annoyingly erudite sermons stretching into the infinity of his exile in Shropshire.

The earl had also deigned to dine at the squire's, a duty he could not avoid, and, indeed, his mama had pointed out with some asperity that he should get down on his knees and thank Matthew and Tabitha Houghton for arranging a dinner that included the four leading families of the area, a definite fillip to his wife's efforts to take her proper place in society. But Jason could not help but note that the dinner had been an ordeal for his countess, even though Penny had put on a gracious social façade that had never slipped under the guests' blatant scrutiny. (Not unlike the night, he thought in sudden reminiscence, she had enacted an erotic play before the avid eyes of the sultan and his court.) A game one, was his countess, he had to give her that.

Yet when he had come to her bed the night of the squire's dinner party, she had lain like a stone frozen at the bottom of an icy stream. So he had taken her in his arms and simply held her until her poor stiff body nestled into his and, at last, he held a woman and not a carving of ice. Was that the night, the earl wondered, when the Jason Lisbourne he should have been had begun to make himself known? When he had begun to doubt that his odd mix of pragmatic fatalism, interspersed with moments of erotic fantasy, were a proper approach to marriage?

Jason groaned, slumping into his saddle, from which he had been gazing out over his acres from a vantage point well up the steep hill above Rockbourne Crest. He had ridden up the winding rocky path in a quest for the solace this particular view always brought. Yet now that he was here, he was so lost in thought he scarcely saw it.

There was something that hovered just out of his grasp, something his wife expected from him that he had not been able to give. Yet, for the life of him, he was unsure what it was. She was so *determinedly* willing. She had given him Gulbeyaz—achingly lovely, accommodating, skilled—but the . . . eagerness was gone. Yes, that was it. Impossible as it seemed, there must have been a time at the beginning when she had loved him. Worshipped him as a hero. Waited for him to come to her.

And he had not.

So his once-shining Penny, now his tarnished bride, had settled for what life had dished out to her—a rakish earl who now wished to set up his nursery. Rather than live the life of a lonely recluse, she had agreed to be his brood mare. And even though her actions gave evidence that she was not adverse to the process, his wife now held her heart close, encased behind an iron wall of his own construction.

Surely such a calculated arrangement was sufficient, the earl grumbled. Many men must deal with wives who showed no interest in bedchamber activities at all. That was the way of the *ton.* Marriages were made by bloodlines, titles, land, and wealth. In society, love was more apt to presage disaster than happily-ever-after. Look at the current disgrace of the very much married Caro Lamb chasing after that idiot Byron. And there was always the sad example of the Prince of Wales—surely the most foolishly romantic prince of all time—who had married for love a woman thrice condemned by society's rules—a commoner, a widow, and a Roman Catholic. A sorry affair that had ended in his formal, *approved* marriage to a woman who so disgusted him they had lived apart almost from the moment of conception of their only child.

So he should be grateful, should he not? Jason mused. He was better off than most of his acquaintances. Penny was a delightful armful. Even if he had not been able to touch her heart.

And whose fault was that? For she had once laid it out on a platter and thrust it under his nose, while he had set his eyes on far horizons and not even looked down to see her precious gift.

His mama underfoot, eagle eye trained on his dealings with his wife. Stanmore prating away on Sunday and altogether too visible the remainder of the week. Dinner at the squire's. Musical evenings. *Hell and the devil, how was a man to have time to think?*

And what, declared his once-silent conscience that now troubled him daily, required so much deep thought to discover the obvious? To regain his wife's love required only that he give love in return. But that was more than a bit of a struggle, for by day his wife was as cool and tart-tongued as the woman who had arrived on his doorstep one icy February night. A second Cassandra Pemberton in the making. And she was far too much in the company of that blasted round-collared Don Juan, the vicar. How could he have been such a fool as to have appointed a young, unmarried man to such a position? Just another example of his careless rakish ways, Jason supposed. And now he was paying for it, for every woman in the area was making eyes at Mr. Adrian

Stanmore, even spinsters twice his age. Outrageous, that's what it was.

Instantly recognizing the supreme irony of his wayward thoughts, the earl let out a rueful chuckle, then patted his horse's neck when the animal sidled and snorted, startled by his owner's mirth. "It's all right," he whispered to the stallion. And then, more thoughtfully, "Yes . . . somehow it will all come right." Jason Lisbourne took one last look at the spring beauty of his acres, then turned his horse toward the path leading down to the problems that waited below.

From the age of nine, Penny had spent her life solely in the close company of her Aunt Cass. Traveling constantly, she had never had the comfort of a friend her own age. Nor had she had the benefit of the wisdom of a woman who had borne and raised three children, as had the Dowager Countess of Rocksley. Except for one or two inevitable skirmishes over which Lady Rocksley was head of the household, Penny was well pleased with Jason's mother. That lady had, in fact, taken the news of her son's irregular marriage exceedingly well and was spending long hours at the secretaire in the morning room writing letters to a vast number of friends, imparting the "true" story of her husband's marriage and his wife's impeccable antecedents. And at the same time the dowager had found time to support her daughter-in-law's plunge into county life. For Penny had rushed to renew her brief acquaintance with Mary Houghton, daughter of the local squire, and with Helen Seagrave, the young gentlewoman so impoverished she was obliged to earn a few extra shillings by providing lessons on the harp and pianoforte.

Not only did Penny enjoy the rare treat of developing friends her own age, but she had long since determined that one of her new friends would make an excellent wife for Mr. Adrian Stanmore, for whoever had heard of a bachelor vicar? Particularly one who was almost sinfully handsome? Mary, the downtrodden daughter of the loquacious and overpowering Mrs. Houghton, very much needed a home of her own, and Helen Seagrave also needed some means of raising herself above the level of genteel poverty. Both women were well brought up and kindhearted, although Miss Houghton was far too much of a mouse, to Penny's way of thinking. She could only hope, freed from her mama, Mary Houghton would develop a bit of backbone.

If the younger Countess of Rocksley ever gave a thought to whether her compulsion to be so busy about the affairs of others might be due to having less time to consider her own unsatisfactory situation, she gave no outward sign.

It seemed, however, that the earl could not share his wife's interest in the vicar, for he scowled mightily whenever Mr. Stanmore's name was mentioned. A fact that brought a positive gleam to his mother's eye and which Penny found puzzling, for she could not imagine any fault Jason could find in Mr. Stanmore, nor why his obvious annoyance seemed to please the dowager.

A bustling at the front entrance drifted down the hall to the cozy parlor where Penny had been sitting, a novel abandoned at her side. Callers? There had been so few of these in their weeks of rustication that Penny did not wait for Hutton's summons. She arrived in the foyer in time to see Gant Deveny handing his many-caped driving coat to Hutton. "Lord Brawley!" she exclaimed, then, recovering quickly, added with surprising truth that she was delighted to see him. As well as the softer, gentler Mr. Dinsmore, who accompanied the viscount.

Gant Deveny turned to greet her, white teeth flashing into a lopsided grin. The irony of the situation—the contrast with the night when he had been the one to greet her under such inauspicious circumstances in the same entry hall—struck them both at once. Penny glanced at Hutton, who stood ramrod-straight, very much on his dignity, then back to Lord Brawley. She giggled. He chuckled, then, green eyes dancing, burst into an open guffaw. Hutton let out an audible huff. Penny and Gant Deveny attempted to stifle their laughter, only to bend nearly double in paroxysms of hopeless mirth, while Harry Dinsmore looked on, thoroughly confused.

"Good God, whatever can be so amusing?" the earl demanded, from halfway down the stairs.

"We were . . . remembering . . ." Penny began.

"The night your lady arrived last winter," Gant Deveny finished.

Jason immediately glanced at the obviously outraged Hutton. A slow grin spread over his face. In retrospect, in spite of his own reprehensible conduct that night, it *was* rather funny.

It also marked how very far his marriage had come in a remarkably short space of time. If they could all laugh about that disastrous night, perhaps there was hope for them yet.

Chapter Nineteen

Hope was fleeting. In spite of the flurry of assigning rooms to their unexpected guests and ordering the luggage taken up, the Countess of Rocksley caught the speaking look Lord Brawley exchanged with her husband. *Merciful heavens, what now?* With the certainty of some new disaster come upon them, Penny excused herself, saying she needed to be certain the rooms were properly turned out (a slight that would undoubtedly incense Mrs. Wilton, if Hutton were foolish enough to tell her), and left the gentlemen to closet themselves in the earl's study.

"Well?" Jason demanded, as soon as they all had glasses of Madeira in hand and were sprawled in the room's comfortable chairs. "And do not tell me you are merely passing through Shropshire on your way to Brighton."

His listeners paid the earl the compliment of chuckling at this feeble attempt at humor. Harry Dinsmore sank further into his bergère chair, his legs stretched out in front of him. Gant Deveny's rather prominent Adam's apple convulsed as he swallowed the bald statement he had been about to make. "Ah . . . you recall the scandal between Lord Byron and Caro Lamb while you were in town?" he inquired rather obliquely. At the earl's abrupt nod and impatient scowl, Lord Brawley ventured, "As you can well imagine, no man could be faulted for tiring of such a surfeit of adoration, and any normal woman might take the hint—"

"But not Caro Lamb," Harry Dinsmore contributed eagerly, catching the purpose of Brawley's circumlocution. "Byron wants nothing more to do with her, but she follows him everywhere, camps in the street outside places she ain't invited, throws herself at his feet."

"Worse than a leech," Gant declared. "The chit's gone mad, fit for Bedlam. Can't stand Byron myself, but I have to admit it's enough to make me feel sorry for the poor devil."

"Feel sorrier for Charles Lamb," Harry Dinsmore grunted. "Imagine having such a wife."

There was a decidedly awkward silence as all three men contemplated Mr. Dinsmore's words. "Is that the point you are trying to make, gentlemen?" the earl intoned. "That I should be grateful my wife's reputation is not in worse shreds than it already is?"

Lord Brawley looked at Mr. Dinsmore, who raised a hand to cover his lips and slowly shook his head. Gant Deveny, obviously elected to be the bearer of bad tidings, emitted a heartfelt sigh. "Never thought any such thing, Rock, I assure you. Your countess is a fine woman. No one who meets her can fail to recognize her for the lady she is. Whole thing's a misunderstanding, blow over in no time, without a doubt."

"Then . . . ?" The earl raised an eyebrow, and waited.

"It's Daphne!" Mr. Dinsmore burst out, forgetting his intention of letting Brawley take the brunt of the earl's displeasure.

"She has decided to emulate the antics of Caro Lamb," said Gant. "We caught wind of her intentions and have come to warn you. She has leased a house near here and plans to lay siege to the citadel, as the Lamb has done with Byron!"

"She cannot think I will take her back!" the earl barked.

Harry Dinsmore cleared his throat. "She wants a good deal more than that, I fear."

"It seems," Brawley said, "she has convinced herself that your marriage is totally invalid and that she will rescue you from the harem harpy. As she puts it," he added hastily, when Jason Lisbourne appeared on the verge of erupting from his chair with the purpose of throttling his best friend.

"Or else she simply plans to drive a wedge between you and your wife," Mr. Dinsmore said, "so that you will divorce Lady Rocksley and be free to marry her."

"Has the whole world gone mad?" Jason groaned. Jumping to his feet, he paced the room, hands behind his back, head down. "Is she here now?" he demanded at last. "Am I to expect her to arrive at my door, hard on your heels?"

"Unknown," Lord Brawley responded. "She has effected a short-term lease for something called Fenwick Manor, I'm told—a property belonging to some cit in Bristol."

The earl swore with grim fluency. "Not two miles from here," he muttered, "less as the crow flies. I'll wring the blasted woman's neck. Just let me get my hands on her—"

"Can't do that, old chap," Harry Dinsmore advised. "Bad *ton.* And I daresay the countess would not care to see you hanged."

The earl's profanity grew even more inventive, causing his friends to view him with undisguised admiration. "Hutton!" the earl bawled. When the butler answered with suspicious alacrity, all three gentlemen realized he must have had his ear to the door. "Send a footman to Fenwick Manor at once to inquire if a Mrs. Daphne Coleraine is in residence.

"And now, gentlemen," the earl added after Hutton's departure, "let us anticipate the uproar when my mama and my wife discover this catastrophe. And plan how we may come out of it with our skins intact."

"I say!" protested Mr. Dinsmore. "Ain't fair to say '*our* skins,' you know. Deucedly unfair, in fact. Tell him, Brawley."

But Gant Deveny was slumped glumly in his chair, thinking of the ancient tale about death being the reward of the messenger bearing bad tidings. At the moment death seemed almost preferable to the storm that was about to break over Rockbourne Crest. Yet, as good friends should, he and Harry were here to support Jason in his time of need. And Jason's countess as well. For no one, particularly a bride on such shaky ground as Penelope Lisbourne, deserved as formidable an adversary as Mrs. Daphne Coleraine.

On the following day the younger Lady Rocksley left the gentlemen to their own devices and, blithely unaware that the footman had returned to impart that Fenwick Manor was in hourly expectation of Mrs. Coleraine's arrival, set off for the village, driving a gig, with Noreen O'Donnell up beside her. During the long years of her Aunt Cass's illness, a visit to the village had been her only freedom. Before haring off on what proved to be a wild goose to London, Penny had initiated this practice in Shropshire and re-embraced it with alacrity upon her return. Though Old Betsy was anything but a high-stepping prad, Penny reveled in being in full control of the reins and in her ability to direct the aging animal wherever she and Noreen might wish to go.

Today, in addition to errands for her mama-in-law and for herself, she planned to call on Helen Seagrave, whose struggles to support herself, her ailing mother, and a querulous aunt on the pension of her father, a colonel who had died in the army's brave stand at Corunna, had brought her to giving lessons on the harp and pianoforte. Although Penny also enjoyed the quiet companionship of Miss Mary Houghton, the squire's daughter was a mere nineteen and so painfully shy that Penny was already coming to the conclusion that it must be Helen Seagrave for the vicar. Though how the burden of Miss Seagrave's relatives was to be managed, the countess was, as yet, uncertain. But the determination that there should be at least one happy pair of newlyweds, other than Blossom and her Ned, in this particular part of Shropshire was firmly fixed in her mind. She would see Mr. Adrian Stanmore properly wed before the year was out!

But any opportunity Penny might have had for a private coze with Helen Seagrave was soon knocked to flinders, for no sooner had the countess accepted a cup of tea from Mrs. Seagrave than the elderly maid of all work opened the door to Mrs. Tabitha Houghton and Mary. The squire's wife burst into the small but nicely appointed salon like a ship under full sail, Miss Mary trailing like a dinghy in her wake.

As befitted the wife of the local squire, Mrs. Matthew Houghton dominated village life. Although she gave proper deference to the county's noble landowners, no one was left in doubt about who ruled the roost during the many months her titled neighbors spent in London, Bath, and Brighton, or enjoying hunting with the Quorn or shooting in Scotland. Tabitha Houghton's appearance was as imposing as her voice, a stentorian cry of which a parade sergeant might have been proud. In combination with her height and a sturdy girth that seemed twice that of her daughter, Tabitha Houghton presented an altogether intimidating presence that eclipsed Mary's quiet attractiveness.

There was a flurry of shifting seats as Helen Seagrave and her spinster aunt, Miss Ainsley, promptly effaced themselves to allow Mrs. Houghton and Mary to sit beside Helen's mother on their somewhat threadbare sofa. "Have you heard?" the squire's wife boomed, casting but the slightest of nods at the four ladies already seated in the room. "Fenwick Manor is let at last. A widow from the city, I'm told. The squire says I may send her a card for my musical evening, for he has been assured she moves in the first circles in London. A fine addition to our society, I am sure, for I fear we are much too quiet," she added with patently false modesty. Then recalling that one of those present was the Countess of Rocksley, Tabitha Houghton smiled thinly and declared, "Of course we are much livelier now that Rocksley is, at last, spending time at Rockbourne Crest." She flashed the countess a wolfish smile. "Lord Rocksley plans to attend my musical evening, does he not, my lady? We should be quite desolate, I'm sure, if he did not join us."

Penny, who was certain Jason would part with a goodly number of guineas if only he could buy his way out of this social obligation, smiled blandly and assured Mrs. Houghton that not only would the earl attend but so would his two guests, if the squire's hospitality could be stretched to include two single gentlemen just down from London.

This exciting news immediately diverted all thoughts from Fenwick Manor and its new resident. *Two London gentlemen!* While Tabitha Houghton held forth to Mrs. Seagrave and Miss Ainsley on the immense possibilities of such an addition to their social circle, the three younger ladies put their heads together, speaking in whispers.

Miss Helen Seagrave, at three and twenty, had been on the verge of conceding that life had passed her by when Adrian Stanmore had introduced her to the Countess of Rocksley and, for some unaccountable reason—similarity of age or perhaps a recognition that the drab façade of each hid a liveliness of spirit—Penelope Lisbourne had instantly taken her up. The younger Lady Rocksley had even gone so far as to discuss her venture to London with her new friend and to accept her commiserations when Penny's stay in town had been brief.

Miss Seagrave possessed a pair of speaking gray eyes, set in a serene face that was seldom allowed to shine, as, in an effort to appear old enough to be an instructor of music, she had confined her lustrous brown hair in an unbecoming coif and put on her caps at a very early age. A disguise that had not fooled the countess one whit, perhaps because she, too, knew what it was to hide her light beneath a bushel. Helen Seagrave was a woman of lively mind and ready wit, and the Countess of Rocksley was quite determined to improve her new friend's status in the world. Helen would make a splendid vicar's wife, she was certain of it.

Though what she could do for poor Mary, who did not have the gumption to say boo to a goose, she was at a loss to imagine. As Penny imparted what she knew about Lord Brawley and Mr. Dinsmore to the avid ears of her two listeners, she re-examined her plans. Mr. Dinsmore *might* do for Mary, though Lord Brawley was, of course, quite hopeless. Although she could not help but like him—for she knew a genuine sympathy lay beneath his cynical demeanor—she could not envision him as anything other than a lifelong bachelor.

"Ah, look!" hissed Miss Ainsley, as the sound of a four-horse team caused her to peer out the window. Without a thought to their dignity, five of the six ladies (for Mrs. Seagrave remained languidly displayed upon the sofa) rushed to the window, where a glossily painted, though heavily laden, coach was passing by, revealing a glimpse of what appeared to be a grand London lady in a modish bonnet topped by a marvelous curl of matching ostrich feathers.

"Headed for Fenwick Manor, no doubt," declared Mrs. Houghton. "And very grand she is, I'm sure. Yet I daresay she will attend my musical evening as long as *you* do so,

Lady Rocksley. To be sure, the squire must call upon her this very day."

"Do you know the lady's name, ma'am?" Penny inquired.

Mrs. Houghton frowned. "Crimshaw . . . Calworthy . . . no, Colby . . . Cole . . . something of that nature. I fear I did not properly attend. Mr. Houghton will impart the whole of it soon enough. Come, Mary, it's time we finished our errands." So saying, the squire's wife swept out of the Seagrave cottage, with every intention—as they all knew—of visiting each and every one of her cronies to impart the exciting announcement of the newcomer's arrival.

Penny, with a touch of Lord Brawley's cynicism, realized for the first time how great the furor must have been when news of the earl's marriage had burst upon the village. But that was a subject she wished to avoid. With something that might have been termed mutual sighs of relief, Penny Lisbourne and Helen Seagrave settled down to a pleasant exposition of the fine qualities of Cranmere's vicar, Adrian Stanmore, as opposed to the somewhat dubious reputations of the two gentlemen from London. If Miss Seagrave had so much as a soupçon of curiosity about Lord Brawley or Mr. Dinsmore, she gave no hint of it.

The Countess of Rocksley returned from the village with a scant half-hour to dress before dinner, so it was only when all were gathered for sherry that she was able to recount the tale of the new arrival to her mama-in-law. "You would scarce credit it, ma'am," Penny declared with a self-deprecating grin. "There we were, the five of us, attempting to peer out the window at the same time, standing on tippy-toes, craning our necks, while keeping far enough back from the lace curtain to hope we might not be seen. Later, I fear Miss Seagrave and I were overcome by a mix of hilarity and chagrin when we realized how shockingly provincial our behavior must have seemed if the lady had but looked in our direction."

"Are you quite certain she was a *lady?*" the dowager inquired.

"Oh, yes. Mrs. Houghton seemed to know all about her. She plans to call on her and leave a card for her musical evening."

"If she has the squire's approval, then I suppose we must call upon the lady as well—"

"No!" The roar of disapproval came simultaneously from three male throats.

The Dowager Countess of Rocksley turned a basilisk stare on her son, whose look of anguished embarrassment was all too clear before he dropped his eyes to the complex pattern of the Persian carpet.

"I believe," said Lord Brawley, stepping smoothly into the breach, "that we thought you might wish to reserve judgment until you have met the lady at the squire's musical evening."

The dowager knew a faradiddle when she heard it. And sincerely hoped her daughter-in-law did not. For she very much feared the identity of the newcomer was neither unknown to the three gentlemen present nor did it bode well for her son's fledgling marriage. Truly, he had been in short coats the last time she had seen him look so guilty.

With exquisite timing, Hutton announced dinner. If a slight frown creased the lovely countenance of the younger Countess of Rocksley as she went in to dinner on Lord Brawley's arm—a look that indicated she was attempting to solve a puzzle—the others could only be grateful she had not yet reached the correct conclusion. Mr. Dinsmore, his voice somewhat louder and higher than usual, carried the brunt of the dinner conversation, recounting the latest *on dits,* including some of the more colorful incidents in Caro Lamb's pursuit of Lord Byron. Lord Brawley interjected his usual sarcastic jibes, but even Penny could see his heart wasn't in it. Jason's demeanor throughout the several removes seldom relaxed from an outright scowl. The dowager made several attempts to converse in a normal manner, but a strained aura hovered over them, like the heaviness before a thunderstorm. And it all had something to do with the stylish newcomer in the elegant coach. Of that Penny was certain, although her duties as hostess at this awkward meal precluded her analyzing just what the problem could be. When she had Jason alone . . .

But he might not come to her tonight. After all, he had not come the night before, though she had not found this surprising, as it was inevitable he would stay up late talking with his friends. But tonight? Perhaps she should be greatly daring and go to him, for there was a mystery here, and, even though she was nearly certain she would not like the answer, she was determined to solve the riddle.

But the Earl of Rocksley did not linger with his friends that night. Although he was still roundly cursing Fate for saddling him with so many disasters, he left his friends to amuse themselves at billiards and—after enduring slaps on the back and pithy comments on how to divert his wife's wrath—he changed into his dressing gown and dismissed his valet. Perhaps if he selected a bit of jewelry from the family vault . . . ? No, gentlemen bought off their mistresses, not their wives. Jason then recalled all the fine new pieces of jewelry worn by the wives of acquaintances who were blatantly engaged with a ladybird or with other men's wives, and sighed. Jewelry, it seemed, was tantamount to an admission of guilt. Therefore, he must go to his wife empty-handed.

The trouble was, he was also empty-headed. For all his much vaunted wit and savoir faire, he could think of no satisfactory way to inform his wife that his mistress had followed him to Shropshire. *Hell and the devil confound it!* He had enough problems with his marriage without Daphne taking a page from Caro Lamb's book.

The earl could hear the drum tattoo and rattle of the tumbril as he made the long walk through the dressing rooms to his wife's bedchamber. Halfway across Penny's dressing room, Jason paused, his single candle casting wavering light over his wife's colorful new gowns and rows of matching slippers. The scent of lavender wafted past his nose, yet he could almost swear he detected the more exotic perfumes of the East, tantalizing his senses beneath the solid odors of a proper English garden.

Penny Blayne. A charming young bud of femininity

transformed into the enchanting seductive odalisque, Gulbeyaz. Then, with a snap of Cassandra Pemberton's man-hating fingers, into a forbiddingly proper, stiff-spined Englishwoman only grudgingly willing to perform her wifely duties. For years the blasted chit had been a millstone about his neck, a most inconvenient match. Yet, as females went, she was a good sort. She had done her best in an impossible situation and now . . . now she had once again transformed herself in an almost pitiable attempt to adapt to yet another blow to her life.

And he? He, Jason Victor Granville Lisbourne, had walked into their marriage knowing full well what he was doing. Though he certainly had never expected it to come to this. If they had been allowed to be truly married from the beginning, what would their life be like now? Would he have resented being tied down so young? Would he have taken a mistress? Would they now be playing this same scene, even though the third-floor nursery was well occupied with so-called pledges of their affection?

Unfortunately, the answer to all three questions was very likely *yes.*

Though guilt is difficult to erase, the Earl of Rocksley made a valiant effort to paste a pleasant expression on his face. He completed his walk across the dressing room and opened the door.

Chapter Twenty

At first he did not see her. Plainly, the bed, so carefully turned down by a chambermaid, was empty. Ridding himself of the glare of his candle by setting it on his wife's dressing table just inside the door, Jason allowed his eyes to adjust to the gloom. And there she was . . . tucked up on a cushioned window seat, bathed in moonlight, the flounces of that remarkable dressing gown tumbling in a cascade to the carpet. Dear God, he had never felt less like forcing himself to a serious discussion. All he wanted—all any man could want in such a situation—was . . .

Grimly, the earl picked up the delicate chair that matched his wife's dressing table and moved it to within a foot of her elaborate flounces. Without a word, he sat, noting with some trepidation that her gaze was still fixed on the gardens below, shimmering in all the beauty of a warm June night.

"You suspect the worst, do you not?" he said at last.

"I am not a complete fool, my lord, although my laggardness in understanding what should have been as plain as a box to the ear shames me. Such a sad length of time for me to make sense of Mrs. Houghton's attempts at the lady's name. Your friends' arrival, their sly looks and whisperings, your mama's shock and valiant attempt to recover. Yet there is nothing new in my ignorance, is there, my lord? As always, in spite of my advanced age, I am the naive child; you, the sophisticated rake—"

"I did not invite her here!"

Jason's roar brought his wife's head round in a slow turn,

every fiber of her being bristling with wounded dignity. "You have known her a long time, have you not?"

"Yes," the earl ground out.

"And for how long has she been your mistress?"

"Close on to two years. But," Jason added swiftly, "I have not been in her bed since you and I renewed our vows."

"Really?" The countess sounded surprisingly indifferent. "Have you, I wonder, made your feelings perfectly clear to Mrs. Coleraine? And do you not feel you have some obligation to this woman of good family?"

"Do not be absurd, Penny. She was an obliging—nay, eager—widow, and I was glad enough to sample her charms. What else did I have?" the earl added a trifle petulantly.

"It seems to me you have had a great deal," his wife returned. "Every privilege of your title and your wealth, while I . . . But pay me no mind. Feeling sorry for myself will pay no toll."

Jason raised his hand to touch her, tell her there was no need to flail herself in this manner, but his fingers fell back, clenching into a fist as Penny added, "It is most inconvenient that the Sultan Selim is dead or you could sue him for criminal concupiscence, as Lord Elgin did with Robert Ferguson. Elgin received a mere ten thousand pounds. Just think, my lord, what *you* might have pried from the Turkish treasury."

"Penelope," the earl intoned, most awfully.

"But since you cannot sue poor Selim," his wife continued in carefully reasoned tones, "perhaps you may choose some wealthy gentleman you do not like, and I shall write him most frightfully incriminating letters, as poor foolish Ferguson did to Lady Elgin. Then you will be able to collect from him a satisfactory sum to compensate you for the years you have endured this most inconvenient match—"

"If I had ever wanted a divorce," a thoroughly incensed Lord Rocksley broke in, "I would have told you so. And if I did get a divorce, I swear to you I would not marry Daphne Coleraine. I am," he added in softer, almost cajoling tones, "quite content with the wife I have."

Merciful heavens, his insouciance must well be one of the wonders of the world! "If Aunt Cass had allowed us to be truly married," Penny managed, "do you think we might be playing this same scene, rebelling against the inevitability of fate and wishing we had waited?"

For the first time since he had heard of Daphne Coleraine's arrival in Shropshire, Jason felt a bubble of humor pushing its way through the gloom. "Very likely," he agreed, "but, hopefully, our nursery would be full of young Lisbournes, and we would each know we were merely encountering a bump on the long road of marriage. We would, I think, hold hands"—Jason's action followed his words. "I would touch your cheek, put my finger to your lips, and tell you we have both made mistakes and must learn to forgive. I would"—he moved within a hair's breadth of her mouth—"kiss you." A longish pause while the earl did just that. "And then we would go to bed." Gently, ever so gently, the Earl of Rocksley handed his wife down from the window seat and walked with her toward the waiting bed, careful to keep his arm only loosely about her, never pinning her down, making it clear the choice was hers.

And Penny walked with him, giving no indication of the unresolved turmoil inside her. *Content.* Jason Lisbourne was content with the wife he had. How very gratifying. Though, she had to admit, it was a step up from *her* wedding-night announcement that she was *reconciled* to being his wife. What fools they both were. Yet who was to provide the sword to cut the Gordian knot of their marriage?

"I beg you will not do this!" Penny declared fervently the next morning as the dowager tied her bonnet and pulled on her gloves.

"Needs must when the devil rides," said the elder Lady Rocksley with grim determination. "I will not have that ineffably foolish Tabitha Houghton sending cards to *that woman*!"

"But I understand Mrs. Coleraine is received everywhere," Penny protested. "Attempting to shut her out only emphasizes the . . . the—ah—unfortunate association."

"Unfortunate association! Dear God, child, how can you be so charitable? Unnatural, that's what it is. Positively unnatural."

"Is that . . . is that not what is expected in the *ton,* my lady? A wife must accept the inevitable . . . and have the courage to make the best of what life puts on her plate?"

The Dowager Countess of Rocksley gave one last tug on her glove, then waved her hand toward the morning room's comfortable striped settee. "Sit down, Penelope," she said. The elder Lady Rocksley then proceeded to remove her bonnet and, setting it on a side table, took a seat beside her daughter-in-law. "You may stare when I tell you, my dear, but Jason's father was faithful to me for all the years of our marriage. And, no, I was not some silly ostrich with my head in a hole. And *your* Jason is made of the same cloth. You may take my word for it, he was never cut out to be a rakehell. I believe him when he says he has not been with Mrs. Coleraine since you came to him here in Shropshire. And so should you. Therefore, we have only to rout this contemptible creature, who would chase after him like a hound after a fox, and you may be free to enjoy your marriage to its fullest." The dowager, deciding she had made her point quite well, reached for her bonnet.

"My lady," Penny said swiftly, even though her solemn expression indicated she was considering the dowager's words with care, "I still wish you would not speak to Mrs. Houghton. The poor woman cannot, in all conscience, retract her invitation. There would be enormous embarrassment on all sides, not the least of which would be mine, as such a cut to Mrs. Coleraine could only precipitate the kind of gossip we wish to avoid. I am so grateful," Penny added on an urgent note, "so very grateful you wish to go off and do battle for me, truly I am. But I beg you not to stir the waters. I will—indeed, I *must*—face Mrs. Coleraine and make the best of it."

Penny ducked her head, a blush creeping up her neck to suffuse her face a glowing pink. "Last night . . ." She broke off, made another attempt. "Jason has assured me their liaison is at an end. At some time in the near future, I must meet her in town. It is best, I think, to endure the initial introduction here, rather than under the avid scrutiny of the entire *ton.*"

"Oh, my dear child," cried the dowager. "I doubt I should ever have the strength to be so shockingly brave." But, slowly, with resignation, Eulalia Lisbourne, Dowager Countess of Rocksley, began to work her fingers free of her fine kid gloves.

Two hours later, as Lord Brawley and Mr. Dinsmore once again indulged in a desultory game of billiards, they paused, eyebrows raised in query as Lord Rocksley entered the room. Gant Deveny rested his cue against the soft carpet, eyeing his friend's gloomy face with sympathy. "The lady was not cooperative," he intoned. It was not a question.

"She was not," the earl concurred flatly.

"But how can she wish to stay where her name is anathema?" Harry Dinsmore demanded.

"She has, it seems, convinced herself that my wife's reputation is so thoroughly ruined that I *must* divorce her, leaving the ever-faithful Daphne to assuage my wounded pride and provide me with the necessary heir."

"Elgin has what?" Gant Deveny drawled, deliberately goading his friend. "At least two brats in his second marriage, after four or five with the first. Swear the man breeds like a rabbit."

The Earl of Rocksley grabbed the billiards cue from Brawley's hand and snapped the birds'-eye-maple stick into two pieces, while looking very much as if he wished to break it over the viscount's head. "I have told you," Jason ground out, "I do not want a divorce. I do not want Daphne as mother of my children."

"She wasn't 'ever-faithful' either," Harry Dinsmore commented. "Must have seen her with Ormsby or Haliburton a dozen times or more, Rock, since you sent us all packing last winter."

"So the squire's musical evening is likely to feature fireworks," murmured Lord Brawley, enjoying, as always, his role of *provocateur.*

"Perhaps we should all be afflicted with the influenza," Mr. Dinsmore offered.

"Cut line, Harry," the earl snapped. "I fear we must, quite literally, face the music." While his friends groaned at this sally, Jason tossed the pieces of the broken cue into a corner, then lifted a fresh stick from the rack on the wall. "And do not forget," he added with savage satisfaction, "I believe my wife expects you both to do the pretty with the village maidens, who are, I believe, all aflutter at the thought of having such fine London gentlemen among them."

With that Parthian shot, the earl tossed the stick at Brawley, who caught it in mid-flight. Rocksley then strolled nonchalantly from the room, paying no heed to Mr. Dinsmore's sputtered, "Oh, I say, Rock!"

The younger Countess of Rocksley brought up her heavy guns for the Houghtons' musical evening. With Wellington winning battles at last on the Peninsula, military terms were on everyone's tongue, and Penny Lisbourne was no exception. If the Houghtons' attempt at culture could not qualify as a battle, it was most certainly a skirmish, and the wife of the Earl of Rocksley would dress accordingly. Yes, Penny admitted to herself, as Noreen entwined a strand of small but finely matched pearls in her hair, she might be a wee bit overdressed for a country musicale, but—as she had known when "Mrs. Galworthy" slipped off to London to acquire a new wardrobe—fine clothing was armor. And tonight she very much needed it. Her high-waisted gown of French blue was beautifully understated, falling in a graceful column topped by a half-skirt of delicate white lace. Lace also peeped out from beneath her hemline and from the cuffs of her tiny puffed sleeves and at the edge of her daring décolletage. A single sequin, glittering iridescently, winked from the center of each pristine flower woven into the white lace. In addition to the pearls in her hair, Penny wore a modest aigrette of sequined feathers on one side of her head. The aigrette was sheer defiance, a reminder of the jeweled feathers that distinguished the turbans of the Ottoman sultans.

After Noreen had fastened the diamond necklace the earl

had given his wife and helped affix the matching earbobs, Penny turned to her long-time companion. "Will I do?" she inquired.

"Indeed you will, me darlin'. There's none can touch ye," Noreen affirmed, her Irish even more broad than usual.

The eager light faded from Penny's eyes. "If only that were true," she sighed. "I may look quite splendid, but I am all aquake inside."

"She canna hold a candle to ye, love," Noreen declared.

"*You* have not seen the woman," Penny sighed.

"She could be that Venus they talk about, but you're the wife, and never forget it!"

Penny gave Noreen a hug, squared her shoulders, and went to war. Somehow, the poor bachelor vicar, Adrian Stanmore, and his possible brides, Miss Mary Houghton and Miss Helen Seagrave, had vanished from her mind.

When the party from Rockbourne Crest arrived at Squire Houghton's, Penny was, however, instantly reminded of her broken vow to concentrate on the problems of her friends so she might not have time to contemplate her own. For as the guests were ushered to the fragile-looking chairs Tabitha Houghton had had set up in her drawing room, Helen Seagrave was just finishing the tuning of her harp, which had been brought by wagon from Cranmere several hours later than the carter had originally promised.

Such a lovely picture Helen made, Penny thought, for Miss Seagrave had been persuaded she could not perform while wearing anything so old-cattish as a cap. Her gown of rose lustring added color to her pale cheeks and her brown hair glowed with vibrance under the light from two tall candelabras placed to illuminate the performance area. Miss Seagrave's fingers were long and graceful, her lovely gray eyes tantalizingly hidden beneath long lashes as she kept her eyes fixed on her strings, their tuning pegs, and the chromatic pedals that were the very latest addition to harp design.

Helen looked up, glanced at the earl and his guests, and, with the briefest of smiles to the countess, she effaced herself, slipping out of the room before anyone else might see her at her plebeian task. Penny looked around for Adrian Stanmore, pleased to discover him in the third row on the left, though he was barely visible behind the bevy of women surrounding him. Continuing what she hoped was a subtle inspection of the room, while nodding and smiling to acquaintances, Penny was infinitely relieved when she did not see the dashing beauty of Daphne Coleraine. Could it be someone had persuaded the dratted woman not to come? For as much as she could not blame Mrs. Coleraine's obsession with the earl—even to the point of feeling sympathy with the poor creature to whom Jason seemed so coldly indifferent in spite of their long-time association—Penny truly did not care to be reminded that little Penny Blayne was no competition for an accomplished courtesan (no matter how gentle her birth).

With much fluttering, and far too many words from both the squire and his wife, the musical evening finally began, with the absence of Mrs. Daphne Coleraine an unexplained mystery. Just prior to the squire's lengthy speech of welcome, Penny had seen Lord Brawley and Mr. Dinsmore with their heads together, whispering, and had no doubt about the subject of their conversation. Penny, smiling just a bit smugly, settled into her chair, prepared to enjoy the music far more than she had anticipated. Beside her, she could feel Jason begin to relax as well. It would seem, praise be, that they had been spared.

Miss Mary Houghton, though looking as if she wished the floor would open and swallow her up, was a credit to her teacher, Miss Seagrave, not only playing pieces by Haydn and Scarlatti, but accompanying Mr. Jeremy Tate, tutor to the squire's younger children, while he performed a lively variety of country songs. Helen Seagrave then offered a thundering piece by Mr. Beethoven, which was met with enthusiastic applause, after which she surprised everyone by coaxing a suddenly shy Adrian Stanmore to the makeshift stage to join her in a decorous Italian duet.

Jason, Penny noted, seemed singularly indifferent to the absence of Daphne Coleraine. While his wife was burning with questions about the lady's absence, the earl circulated during the interval, carrying Penny with him by virtue of keeping a hand tightly clamped around her arm. Together, they smiled themselves silly, positively oozing marital congeniality, until the countess thought she might be quite nauseous. Jason was overdoing it, she knew he was. Possibly because he, too, was relieved at his mistress's absence.

Or did he know all about it? Had he strangled her then? Buried her body in the Fenwick Manor gardens? Dropped her down a well?

The idea was so absurd Penny had to choke back a near hysterical giggle. Nor did she dare ask her hostess what had happened to Cranmere's elegant newcomer. For when Tabitha Houghton heard of Daphne Coleraine's connection to the earl—if she had not already done so—Penny's mortification would be unbearable. Beyond the most civil of nods, never would she acknowledge Mrs. Coleraine's existence. But tomorrow—oh, yes, tomorrow—she would get the entire story from Helen, who must have heard all the gossip while waiting in the wings.

The second half of the program featured Miss Helen Seagrave with her harp, and a virtuoso performance it was. Even Penny forgot her anxieties in the nimble grace and power of Helen's skill. It was almost a misfortune Miss Seagrave had been born a gentlewoman, Penny realized, for her talent would earn her far more money upon the stage than she would ever earn as a sometime teacher in the Shropshire village of Cranmere.

And then, of course, just as the countess had forgotten her fears and was caught up in contemplating the affairs of Helen Seagrave, the other shoe dropped. The mystery resolved itself, taking Penny's burgeoning, yet vulnerable, hopes with it.

Chapter Twenty-one

After gracefully accepting the long and genuinely enthusiastic applause that erupted after her final rippling chord, Miss Seagrave removed herself to the pianoforte where she sat on the tapestry-covered tabouret, bowed her head, folded her hands, and retreated into her more usual role as nameless, faceless accompanist.

Tabitha Houghton bustled forward, her gown and turban of purple taffeta doing little for either her hearty coloring or her sturdy figure. Beaming, she announced, "We have a splendid surprise this evening. The newest addition to our society, Mrs. Daphne Coleraine, has kindly agreed to render a few selections. After her performance, I know you will wish to greet her at the supper that is laid out in the Red Salon." With a gesture worthy of Mrs. Siddons in her prime, the squire's wife swung a plump arm toward the side door through which each performer had entered. "Mrs. Coleraine!" she boomed.

Penny heard, quite distinctly, Jason's breath whistle between his teeth. She most sincerely hoped he was as surprised as she. If not . . .

No, that was a thought she did not wish to have.

She sat perfectly still, hoping her face was as bland as her mind was in turmoil. She had *known* the blasted woman was to be here. She should not have allowed herself to hope . . .

There was, of course, one good thing to come from this, Penny realized. One look, and she no longer felt the slightest sympathy for Daphne Coleraine. One look, and, as she had feared, the Countess of Rocksley was reduced to the sixteen-year-old Penny Blayne. Young, naive, and utterly unable to compete with the siren before her. For Daphne Coleraine was garbed in black spider gauze opening over an undergown of silver, the gauze caught up in scallops, each fastened with a silver rose, sparkling with brilliants. Twisted into the lady's black hair was a scarf of the spider gauze, also sparkling with brilliants. And her face—*oh, dear God,* Penny groaned—the brief view she had had of Mrs. Coleraine in Hyde Park had not revealed the whole. The elegant widow—not more than a year or two older than herself—was a stunningly beautiful woman well able to provide Jason with an heir and several spares. A woman who was, Penny speculated, endowed at birth with more sophistication and ability to entice than the younger Countess of Rocksley would ever know. And the spectacular diamonds around her neck, around her arm, and in her ears—the heavy parure that would have overwhelmed Penny's delicate English beauty—looked perfectly splendid on Mrs. Daphne Coleraine's more voluptuous stature. Were they a gift from Jason? A *parting* gift? *Goodness knows the tart had earned them,* the countess thought rather nastily.

If she had been up to continuing that thought, Penny might have expected Mrs. Coleraine to break into the Queen of the Night's aria from *The Magic Flute,* for the role of villainess suited her well. But the miserable female suddenly transformed herself into the coquettish Zerlina, launching, in a sultry and altogether too fine mezzo-soprano, into *"Batti, batti, o bel Masetto."*

Seething, Penny sat, cursing Mozart for writing the blasted piece, while Daphne Coleraine directed every last note of this tempting siren song at the modern-day Jason sitting at his wife's side. Never had Penny, who truly loved music, been so happy to have a song come to an end. After the applause had faded, Mrs. Coleraine, looking very smug, launched into an Italian song. *"Vittoria, mio core!"* she sang, this time directing her attention to Penny, as well as to the earl.

Victorious, my heart. A challenge, an out-and-out challenge. The witch! But worse was to come. After bowing, and flashing her fine white teeth at every male in the room (or so Penny would have sworn), Mrs. Coleraine announced that she would need help for her next song. Surely there was a gentleman willing to join her . . . perhaps Lord Rocksley, who had performed this particular piece with her so many times before . . .

To give Jason credit, Penny thought, he had stiffened into a block of ice the moment Daphne Coleraine had swept onto the stage, and even now he did not move. It was almost as if he had not heard Mrs. Coleraine's oh-so-charming plea. Penny moved her lips to his ear. "You will have to do it, you know," she hissed. "There will be too much talk if you refuse."

And a very great deal if he did not. But no time to think of that now, as the earl added a surprisingly rich baritone to a rendition of an old English patter song. As the song progressed, Penny took due note of her husband's transformation from stiff-necked nobleman to outrageous flirt, grinning, teasing, leering, and sending the audience into whoops. The Countess of Rocksley smiled. And smiled, while a full ten years of hurt swelled in her heart, swelled so far it shattered, the myriad pieces blown away on the storm winds of her soul.

Yet, somehow, the earl and his countess survived the evening, as the Jason and Penelope of Greek legend had survived their own peculiar trials. Penny even managed to be gracious, if cool, during her inevitable introduction to Mrs. Coleraine. Although how to greet one's husband's mistress had not been included in Aunt Cass's training, she thought she managed it rather well.

With five squeezed into the carriage on the way home, there was no opportunity for the earl to say what was foremost in his mind. No opportunity to assure his wife he had indeed made a formal, final break with Daphne Coleraine. Was not that spectacular parure evidence enough as his lavish parting gift? Surely Penny must have realized . . . No, it was quite possible she did not. Yet it was she who had urged him to sing with Daphne, was it not? And had she not smiled quite brilliantly during the applause that greeted their duet?

Jason peered at his wife in the dim light of the carriage lantern. She was responding lightly to his mama and to Brawley and Dinsmore as they made polite conversation about the performers and the Houghtons' lavish hospitality. And yet . . . he was nearly certain she was furious . . . or hurt. Could she not see that he, like all the other performers, had been required to play the game? To act a part—to smile and flirt and appear to be enjoying himself? It was not as if he *wanted* to stand up before every last family of importance in the neighborhood and sing a duet with his mistress?

Ex-mistress.

He would have to speak to Penny, of course. Explain that he truly had not enjoyed himself. Yes, that was it. As soon as he had her alone, he would make her understand . . .

But shortly after their return to Rockbourne Crest, Noreen O'Donnell delivered a message to Kirby, the earl's valet. Her ladyship was not feeling well. She trusted the earl would understand his lady's desire to be alone.

What choice did a gentleman have? Though Jason burned to speak to his wife, he was not prepared to break down the door. Perhaps Penny was right. A night to cool their heads might benefit them both. Or . . . possibly there was nothing more to the message than the arrival of her monthly, and he was making a mountain out of a molehill. But, surely, no matter the circumstances, she would wish to speak to him tonight. Should he not go to her anyway?

And thus play the sultan, giving her no choice?

With a sigh that was close to a groan, the Earl of Rocksley climbed into his bed, where, after a quarter-hour of rationalizing and justifying his behavior, he fell into a deep and dreamless sleep.

But on the morrow he did not find his wife at breakfast. Nor in the morning room conferring with Mrs. Wilton. Her ladyship was not feeling well, Hutton told him, and had asked not to be disturbed. Nobly, Jason refrained from tapping on his wife's door, although he engaged in a sharp colloquy with the butler about whether or not the doctor should be called. Hutton swore quite solemnly that Mrs. Wilton had assured him, going by the word of the O'Donnell herself, that no doctor was needed. His mama, though looking more grave than was customary, counseled him to patience. So it was teatime before the earl, now thoroughly frustrated as well as concerned for his wife's health, tapped on her door, urgently requesting entry.

Silence.

"Penny? O'Donnell?" Jason turned the handle and stepped inside.

The room was empty. Nothing but a folded parchment perched on the mantel to greet him. He did not need to open it to know what had happened. His entire household had conspired to dupe him. Every last one of the traitorous devils. Even his mama.

He supposed he deserved it. If only he had not been such a gentleman last night . . . If only he had barged in and *handled* the situation . . .

What was that ancient expression about fools rush in where angels fear to tread? Yes, honesty forced him to admit he might have made things worse . . . though what was worse than a runaway wife he could not, at the moment, imagine. He picked up the letter and broke the seal.

My dearest Jason. Yes, I may address you so in this darkness of the night and in the certainty of knowing I will be gone when you read this. I have, you see, decided I must be the one to cut the Gordian knot we have made of our marriage, for it has become plain that renewing our vows was not enough to make us one. I assure you I am not making a dramatic run to the ends of the earth where you can never find me. I am merely going into isolation so I may think about our marriage, and you may have time to do the same.

I confess, here and now, that I have loved you almost from the very moment of our first meeting at Lord Elgin's embassy. But I know now my emotions were childish. I fantasized a great love, as young girls are wont to do. I endowed you with every virtue, every heroic quality of legend. I even fancied you loved me as I loved you. Perhaps I may be excused a bit since my situation was so dire, and a hero so greatly needed.

Even after your disinterest became apparent, I clung to my convictions of our mutual love. (You were, I told myself, merely waiting to express your love until I was older.) And even after disillusionment set in, I never stopped loving you. I recognized that I—a soiled dove, if you will—was quite inadequate to attract your love, yet I could not cease to love you.

And then when you finally said you wanted me . . . I thought being truly married to you, being mother of your children, would be enough. I had already proved I had courage. Therefore, I knew I could manage.

But I have made a sad discovery. I am a jealous, selfish female. I want all of you. I will not share. I demand your love, complete and unreserved.

And, Jason, do not, I pray, leap into your carriage and follow me because of pride, because I am an absconding wife—your property to do with as you will. I beg of you, take time to think about what I have said. If you can find it in your heart to offer me love, you will discover word of me at O'Shea's, a pub in the village of Dingle, where Noreen was born. If, at the end of six months, I have not heard from you, I will consider our marriage at an end. You may petition Parliament for a divorce and live the life Jason Lisbourne was destined to have before he met Penny Blayne and the White Rose, Gulbeyaz.

Your loving wife, Penny

The Earl of Rocksley sat down hard on a blue brocade chaise near the fireplace before reading his wife's letter a second time. He was conscious of immense relief that Penny had left word where to find her. And abject horror that his young man's single-minded rejection of encumbrances, combined with his own puerile fantasies of Gulbeyaz, had somehow kept him from seeing the wonder of the woman right under his nose.

Ireland. The thrice-damned *west* coast of Ireland!

Hell and damnation, the poets had it right. Not even a belated and abject realization of love could keep him from thinking that women could be a great deal of trouble.

Chapter Twenty-two

The Dingle Peninsula, Ireland

The barefooted girl on the beach at the edge of Dingle Bay quite shamelessly clutched the folds of her brown fustian skirt, raising the hemline so high it barely covered her shapely knees. Not that she was so lost to all propriety that she had failed to examine the deserted shoreline with care before indulging in such extreme behavior. With something close to a chortle, Penny Lisbourne waded into the blue-gray water lapping at the fringe of the pale yellow sand. She gasped, and stepped swiftly back from a foaming whitecap as water that must have come straight from Iceland nipped her toes.

Once again standing on the warm sand, Penny gazed thoughtfully toward the west—past the town of Dingle, its sheltered harbor—filled with colorful fishing boats—and on down Dingle Bay, past Great Blasket Island, to the open Atlantic, where there was simply nothing between the western Irish coast and the Americas. Nothing at all. Perhaps there lay her destiny. It was not an unknown, for she and Aunt Cass had spent nearly two years in the former colonies and in the Upper and Lower Canadas. She could easily afford to emigrate—Jason had seen to that.

A stubborn line formed about her mouth; her chin firmed, and her eyes sparked. Such a generous, thoughtful husband. Too little, too late. And once again a laggard. Seven weeks! He needed seven weeks to think about their marriage! Of course, the journey itself was arduous, as Penny very well knew. Boats could not put out to sea in stormy weather, and the overland trip from Waterford to Tralee had been as rough and difficult a journey as she had ever undertaken.

Therefore . . . he was not coming. She should admit as much by now.

I'm a survivor, Penny told herself. *I will live through this, as I have through all else. If Jason does not come, I shall emigrate, become part of the brave new world. Is that not where the most courageous of the ruined or destitute pin their hopes?* Boston, Atlanta, perhaps New Orleans. Or would she be truly daring, making the dangerous journey around Cape Horn to join that exotic settlement, San Francisco? Why not? If she did not care for the burgeoning civilization on the East Coast . . . if it were too much like what she had left behind, she would take ship for California. What was one more voyage to a girl who had seen Bombay and Constantinople?

Penny eyed the foaming water as if it were another enemy to be conquered. Once again raising her skirts, she plunged in, defying the waves as they splashed up, dampening her gown all the way to her waist. Defying the bone-chilling cold. Defying the icy heaviness of her heart. Defying her urge to run away, as she had so many times before. To take the first ship headed for the Americas, put Jason behind her, and be done with all this anguish.

But seven weeks was not the six months she had so rashly promised. And she would, of course, be true to her word. But that meant a winter in Dingle, and if she had thought Pemberton Priory or Rockbourne Crest isolated, it was only because she had never encountered anything so out of the way as the Dingle Peninsula. Lady Rocksley sighed and retreated from the Atlantic, which was icy even in August. She could not begin to imagine how it would be in January. She shivered even thinking on it.

As Penny drove her gig back toward the village of Dingle, she breathed deeply of the clean Irish air, so deeply tinged with salt and seaweed mingled with the earthy odors of damp greenery and barnyard animals. It was a beautiful place, the Dingle Peninsula, with its central mountains rising so precipitously from the narrow strip of land around its edges that Penny had once declared to Noreen that the sheep, in order to graze upon the hillsides, must have legs shorter on one side than the other. And the neatly hedged fields seemed even smaller, rockier, and more intricately tangled into mazes than those of England.

Surprisingly, the people were kind, if still a bit doubtful about the Englishwoman who had come among them. But if Noreen O'Donnell—on whom the Blessed Mother must look with favor if she had guided the colleen home again—vouched for her lady, then the foreigner would be welcome. Or so Noreen had repeated to Penny, even as she was taken with an odd bit of blushing and stammering as she admitted overhearing this sentiment at O'Shea's Pub. Which was another reason Penny knew she must fulfill her promise of six months in Ireland, for Noreen O'Donnell had acquired an admirer, the publican Michael O'Shea himself, and Penny would not think of dragging her companion away from what might be her sole opportunity for a life of her own.

Penny pulled up in front of O'Shea's, tied her horse to the hitching post, and went inside to collect her long-time companion. O'Shea's Pub was a long, low, whitewashed building, heavily thatched. Inside, its great stone fireplace, blackened by a century or more of roaring fires, filled nearly all of one wall of the low-ceilinged room, and a cluster of men stood at the bar, while their wives had their heads together, gossiping, in a cozy snug fitted into a narrow space next to the fireplace. Noreen, not surprisingly, was behind the bar, helping Michael O'Shea, who, Penny suspected, had been dazzling the ladies with his dark good looks for twenty years or more. Yet she had to admit he appeared to be caught at last.

Penny allowed herself to be persuaded to a glass of O'Shea's own brew, for which she was beginning to develop a partiality, and then she and Noreen were off to their modest cottage, tucked into the side of the narrow valley that led from the village to the Conor Pass. It was only as the cottage came into view that Penny realized there had been an underlying excitement at O'Shea's this day. A glance, a whisper, a light in the eye. But Irishmen were adept at deception, she recalled grimly. They had had to be through hundreds of years of English occupation. *They had known,* Penny fumed. They had sat her down and fed her ale and kept her there just to torment her! Or to give her visitor time to ensconce himself in her parlor.

Dear God, what if the visitor whose fine carriage was pulled up at the door was not Jason?

Who else would come in such fine equipage, undoubtedly the best to be hired in Waterford?

Penny laid her hands in her lap and bowed her head. She could not move. Sean, their young man of all work, had to take the reins from her hands, then Noreen took her in charge, nearly dragging the countess off her seat and through the front door, which opened directly into the parlor. Whereupon, O'Donnell bobbed a curtsy to his lordship and went straight to the kitchen, leaving the stunned Countess of Rocksley alone with her husband.

At the sound of the gig's wheels, Jason had bounded to his feet. He stood now, confronting his wife, his mind nearly blank of all he had intended to say. Only one thought remained. He *must* tell her, must explain . . .

"I recall the terms you dictated quite well," he burst out, "but there are some things I must tell you before we speak of love. Pray be seated," he begged, waving an arm toward a somewhat battered sofa set beneath the parlor's multipaned front window. When his wife did not move, Jason took her by the hand, leading her to the sofa. Then, all his good intentions suddenly scrambled inside his head, he stood as if struck dumb, his eyes fixed on the lace curtains and the rugged Irish countryside beyond.

Where . . .? Where to begin?

"I . . . I wish you to understand," Jason declared at last, standing as stiffly erect as a young miscreant before a headmaster, "that Mrs. Coleraine has not been part of my life—except in her overly active imagination—since the night of your arrival at Rockbourne Crest. Why she should have chosen to emulate Caro Lamb I do not know, but she has now seen my wedding lines—both sets of them—and has spoken at some length with the vicar, who has assured her that only God can put our marriage asunder."

"And Parliament."

"I have assured Mrs. Coleraine," Jason said to his stubborn wife in a tone perhaps a tad more grim than a supplicant should choose, "that divorce is not a possibility. She has decided to winter in Bath, while choosing her new quarry for the coming Season."

Penny's hand flew to her mouth, stifling a sound between a gasp and a chuckle. "Surely, she did not tell you so!"

For the first time since his arrival, Jason managed a tentative smile. "No, but can you think I am mistaken?"

Penny shook her head, once again reduced to silence. The road to this moment had been long and bitter. And now to Jason fell the burden of resurrecting their marriage.

He moved closer, coming to a halt only inches from her knees. "Penny, I beg you to understand that I was a boy with his head full of idealism, as young men so frequently are. Rescuing you put me into the realm of legends, of Arthur, Lancelot, and the search for the Holy Grail. I was every knight who had ever slain a dragon or rescued a fair maiden. And when I . . . when *you* . . ." The earl stumbled to a halt. "On our wedding night," he continued, choosing his words with care, "I was totally caught up in noble ideals. You will recall you appeared even younger than you actually were. To me you were a child with whom I would enact a play for our watchers. There was no question of any genuine passion. No question of any emotion of any kind between us."

Jason managed a rueful smile. "I was an idealistic young fool, my dear. You aroused such passion in me, elicited such responses to your skills that I almost totally forgot myself. Later, I was so ashamed of my failure to be the noble hero of my imagination that I could not face you. I saw myself as completely derelict. And, later, of course, it was all so easy to blame you. To tell myself I had been made a fool of by a well-trained odalisque instead of acknowledging I had spent the night with a naive and innocent girl who had only wished to please her husband."

Through the last part of this speech, Penny had been staring up at him, eyes shining with tears of pity, tears of joy. "Oh, my dear," she said softly, taking both his hands in hers, "why could you not have told me sooner?"

"I was *such* a fool," Jason snorted. "One moment I blamed you, the next you were once again the fair maiden whose innocence I had defiled. I lusted after Gulbeyaz, yet could not forgive myself for touching little Penny Blayne." The earl ran agitated fingers through his bronze hair. "And then, when we were together at last, I made a mull of that as well." Jason sighed, his lower lip quirking into a rueful smile as he gazed down at her.

"I wanted so much for you to love me," Penny confessed, "yet I could not forgive. Outwardly, I made an effort to attract you, yet, inside, I held a grievance far beyond any sin you may have committed. We were star-crossed, I fear."

"Is there hope for us then?"

Penny's gaze now held a hint of mischief. "There is but one more hurdle, my lord," she decreed. "If you will give me a quarter-hour before you follow me up the stairs?" Gracefully, the countess rose, offering her husband a look full of promise before, calling for Noreen, she headed up the cottage's narrow staircase.

The earl, red-faced, was forced to place his hat over his lap while he waited, most thankful that no one came into the room during that tense fifteen-minute wait. By the end of it, he was certain he had put a new polish on his pocket watch from the amount of times he had taken it out to look at it.

When the moment finally came—when he mounted the steep stairs and found the invitingly open door—he came to a halt a step inside the small bedchamber and simply stared. He should have known, of course. The little witch! She stood before the dormer window, every inch of her clearly outlined by the rays of the late afternoon sun, for she was clad in nothing but the full-sleeved white gauze tunic and azure *shalwar,* with the accompanying jeweled satin cap and the long white silk veil, fastened beneath heavily kohl-rimmed blue eyes. Even after ten full years, he would swear he could smell the perfumes wafting from her clothes.

The eyes above the veil gazed at him quite steadily.

Calmly. Coolly. Assessing his veracity, his understanding of what was happening.

"Look at me, Jason," she said. "Tell me what you see."

The Earl of Rocksley, once the heroic but unrealistic boy known as Lord Lyndon, had learned a great deal in the last few months. He had no difficulty at all interpreting his lady's question. "I see Penelope Blayne Lisbourne. My wife," he returned as steadily as her query. "I see the woman I love, the woman I wish to have for the mother of my children, the woman with whom I wish to spend all of my life, cleaving to her and no other."

"And Gulbeyaz?"

A trickier question—the little minx!—but Jason thought he could manage that as well. "The White Rose will always be with us," he told her, "the mistress I do not intend to seek outside my marriage bed."

And, with that, the Earl and Countess of Rocksley forgot the sun was still shining, forgot the servants breathlessly waiting below, forgot the ribald, if good-natured, jokes being passed around at O'Shea's Pub, and tumbled upon the bed, pledging with fervor their devotion to each other.

Their supper, which Noreen finally set down on a tray outside their door before going off to O'Shea's to recount the final happy ending of this long, convoluted tale, was found still there, unnoticed, the next morning.

"May the saints preserve us," O'Donnell murmured to herself. "Sure, and it must be true 'tis possible to live on love."

About the Author

With ancestors from England, Wales, Scotland, Ireland, and France, **Blair Bancroft** feels right at home in nineteenth-century Britain. But it was only after a variety of other careers that she turned to writing about the Regency era. Blair has been a music teacher, professional singer, nonfiction editor, costume designer, and real estate agent, and she has still managed to travel extensively. The mother of three grown children, Blair lives in Florida. Her Web site is www.blairbancroft.com. She can be contacted at blairbancroft@aol.com.